Smells Like Dog

by Suzanne Selfors

SCHOLASTIC INC.
New York Toronto London Auckland
Sydney Mexico City New Delhi Hong Kong

This edition published by arrangement with Little, Brown and Company, New York, New York, USA. All rights reserved.

ISBN 978-0-545-33305-4

Copyright © 2010 by Suzanne Selfors.
All rights reserved. Published by Scholastic Inc., 557 Broadway, New York, NY 10012, by arrangement with Little, Brown Books for Young Readers, a division of Hachette Book Group, Inc. SCHOLASTIC and associated logos are trademarks and/or registered trademarks of Scholastic Inc.

12 11 10 9 8 7 6 5 4 3 2 1   11 12 13 14 15 16/0

Printed in the U.S.A.   40

First Scholastic printing, January 2011

This book is dedicated to
my dogs, past and present:
Lulu, Max, and
most especially **Skylos.**
I can't imagine a life without
muddy paw prints,
soggy tennis balls,
or dog breath.

CONTENTS

"It is a sad truth of human history that those who dare to be different are often judged to be not quite right in the head."

—Drake Horatio Pudding

Dear Reader,

The following story is a dog story, but it is not, I repeat, NOT, a sad dog story. I hate sad dog stories. I bet you do too. How many times have you picked up a book about a dog and just when you start to fall in love with the dog it falls down a well, or gets hit by a car, or somebody shoots it? Then you cry quietly in your bedroom because you don't know if the dog is going to live or die and it eats you up inside because there's nothing worse than not knowing if a dog is going to live or die. And you don't want to go downstairs to dinner because your eyes are all puffy from crying, which is very embarrassing. I hate it when that happens.

So I promise you that you don't have to worry because the dog in this story does not die. But that's not to say he doesn't have many harrowing and exciting adventures.

This is a happy dog story so you don't have to hide in your bedroom to read it. You can read it in the grocery store, or on the school bus, or in the very back of the classroom during a boring multiplication lesson if you're extra careful not to get caught by your teacher. And if any tears fall from your eyes they will be tears of laughter and joy, and those kinds of tears are never embarrassing.

Happy reading.

PART ONE

THE PUDDING FARM

1

Breakfast with the Puddings

What Homer Pudding didn't know on that breezy Sunday morning, as he carried a pail of fresh goat milk across the yard, was that his life was about to change.

In a big way.

What he did know was this: That the country sky was its usual eggshell blue, that the air was its usual springtime fresh, and that his chores were their usual boring, boring, boring.

For how exciting can it be cleaning up after goats?

And that's what Homer had done for most of his twelve years. Each year his chore list grew longer, taking more time away from the thing that he'd rather do. The one thing. The only thing. But it was not playing football, or riding a bike. Not swimming, or fishing, or building a fort.

If he didn't have to rake goat poop, or change straw bedding, or chase goats out of the flower bed, Homer Winslow Pudding would have more time to dream about the day when he'd become a famous treasure hunter like his uncle.

"Daydreaming doesn't have any place on a farm," his father often told him. "There's too much work to be done."

But Homer dreamed anyway.

Mrs. Pudding waved from the kitchen window. She needed the milk for her morning coffee. Homer picked up his pace, his rubber boots kicking up fallen cherry blossoms. As he stumbled across a gnarled root, a white wave splashed over the side of the bucket. Warm goat milk ran down his sleeve and dribbled onto the grass where it was quickly lapped up by the farm's border collies.

"Careful there," Mr. Pudding called as he strode up the driveway, gravel crunching beneath his heavy work boots. He tucked the Sunday newspaper under his arm.

"Your mother will be right disappointed if she don't get her milk."

Homer almost fell over, his legs tangled in a mass of licking dogs. "Go on," he said. The dogs obeyed. The big one, named Max, scratched at a flea that was doing morning calisthenics on his neck. Max was a working dog, like the others, trained to herd the Puddings' goats. He even worked on Sundays while city dogs slept in or went on picnics. Every day is a workday on a farm.

And that's where this story begins—on the Pudding Goat Farm. A prettier place you'd be hard pressed to find. If you perched at the top of one of the cherry trees you'd see a big barn that sagged in the middle as if a giant had sat on it, a little farmhouse built from river rocks, and an old red truck. Look farther and you'd see an endless tapestry of rolling hills, each painted a different hue of spring green. "Heaven on earth," Mrs. Pudding often said. Homer didn't agree. Surely in heaven there wouldn't be so many things to fix and clean and haul.

The dogs stayed outside while Mr. Pudding and Homer slipped off their boots and went into the kitchen. Because the Pudding family always ate breakfast together at the kitchen table, it was the perfect place to share news and ask questions like, *Whatcha gonna do at school today?* or *Who's gonna take a bath tonight?* or *Why is that dead squirrel lying on the table?*

"Because I'm gonna stuff it."

"Gwendolyn Maybel Pudding. How many times have I told you not to put dead things on the kitchen table?" Mr. Pudding asked as he hung his cap on a hook.

"I don't know," Gwendolyn grumbled, tossing her long brown hair.

Homer set the milk pail on the counter, then washed his hands at the sink. His little brother, who everybody called Squeak, but whose legal name was Pip, tugged at Homer's pant leg. "Hi, Homer."

Homer looked down at the wide-eyed, freckled face. "Hi, Squeak," he said, patting his brother's head. Squeak may have been too young to understand Homer's dreams, but he was always happy to listen to stories about sunken pirate ships or lost civilizations.

"Get that squirrel off the table," Mr. Pudding said, also washing his hands at the sink.

Gwendolyn picked up the squirrel by its tail. The stiff body swung back and forth like the arm of a silent metronome. "I don't see why it's such a problem."

"It's dead, that's why it's a problem. I eat on that table so I don't want dead things lying on it."

Confrontations between Gwendolyn and Mr. Pudding had become a daily event in the Pudding household, ever since last summer when Gwendolyn had turned fifteen and had gotten all moody. In the same breath she might

6

laugh, then burst into tears, then sink into a brooding silence. She befuddled Homer. But most girls befuddled Homer.

He took his usual seat at the end of the pine plank table, hoping that the argument wouldn't last too long. He wanted to finish his chores so he could get back to reading his new map. It had arrived yesterday in a cardboard tube from the Map of the Month Club, a Christmas gift from Uncle Drake. Homer had stayed up late studying the map, but as every clever treasure hunter knows, a map can be read a thousand times and still hide secrets. He'd studied an Incan temple map eighty-two times before discovering the hidden passage below the temple's well. "Excellent job," his uncle Drake had said. "I would never have found that at your age. You're a natural born treasure hunter."

But the new map would have to wait because the morning argument was just gathering steam. Clutching the squirrel, Gwendolyn peered over the table's edge. It wasn't that she was short. It was just that she almost always sat slumped real low in her chair, like a melted person, and all anyone saw during meals was the top of her head. "You eat dead things all the time and you eat them on this table so I don't see the difference." She glared at her father.

"Now Gwendolyn, if you're going to talk back to

your father, please wait until we've finished eating," Mrs. Pudding said. She stood at the stove stirring the porridge. "Let's try to have breakfast without so much commotion, like a normal family."

"And without dead squirrels," Mr. Pudding added, taking his seat at the head of the table. "Or dead frogs, or dead mice, or dead anything."

"But I've got to practice. If I don't learn how to make dead animals look like they ain't dead, then how will I get a job as a Royal Taxidermist at the Museum of Natural History?"

"Gwendolyn said *ain't*," Squeak said, climbing next to Homer. "That's bad."

Mr. Pudding shook his head—a slow kind of shake that was heavy with worry. "Royal Taxidermist for the Museum of Natural History. What kind of job is that? Way off in The City, with all that noise and pollution. With all that crime and vagrancy. That's no place for a Pudding."

"Uncle Drake moved to The City," Gwendolyn said, emphasizing her point with a dramatic sweep of the squirrel. "And he's doing right fine."

"How do you know?" Mr. Pudding asked with a scowl. "We don't even know where he lives in The City. All he's given us is a post office box for an address. And we haven't heard a word from him since his last visit. Not a

8

letter. Not a postcard. What makes you think he's doing right fine?"

"No news is good news," Mrs. Pudding said. She set bowls of porridge in front of Mr. Pudding and Squeak, then set a bowl for Gwendolyn. "Now stop arguing, you two, and eat your breakfast. And put away that squirrel."

Gwendolyn stomped her foot, then tucked the squirrel under her chair.

As Mr. Pudding stirred his porridge, steam rose from the bowl and danced beneath his chin. "I told him not to go. The City's no place for a Pudding. That's what I told him. But he said he had *important matters* to tend to. Said he had to find out about that pirate, Stinky somebody or other."

"Rumpold Smeller," Homer corrected, suddenly interested in the conversation. "Duke Rumpold Smeller of Estonia became a very famous pirate. His treasure has never been found. Uncle Drake wants to be the first person to find it."

Mr. Pudding groaned. Gwendolyn rolled her eyes.

"Eat your porridge, Homer," Mrs. Pudding said, setting an overflowing bowl in front of him. Then she planted a smooch on the top of his curly-haired head.

Mr. Pudding motioned to his wife. Though she bent close to him and though he whispered in her ear, everyone at the table could hear. "Why'd you give him so much? Don't you think he's getting kind of...*chunky?*"

She put her hands on her hips. "He's a growing boy. He needs to eat." Then she smiled sweetly at Homer.

Now, Mrs. Pudding loved all three of her children equally, like any good mother. But love can be expressed in different ways. For instance, Mrs. Pudding knew that her eldest child had a mind of her own, so she gave Gwendolyn lots of room to be an individual. Mrs. Pudding knew that her youngest child wanted to be helpful, so she gave Squeak lots of encouragement and praise. And Mrs. Pudding knew, and it broke her heart to know, that her middle child was friendless, so she gave Homer extra helpings of food and more kisses than anyone else in the house.

"Growing boy," Mr. Pudding grumbled. "How's he ever gonna fit in if he can't run as fast as the other boys? If all he talks about is treasure hunting? It's my brother's fault, filling his head with all that nonsense."

It's not nonsense, Homer thought, shoveling porridge into his mouth. So what if he didn't fit in with the other boys? All they cared about was fighting and getting into trouble. He pulled the bowl closer. And so what if he was chunky? A true treasure hunter would never pass up the chance to eat a warm breakfast. Near starvation while stranded on a deserted island had forced more than a few treasure hunters to eat their own toes.

"I like twesure," Squeak said, porridge dribbling down his chin.

"I like treasure, too," Homer said.

Mr. Pudding drummed his calloused fingers on the table. "Could we go just one meal without talking about finding treasure? Or stuffing dead animals? I don't know where I went wrong with you children."

Mrs. Pudding poured herself a cup of coffee, then added a ladle of fresh milk. "There's nothing wrong with having *interests*."

"*Interests?*" Mr. Pudding scratched the back of his weathered neck. "Stuffing dead animals and finding lost treasure—what kind of interests are those? Why can't they be interested in goat farming? Is that too much to ask? Who's gonna run this farm when I'm too old to run it?"

"Me," Squeak said. "I like goats."

As sweet as that sounded, it gave Mr. Pudding no peace of mind. Squeak was only five years old. Yesterday he had wanted to be a dragon-slayer.

"Goat farming's honest, solid work," Mr. Pudding said, dumping brown sugar on his porridge. "You children don't understand the importance of honest, solid work."

Gwendolyn rolled her eyes again. Then she sank deeper, until her bottom was hanging off the edge of her chair. Homer was bored by the conversation again. He tried to dig a hole in his porridge but the sides kept caving in—like trying to dig for treasure in mud.

Now, Mr. Pudding loved all three of his children equally, like any good father. But he didn't believe that giving them extra room to be individuals, or giving extra encouragement or extra food and kisses, did much good. Solid work meant a solid life, which in turn meant a roof, and a bed, and food on the table. What could be more important than that?

Mr. Pudding pushed his empty bowl aside, then unrolled the Sunday *City Paper*. "Wouldn't surprise me one bit if I started reading and found out that my brother had been robbed or had fallen into a manhole. I'm sure something terrible's gonna happen to him. The City's a terrible place."

As he read, muttering and shaking his head, the children finished their breakfast. Gwendolyn carried her bowl to the sink, as did Homer.

"Mom, when I'm done cleaning the stalls, can I go read my new map?" Homer asked.

"Of course." Mrs. Pudding kissed Homer's soft cheek, then whispered in his ear. "I believe in you, Homer. I know you'll find treasure one day."

Homer looked into his mother's brown eyes with their

big flecks of gold—like coins half-buried in the sand. When he became a famous treasure hunter, he'd give all the jewels to her so she could wear a different necklace every day and buy new dresses and shoes. And one of those fancy crowns that beauty queens wear.

But chores came first. He started for the kitchen door when Mr. Pudding waved the newspaper and hollered, "I knew it! I knew something terrible would happen to him!"

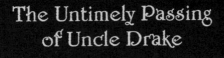

2

The Untimely Passing
of Uncle Drake

Mr. Pudding's hands shook so violently that the paper slipped from his grip. "Page three," he said. "It's on page three."

Mrs. Pudding found the alarming article and read it to her family. The article is included here. You may need to read it six or seven times before the horror fully sinks in.

EDIBLE END FOR COUNTRY BUMPKIN

A peaceful stroll in City Park was shattered yesterday by the sound of screaming. Witnesses said it was the most horrid thing they'd ever seen.

"It was the most horrid thing I've ever seen," said Mr. Portly, owner of Portly's Mustard Shop. "I was taking a stroll and there it was, this monstrous turtle with two legs sticking out of its mouth."

"The monstrous turtle is actually a tortoise," the park's groundskeeper, Morton Bun, said. "A tortoise and a turtle are two entirely different creatures."

From clues left at the scene, City police have deciphered the following: That a man named Drake Pudding, originally from the town of Milkydale, was leaning over the railing to feed the park's famous tortoises, blatantly ignoring the Do Not Feed sign, when one of the tortoises attacked.

"I couldn't believe my eyes," said Mrs. Portly. "That beast swallowed him whole. Only his legs stuck out."

"I tried to pull him free but all I saved was his shoes," Mr. Portly added.

The tortoises have been an attraction at City Park for fifty years. "They usually just laze around and eat lettuce," Bun said. "Sometimes I feed them carrots and cauliflower, but mostly they like lettuce. It's a mystery to me why this one suddenly got a craving for meat."

A veterinarian rushed to the scene and tried to induce vomiting but the tortoise refused to retch anything up. It simply fell asleep. "It's digesting," Bun said.

Plans are underway to remove the man-eating tortoise from the park.

"In all my years of keeping these grounds, no one's ever been eaten," Bun commented. "Guess that's what happens when a country bloke comes to The City."

Mrs. Pudding set the newspaper on the table. Choking silence filled the kitchen. Homer couldn't breathe. He stood stunned, watching as a fat tear rolled down his father's cheek.

"I told him not to go," Mr. Pudding muttered.

Between her own tears, Mrs. Pudding tried to comfort her husband. Squeak started crying too, even though he didn't understand what had happened.

Gwendolyn grabbed the newspaper. She stared at the

article. "That doesn't make one bit of sense. Tortoises don't eat people. That can't be true."

"Of course it's true," Mr. Pudding said, wiping his nose on his sleeve. "It's in the paper."

"Poor, poor Drake," Mrs. Pudding said. "He was such a nice man."

Mr. Pudding's sorrow swelled into outrage. "He was a dreamer. Searching all the time for things that aren't real. Look where it got him." He turned his reddened face to Homer. "Do you see, Homer? This is what happens to people who waste their lives looking for treasure. He'd be right fine if he'd stayed on the farm like he was supposed to. Do you see?"

But Homer didn't see. The kitchen had turned blurry. Blackness closed in, bubbling and churning like the inside of a tortoise's stomach. Homer backed into the corner. Uncle Drake was dead. DEAD. There'd be no more late nights talking about Egyptian tombs or Babylonian temples. No more trips to the map store to search through dusty boxes. No more decoder rings or metal detectors or titanium shovels under the Christmas tree. Homer slid down the wall and sat on the cold kitchen floor. *Why?* his mind cried. *Why, why, why?*

"This is a terrible shock," Mrs. Pudding told her husband, leading him toward the stairway. "You should go lie down. I'll bring you some tea."

"I don't want any more talk about treasure," Mr. Pudding said.

"Yes, dear."

"No one in this family is going to become a treasure hunter. I won't allow it. It's too dangerous."

"Yes, dear. Go lie down. Gwendolyn and Squeak will take care of the goats and the chickens."

For the first time since anyone could remember, Mr. Pudding did not finish his morning chores. He climbed the stairs to his bedroom, mumbling with each sad step.

"Mom," Gwendolyn said. "Something's not right. Tortoises don't eat people. I know because there's a picture of a stuffed tortoise in the Museum of Natural History's guidebook and it says that it ate bugs and water plants."

"We can talk about that later." Mrs. Pudding pulled Squeak's jacket off its hook and handed it to Gwendolyn. "Go feed the chickens and let the goats into the pasture. And keep an eye on your little brother."

After the front door closed, Mrs. Pudding knelt beside Homer. Of all the people who would be saddened by Drake Pudding's death, her middle child would grieve hardest. "I know," she whispered, hugging Homer to her chest. "I know, I know, I know," she cooed. "You loved your uncle with all your heart. And he loved you most of all."

He had. Everyone knew that.

Homer may not have looked anything like his tall, athletic uncle. He may not have been a rugged outdoorsman or a born risk-taker. But in Homer, Uncle Drake had found a kindred soul—a dreamer who preferred the world of myths and mysteries to the real world.

Homer buried his face in his mother's apron. "Why?" he asked. "Why did he have to die?"

Mrs. Pudding tightened her hug. "I don't know, sweetie. I wish I knew. I wish I could make it go away, but I can't. We'll all just have to feel sad for a while. For a long while."

And that's when someone pounded on the kitchen door.

3

A Snooty Delivery

When Mrs. Pudding opened the door, she found a short man dressed in a gray pin-striped suit standing on her porch. The man removed his black hat, revealing a shiny shaved head. "Good morning. My name is Mr. Twaddle. I have a delivery for the Pudding family. Are you Mrs. Pudding?"

"Yes. What sort of delivery?"

"This will explain everything, ma'am." His face was taut with seriousness as he handed her a white envelope.

Mrs. Pudding opened the envelope and pulled out a letter. Then she read it aloud so Homer could hear.

Dear Mr. and Mrs. Pudding,

The law office of Snooty and Snooty regrets to inform you that your relative, Mr. Drake Pudding, has been declared dead due to the carnivorous appetite of a reptilian beast. As the sole heirs of Mr. Pudding's estate, all of his worldly possessions are hereto delivered to you on this Sunday morning.

Yours respectfully,
Mr. T. Snooty and Mr. C. Snooty,
Attorneys-at-Law

"Here you go," Mr. Twaddle said, holding out a pair of brown loafers.

Homer crept toward the door as his mother took the shoes. "What are these?" she asked.

"Drake Pudding's worldly possessions."

"A pair of shoes?"

"Yes. They were pulled off his feet before..." He grimaced. "Well, anyway, they are the only items that he left behind." Mr. Twaddle plunked his hat on his head, then held out a clipboard. "If you would be so kind as to sign on the dotted line then I can be on my way. I'm very busy, you see. And I'm sure you'd like some privacy on this sad occasion." He tapped his two-toned shoe.

"Surely my brother-in-law left more than a pair of shoes? What about clothes or furniture? What about a bicycle or some dishes?"

"What about his maps and books?" Homer asked. He stood close to his mother. A faint scent of leather rose from his uncle's shoes.

"I'm sorry to say he didn't even leave his body. Just the shoes." Mr. Twaddle pulled a shiny fountain pen from his jacket. "I have other Snooty and Snooty business to attend to. If you'll sign, ma'am."

Homer held back tears as the words *didn't even leave his body* echoed off the kitchen walls. He stared at the loafers. They had no laces or ankle support or leech protection—definitely not the type of shoes his uncle would wear while hunting for treasure. He must have been out for a casual stroll in the park. Who would have thought that such a horrid thing could happen during a casual stroll?

After Mrs. Pudding signed for the shoes, Mr. Twaddle collected the clipboard and pen. "My condolences, ma'am," he said with a stiff bow. "Good day." Then he hurried toward a black sedan that was parked in the driveway. Max, Gus, and Lulu circled the automobile, sniffing eagerly. "Shoo," Mr. Twaddle said. Max jumped at the back door, scratching it with his paws. "Shoo." Max scratched harder. "Ma'am, would you be so kind as to call off your dogs?"

"Max, Gus, Lulu, come here." But the dogs didn't obey. "That's strange," Mrs. Pudding said. "Max! Gus! Lulu! Whatever is the matter with them? Do you have something in your car?"

Mr. Twaddle smacked the clipboard against his pin-striped pant leg. "I'm in such a hurry I almost forgot." He ran back to the front porch. "My apologies, ma'am, but I have a second letter." He pulled an envelope from his suit pocket. "This one is addressed to Homer W. Pudding."

"Homer?"

"Yes. Is he here?"

Homer's chest tightened as he stepped forward. "I'm Homer." He pushed his curly bangs from his eyes. Sure enough, his name was right on the envelope.

"Go ahead," his mother said gently. "Read it."

With a trembling hand, Homer opened the letter and read it aloud.

Dear Homer W. Pudding,

The law office of Snooty and Snooty regrets to inform you that your late uncle Drake left an item in your care, which he referred to as his "most treasured possession." According to the laws of inheritance, if you decide that you do not want the item, you have five days to return it to our office, whereby the item will be disposed of.

Under no circumstances will we accept the item's return after the five-day grace period.

If you choose to keep the item, any trouble that the item causes is your responsibility, though we will be happy to offer legal representation at a premium fee if you should incur any lawsuits because of the item.

Yours respectfully,
Mr. T. Snooty and Mr. C. Snooty,
Attorneys-at-Law

Mrs. Pudding smiled warily. "Oh, Homer, isn't that nice? Your uncle left you an...*item*."

Homer nodded. Could it be his uncle's gold-panning kit? Maybe it was his night vision goggles or his echo-locating gyroscope. Something, anything that would remind him of his uncle. He looked hopefully into Mr. Twaddle's squinty gray eyes.

"You sure you understand the five-day clause?" Mr. Twaddle asked. "Because we won't take the item back on the sixth day, no matter how much you beg or plead."

"Beg or plead?" Mrs. Pudding asked while wringing her hands. "Why ever would we beg or plead?"

"Oh, no reason. No reason at all." He coughed. "So, if you'll just sign here then I can be on my way. Other business, as I mentioned." He handed the clipboard and pen to Homer, who signed his full name, Homer Winslow Pudding. "Fine. I'll get the item for you."

Max, Gus and Lulu ran around the car, wagging their tails and barking. "Shoo," Mr. Twaddle said as he scurried toward the sedan. Then he opened the passenger door. Homer and Mrs. Pudding leaned over the porch railing, trying to see into the car's dark interior.

Two eyes stared back.

"Come on," the man said. He reached in. "Come on." He tugged, then tugged again. "Come on, come on." He tugged some more, then stepped aside.

A long nose emerged from the darkness, followed by the saddest face Homer had ever seen.

4

Droopy Dog

In the beginning of this book, a promise was made that this would NOT be a sad dog story. Nothing was said, however, about the dog not *looking* sad. That's an entirely different situation.

The dog slid out of the automobile, then just stood there, staring at the ground.

"What's the matter with that dog?" Mrs. Pudding asked as she and Homer walked down the porch steps.

The dog looked nothing like the Puddings' farm dogs. Its legs were way too short, its brown and white body was way too long, and its skin was a couple sizes too big. A pair of brown ears hung to the dirt like heavy curtains. A pair of brown eyes sank into fleshy folds. Homer had never seen anything like it.

Mrs. Pudding searched for the right word. "Why's that dog so . . . so . . . so *droopy*?"

"You have five days to return it," Mr. Twaddle said as he closed the passenger door. Then he looked down at the dog. "Most treasured possession," he said with clear disdain. "I'll never understand the way people carry on about their mutts. Well, good day." He tipped his hat, then ran around the car, jumped into the driver's seat, and drove off.

The dog didn't move. It moaned. "Urrrr." Just like that. Real low and grumbly. The farm dogs sniffed it a few times. It didn't sniff back. It didn't even wag its tail. The farm dogs nudged it, then, after finding it to be the most boring dog they had ever encountered, they wandered off to the field to check on the goats.

"Urrrr." The dog's jowls swayed as it moaned.

Homer felt like moaning too. A giant tortoise had eaten his uncle and all that was left was a pair of shoes and a weird dog. If ever a situation called for serious moaning it was this situation—this strange situation that didn't make any sense. But what if the moaning turned into crying? He held the letter in front of his face. His uncle wouldn't have cried. Uncle Drake had been the bravest man Homer had ever known.

Gwendolyn and Squeak ran from the barn. "Whose dog is that?" Gwendolyn asked, clutching a basket of chicken eggs.

"It's Homer's dog," Mrs. Pudding said. "Your uncle Drake gave it to him."

Squeak knelt and patted the dog's broad head. "How come it looks sad?"

"That's a basset hound," Gwendolyn said. "There's a whole section in the Museum of Natural History's guidebook about dog breeds. Basset hounds always look sad."

Squeak flattened himself against the ground and peered under the dog's belly. "It's a boy," he announced. "Just like me."

"Hey, how come Homer gets a dog?" Gwendolyn asked. "What do I get?"

Mrs. Pudding shook a finger at her daughter. "Gwendolyn Maybel Pudding! Your uncle just died. This is not the time to be worrying about who gets what. Now go put those eggs into the icebox."

Gwendolyn narrowed her eyes until they looked like minus signs. "Fine, but I ain't feeding that dog or giving it a bath just because Homer's too busy reading his stupid maps. I'm busy, too, you know. I've got a squirrel to stuff." She stomped back to the house, her hair swaying with each uppity step.

Still fighting his tears, Homer pressed the letter closer to his face. *Don't cry, don't cry.*

"I didn't know that Drake had a dog," Mrs. Pudding said. "But then again, he was so secretive about his life. Well, your father's not going to be too happy about this. We certainly don't need another dog around here. I'll break the news to him after his nap. In the meantime, try to keep that dog out of trouble." She slid the letter from Homer's fingers, then kissed his head. "Isn't it nice that Drake gave you his most treasured possession?"

Homer nodded.

Mrs. Pudding took her youngest son's hand. "Come with me, Squeak. I could use your help clearing the breakfast table. You're such a good helper."

The air stilled as the morning breeze floated away— off to tickle the neighboring farm's trees. Spring sunshine warmed Homer's face as he stood in his driveway, a weird dog at his feet. The dog gazed up at Homer. Half-moon lids, red and wet, hung beneath his sorrowful eyes. He twisted his long body so that his short hind leg could reach his ear. He scratched. Then he went back to looking sad.

Even though he stood in his own front yard, Homer suddenly felt lost. He pulled out his Galileo Compass, the one he always wore around his neck. It had been a gift from Uncle Drake last Christmas. The back of the compass was engraved with one of Drake's favorite sayings:

ONLY THE CURIOUS HAVE SOMETHING TO FIND.

Homer clutched the compass. "Uncle Drake is dead," he whispered, his lips trembling. His eyes got all misty. No longer able to fight the pain, he sat on the gravel and cried, sobs rattling his body like earthquake tremors. His jaw began to ache and his nose filled with snot. "Uncle Drake is dead."

"Urrrr."

At the end of the driveway, some kids bicycled past with nets slung over their shoulders—on their way to Frog Egg Pond. Homer wiped his nose on his sleeve. No one called out or waved to him. None of his classmates ever asked him to go catch pollywogs or to do anything at all. To put it nicely, they thought he was weird. And if they caught him crying, he'd never hear the end of it.

But no one noticed. The bikes disappeared around the bend on Grinning Goat Road. Dog stopped staring at Homer and instead, stared at the ground. Homer tilted forward to see what the dog was looking at. A black beetle was making its way between chunks of gravel, off to do something on that warm spring morning. The dog opened his mouth. The beetle's little black legs wiggled furiously as a long tongue scooped it up. The dog swallowed it whole, just like that. Homer grimaced. Had it wiggled its legs on the way down?

The dog then ambled over to a cherry tree and started eating some of the fallen blossoms. *He must be starving*, Homer thought. Max, Gus, and Lulu's kibble was kept in the barn, along with the chicken and goat feed. Homer stood and wiped gravel off his pants. "Come on," he called. "I'll feed you." But the dog stretched beneath a cherry tree and began to eat a stick.

Why would Uncle Drake have kept such an odd dog? A treasure hunter's dog needed to be fast enough to outrun thieves. This dog's legs looked like they had been cut off at the knees and some oversize paws had been stuck on. A treasure hunter's dog needed to be strong, to help pull sleds of equipment. This dog was fat. But most important, a treasure hunter's dog needed to be smart in case the unexpected occurred. This dog ate sticks.

Homer shrugged, then sat next to the dog. For the first time in his memory, he didn't feel like rushing upstairs to read his new map. He didn't feel like reading, or decoding, or even daydreaming. Every part of his body felt heavy and tired. He leaned against the tree trunk and sighed.

"Urrrr."

The dog draped himself across Homer's lap. He

whimpered, staring at Homer with his watery eyes. Even though Homer's legs started to go numb beneath the dog's weight, he didn't mind. There was some comfort in knowing that they had each loved Uncle Drake. They could be sad together.

Homer gently patted the dog's back. "What's your name, anyway?"

The dog cocked his head.

Homer ran his hand over the dog's neck, then slipped his fingers beneath a fold of skin where a collar lay hidden. He followed the collar around the dog's neck until he came to a tag. He leaned closer to get a better view. The tag wasn't the usual rabies tag, like the ones Max, Gus, and Lulu wore. This tag looked like a gold coin. A small hole had been drilled into the coin and a clasp fed through the hole. Homer released the clasp and held the coin up to the sunlight. One side had an engraving of a treasure chest. The other side had four letters, each separated by a period.

L.O.S.T.

"Is that your name? Is your name *Lost*?" The dog didn't wag his tail the way most dogs do when you say their names. Homer pushed the dog off his lap, then crawled a few feet away. "Here, Lost. Come here, Lost," he called. But the dog went back to eating the stick.

Homer looked at the coin again. Clearly it wasn't the

dog's name. Dog tags aren't usually made of gold, and names aren't usually separated by periods.

So what did *L.O.S.T.* stand for? And why had his uncle attached the unusual coin to a dog's collar?

Through the sorrow and gloom of the morning's events, a tiny spark flickered deep inside Homer. A pair of shoes and a droopy dog weren't the only things his uncle had left.

Drake Horatio Pudding had left a mystery.

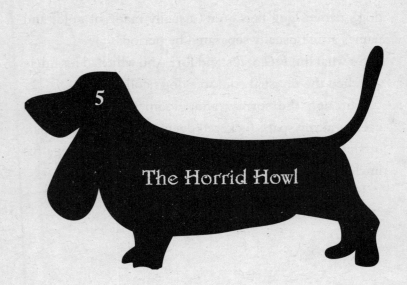

The Horrid Howl

Late that Sunday night, a spine-chilling, ear-splitting, headache-inducing howl arose from the barn. The farm animals panicked—the chickens laid warped eggs, the donkey got diarrhea, and the goats' milk turned sour. Max, Gus, and Lulu joined the howl because that's what dogs do. It's like if someone standing next to you yawned, you'd yawn, too.

The source of the howl was the new dog. He'd been shut into the barn because that's where dogs were supposed to sleep on the Pudding farm.

"Homer!" Gwendolyn yanked a book from Homer's hands. "You'd better shut that dog up. I can't sleep with all that racket and I got an oral report tomorrow on frogs."

"Huh?" Homer was sitting on his windowsill. Oatmeal cookie crumbs dotted his red bathrobe. He'd been reading a book on old coins that his uncle had given him for his tenth birthday. Having a mystery to solve had kept his mind occupied—kept him from imagining what it would be like to be eaten alive by a reptilian beast, which is a horrible thing for anyone to imagine.

Gwendolyn tossed the coin book aside. "Don't you hear that?" She opened the window. The howl shot into the room. "It's your stupid dog. Do something!"

"My dog?"

"What's the matter with you, Homer? Are you asleep or something? Yes, *your* dog. The dog that came today. The weird dog that Uncle Drake gave you."

"Oh. Right." Homer wasn't yet used to having a dog. He tightened his bathrobe and looked out the window. Then he smiled. Mr. Twaddle had believed that the "most treasured possession" mentioned in the letter was the dog. Clearly, the most treasured possession was the mysterious gold coin. If the coin had been sent in an envelope or a box, any run-of-the-mill thief might have found it. Hiding it in the folds of the dog's droopy skin had been a brilliant maneuver by Uncle Drake. The dog had been the perfect delivery boy. Homer stopped smiling. But now the delivery boy was howling.

Mrs. Pudding hurried into Homer's bedroom, the hem of her nightgown swishing across the floor. "Oh dear, what a fuss he's making. We'd better do something about that racket before it wakes your father." Mr. Pudding's nap had lasted all day and into the night. Sometimes, when sadness is overwhelming, a person needs a place to hide and sleep can be the perfect place. "Go out to the barn, Homer."

Homer slid off the windowsill. "What should I do to make him stop howling?"

"Oh for goodness sake, Homer, stop being such a knothead!" Gwendolyn said.

"I'm not a knothead." Homer scratched his ear. "I've just got a lot on my mind."

"You've got a lot on your mind?" Gwendolyn flung her arms in the air. "I've got an oral report tomorrow. How am I supposed to get an A if I'm exhausted?"

Homer had never discussed the subject of older sisters with anyone, but he was willing to bet that Gwendolyn was one of the worst older sisters in the world. Always bossing him around and calling him names. He was also willing to bet that when he did finally find some treasure, she'd change her tune. *That giant ruby's for me? Oh, Homer, you're the best brother in the world!*

"Go out there and give him some attention," Mrs. Pudding said as she adjusted her sleeping bonnet. "He's in a new place. He's probably a bit frightened."

Homer went downstairs and out the front door, where he slid his feet into his rubber boots. Clutching a flashlight, he started across the yard. A full moon hung high over the farm, casting creepy shadows. He didn't like walking across the yard at night. Thanks to his sister's hobby he knew all about the predators that stalked the farm. Gwendolyn had stuffed a fox, a raccoon, and a possum after they'd been killed by the farm dogs. Each of those critters had nasty sharp teeth. Sometimes Gwendolyn used the raccoon as a hole punch.

Homer raked the flashlight beam across the yard. Over the hill, the neighbor's dogs began to howl, a sure sign that coyotes were out and about. Coyotes often traveled in packs. Mr. Pudding hated coyotes because they'd snatched quite a few goats over the years. Homer had the sudden urge to turn back but what would Uncle Drake have thought about that? Professional treasure hunters can't be scared of the dark, not with all those caves, tunnels, and tombs to explore. And night was the best time for treasure hunting. "A treasure hunter must always cover his tracks and night provides the best cover of all," his uncle had told him.

The new dog's howl pierced the night air. Homer

thought of his dad who was trying to sleep. He forged ahead and pushed open the barn door. Max, Gus, and Lulu nearly knocked him over, wagging their black tails and frantically licking his hands. The place was in an uproar. Creatures squawked, stomped, and squealed, trying to get away from the horrid sound. Homer aimed the flashlight at the back of the barn. The new dog stood on his straw bed, his big head thrown back, his jowls flapping.

"HOWOOOOOOO!"

"Hey you," Homer called out. "You'd better stop howling or Gwendolyn's gonna get real mad."

The dog stopped. The chickens settled and the barn fell silent.

That was easy. The dog must have already figured out not to get on Gwendolyn's bad side. "Okay. Bye." Homer turned to leave.

"HOWOOOOOOO!"

The other dogs joined the howl and the chickens got all worked up again. "Uh, you'd better stop that," Homer warned.

The dog stopped and again, the barn quieted. Then the dog stepped off his straw bed and ambled toward Homer.

"Good boy," Homer said, bending to pat the dog's wrinkled forehead. "You'll get used to this place. I know it's kind of smelly in here but it's not so bad. Go on back to bed."

But the dog didn't go back to bed. He moseyed right past Homer and out the barn door.

"Hey, where're you going? Hey…*you.*" What was his name, anyway? "Hey, Rover? Spot? Come here… *Killer?*"

That dog had a mind of his own. No matter how much Homer called, no matter how many times he tried to explain that Pudding dogs were supposed to sleep in the barn, that dog kept right on walking. Across the yard he went, his big white paws pressing into the dewy ground. Homer shut the farm dogs back into the barn, then ran after the new dog. "Wait. You're supposed to sleep in the barn."

The dog stopped in front of the Puddings' porch and started sniffing the ground with his black nose. Then he lay down and started rolling, just the way the farm dogs rolled when they found a fresh patch of goat manure. *Great*, Homer thought. *Now he's gonna need a bath.* "Stop doing that."

Rolling and rubbing, the dog wiggled his rump and wagged his tail.

"Come on. Let's go back." Just as Homer reached out to grab the dog by his collar, the dog scrambled upright and started digging.

"Uh-oh," Homer said, shielding his eyes as dirt flew into his face. "You can't dig there. That's right in front of the porch." Homer had dug plenty of holes over the years in his search for buried treasure and his father had gotten mad plenty of times after stepping in those holes. So digging in the yard was strictly forbidden. Homer stepped back as clumps of dirt pelted his bathrobe. The dog went into a frenzy, digging so fast that Homer had to turn away. *I'm gonna get in big trouble*, he thought. "Cut that out!"

The digging stopped.

"Urrrr."

The dog dropped something on Homer's boot. Homer aimed his flashlight and picked the something up. He shook off a clinging earthworm. The something turned out to be a decoder ring that Uncle Drake had given to him on his eighth birthday. Too big for his eight-year-old finger, it had slipped off that very day and hadn't been seen since. "Neat," Homer said, delighted by the reunion. Even though he owned a professional decoder ring, purchased with saved allowance money, this one had a secret compartment for chewing gum.

Eager to see if the ring still worked, Homer quickly filled in the hole. "You'll just keep howling if I put you in the barn, won't you?" he asked the dog. "Maybe you can sleep on the porch, just this one time." He led the dog onto the porch and closed the porch gate. Then he patted the welcome mat. "You sleep here, okay?" The dog sat on the mat, looking up at Homer with those watery eyes. "I'll come back and check on you."

Homer rushed upstairs with the ring. He sat at his desk and wiped the ring clean with his bathrobe belt. Unfortunately, the decoder dial had rusted shut. But even though it no longer worked, he was thrilled to have it. One more thing to remind him of Uncle Drake.

Homer leaned back in his desk chair and gazed around his room. Thumbtacked maps covered every inch of the four walls and every inch of the ceiling. He'd displayed as many as could fit—the rest were rolled and kept in boxes. The newest map lay open on the desk, beckoning him to study its winding stone passageways and steep golden staircases. Inviting him to journey to a mysterious time when warriors ruled the jungles and sacrificed unlucky intruders to their gods. The warriors were long gone but someday Homer would go to that jungle and search for what they'd left behind.

But for now he was stuck in Milkydale. He yawned and rubbed his eyes. Tomorrow was a school day. He wouldn't tell anyone at school about his gold coin. Wilbur, or one of the other boys, would probably try to steal it. Homer went to turn off his light.

"Urrrr."

The new dog, having pushed open the front door, and having followed Homer up the stairs, stood with his paws on the end of Homer's bed. "What are you doing here?" Homer asked. "You can't sleep here. Dad won't let you." He pointed to the hallway. "You have to go back outside."

The dog threw back its head. "HOWOO—"

"Shhhh."

"HOWOO—"

Homer clamped his hands around the dog's muzzle. "Okay, okay. You can sleep here. Just be quiet." He heaved the dog onto the bed. Then he ran downstairs, shut the front door, ran back upstairs and shut his bedroom door. Dirty paw prints covered Homer's quilt. That dog was going to get him into so much trouble.

The dog, his eyes now closed, had settled on Homer's only pillow. "Hey, that's mine." Homer tried to pull the pillow away.

The dog opened one eye. "Grrrr."

"Fine." Homer took off his bathrobe and wadded it into a ball. Then he crawled under the covers and stuck the bathrobe pillow under his head. "Scoot over, will ya?" He tried to push the dog but it was like pushing a boulder. "How am I supposed to sleep if you're hogging the whole bed?" The dog started snoring. A bit of drool trickled from his droopy lips. "Now I'll have to wake up early just so I can get you out of here before Dad sees you." Homer pulled his bathrobe pillow away from the drool. A big paw pressed against Homer's face so he turned away. He wasn't sure he was going to like taking care of this dog. But the dog had found the decoder ring so one night sharing the bed seemed like a fair trade.

Soon, the snoring had the same effect on Homer as a yawn. Before he could worry too much about the situation, he fell into a deep sleep.

PART TWO

MILKYDALE

6

To School

"WHAT IS THAT?" Mr. Pudding hollered.
Homer, who'd been sleeping at the very edge of the bed, thanks to the new dog's tendency to kick while dreaming about rabbits, woke with a start and fell onto the floor. What was happening? Had morning come so soon? Why were his parents in his room?

Mr. Pudding cleared his throat. "I said, WHAT IS THAT?"

"It's a dog, dear." Mrs. Pudding helped Homer to his feet.

"I know it's a dog. I can see right fine. What I want to know is, *whose* dog?"

"It belonged to your brother but now it belongs to Homer."

"My brother had a dog? He never told me about a dog." Mr. Pudding yanked his overall straps over his shoulders. "That dog's not a border collie. We only keep border collies on this farm."

Mrs. Pudding handed Homer some clothes, then gently pushed him into the hallway. "You'll be late for school, sweetie. Hurry and get changed." Homer took the clothes, then wandered into the bathroom. His brain was still fuzzy with sleep as he looked into the mirror. Shallow lines from his bathrobe pillow crisscrossed one side of his face. Why had he stayed up so late?

"That's one ugly dog," Mr. Pudding told his wife as they walked past the bathroom and down the stairs. "I reckon those stubby legs can't herd worth a darn."

"Maybe we can teach the new dog to do something else," Mrs. Pudding suggested.

"Like what? Fetch my slippers? Squeak does that right fine. What use could there be in a dog like that?" Mr. Pudding's voice faded down the stairs.

What use? Homer remembered the coin. *Where was it?* He pulled a shirt over his head, crammed his legs into a pair of pants, then ran back to his room. With a relieved sigh he grabbed the mysterious coin off the windowsill. As he gazed at it, yesterday's reality crept back. Uncle Drake was dead. And this coin, for some reason, had been his most treasured possession. He had chosen Homer, his twelve-year-old nephew, to take care of it. "And I will," Homer whispered.

After a hearty, yet hurried breakfast of huckleberry pancakes and goat milk yogurt, Homer joined his sister on the front porch for the morning good-bye. Mrs. Pudding checked to make sure they had their book bags, their lunch baskets, and whatever else they needed at school. "Do you have your frogs?" she asked Gwendolyn.

"Yep." Gwendolyn pulled two stuffed frogs from her pocket. "And my notecards in case I forget some of my facts."

"You'll do right fine," Mrs. Pudding said while running her hand down Gwendolyn's long hair. "We're so proud of your interests."

Mr. Pudding stepped onto the porch, shaking his head. "That dog's still in Homer's bed. What was my brother doing with a lazy dog like that? He should have gotten himself a herding dog. He should have stayed here and worked the farm, then he'd be alive today. Do you hear, children? Goat farming's what a Pudding should do." He patted Homer and Gwendolyn's heads. "Be good at school." Then he called the farm dogs and headed toward the field.

Gwendolyn started down the driveway. Mrs. Pudding handed Homer his lunch basket. "I packed an extra cookie because I know you're feeling sad," she said. "To cheer you up, I'll take you to Walker's Department Store this weekend and get you some new clothes." She smiled, the morning sun warming her gold-flecked eyes.

Homer forced a smile. How were new clothes supposed to cheer him up? Nothing was more embarrassing than trying on boxers and jeans in the Husky Boys' section.

"And don't you worry," Mrs. Pudding said. "Squeak and I will take good care of your dog. Now hurry and catch up with your sister."

"Bye, Homer," Squeak said. Still in his pajamas, he held his mother's hand, longing for the day when he would also walk to school.

The goats, lazily chewing tender blades of spring grass, watched from the field as Homer and Gwendolyn started down Grinning Goat Road. "I don't care how many times he says it, I ain't never gonna be a goat farmer. Not in a million years." The morning breeze blew her bangs, exposing a forehead creased by years of serious thought. "I'm way too smart to be stepping in goat poop all day. And as soon as I get a job at the Museum of Natural History, I ain't never eating goat yogurt again. Even if they serve it in the museum's cafeteria, I ain't eating it. I ain't even gonna look at another goat, unless it's dead and stuffed."

Homer wasn't listening because he was reading the coin book.

Homer always walked to school with a map or book in front of his face. It takes great skill to walk while reading. If you think it's easy, go ahead and give it a try. You'll probably fall into a hole, or step on a rake, or tumble off a cliff or something. But Homer could go anywhere while reading. He could cross any terrain without injury—as if his shoes had grown eyeballs.

Because Homer was scanning the pages, searching for a coin with a treasure chest on one side, and the letters *L.O.S.T.* on the other side, he didn't notice that bluebells had sprouted along the road, or that the lilac hedges were in bloom. Or that a lone cloud hovered directly overhead.

"That's a weird-looking cloud," Gwendolyn said.

Homer didn't care about clouds. He had sixty-four more pages to read. His uncle had made sure the mysterious coin was safely delivered so it was Homer's obligation...no...it was his *honor* to figure out why.

"Stop mumbling to yourself, Homer. Here comes Carlotta and you're gonna embarrass me."

Homer peered over the top of his book as Carlotta Crescent ran down her driveway. She was the same age as Gwendolyn and the girls always walked to school together. Two border collies followed at Carlotta's heels. "Hi, Gwendolyn. Hi, Homer," she called.

"Hi, Carlotta," Gwendolyn said.

Carlotta gave her dogs a pat, then sent them back up the driveway. Her yellow plaid skirt reminded Homer of a picnic tablecloth. When she smiled at him, his legs turned to stone. She was the prettiest girl in school and he never knew what to say to her. She swung her lunch basket and started walking alongside Gwendolyn.

"Homer," Gwendolyn called. "Stop standing there. You'll be late again."

Homer hurried to catch up, his book bag thumping against his hip.

"We had puppies last night," Carlotta said.

Neither Homer nor Gwendolyn bothered to ask what kind of puppies. Carlotta Crescent lived on the Crescent Farm and her family kept border collies, just like every other family in Milkydale. "My border collies are the best herders around," Mr. Crescent always said. He had even posted a sign at the end of his driveway.

> **CRESCENT GOAT FARM**
> *Home of the Champion Crescent Border Collies,*
> *Winners of Five County Fair Blue Ribbons.*

"That's *his* opinion," Mr. Pudding had said while nailing a sign at the end of the Pudding driveway.

> **PUDDING GOAT FARM**
> *Home of the Champion Pudding Border Collies,*
> *Winners of Four County Fair Blue Ribbons.*

"Homer got a new dog," Gwendolyn said. "It's real ugly."

"Oh, that's too bad." Carlotta stopped walking and turned to ask Homer a question, but he hurried past. He didn't mean to be rude but talking to Carlotta was kind of like getting the flu—both made his stomach hurt.

With the coin book perched in front of his nose, Homer turned onto Peashoot Lane, a narrow dirt road lined with slender white birch trees. He crossed the bridge over Milky Creek and passed the mercantile and the feed store. Through the town he walked, past the Milkydale Savings and Loan, past the Milkydale Coffeehouse, until his feet led him up the steps of the schoolhouse and into the coatroom, where he closed the

53

book with a disappointed sigh. No success, yet, but he wouldn't give up. Then he placed it on a shelf because that was the rule.

Schoolhouse Rules

1. *Muddy boots must be left in the coatroom.*
2. *Gum, food, and drinks must be left in the coatroom.*
3. *Homer's maps and anything else relating to "treasure hunting" must be left in the coatroom.*
4. *Anything dead must be left in the coatroom.*

Gwendolyn stomped into the coatroom, pulled yesterday's squirrel out of her bag, and set it on the same shelf. Carlotta took off her yellow cardigan and hung it on a hook. Homer made sure his Galileo Compass was tucked beneath his shirt, then he followed his sister into the classroom.

"Find any treasure yet?" Wilbur asked as Homer walked to his desk. He asked that question most every day, in a real nasty tone.

Homer used to answer that question. When he was little, he used to tell the other kids all about how he was going to help his uncle Drake find the lost treasure of Rumpold Smeller the pirate, but that always made them laugh, and not in a nice way. They'd also laugh when they caught him digging holes or searching the fields with his metal detector. "You ain't never gonna find nothing," they'd say.

And that's what Wilbur said that very morning. "You ain't never gonna find nothing."

Homer bit his lip. He hadn't found any treasure because, like most kids, he wasn't allowed to take off and explore places like Egypt, or the Bermuda Triangle, or Dead Man's Island, which is what a professional treasure hunter does. He wasn't even allowed to go into The City on his own.

"Better use your compass or you might not find your desk," Earl said, poking Homer in the leg with a pencil.

Homer hurried past the snickering kids and settled into his seat. Then he picked up his English composition book and stuck it in front of his face.

A bell rang and the class settled. "Homer and Gwendolyn, I was very sorry to hear about your uncle," Mrs. Peepgrass said. Mrs. Peepgrass taught all the grades in Milkydale, since there were only twenty-one students. "Would you like to postpone your oral report, Gwendolyn, on account of the tragic circumstances?"

"I'm ready." Gwendolyn strode to the front of the classroom and pulled the stuffed frogs from her pocket.

Mrs. Peepgrass rapped her fingers on her desk. "Now, Gwendolyn, you know the rule."

"But these are for my report."

"I have told you many, many times that I cannot abide having dead animals in my classroom. It's unsanitary. You'll get germs everywhere."

Gwendolyn squeezed her forehead into one big crease. "I washed these frogs real good before I stuffed them. I bet there's more germs in your nose than what's on these frogs."

Mrs. Peepgrass covered her nose. "Gwendolyn Maybel Pudding, do I have to telephone your mother?"

"Go ahead and call my mother. She thinks that my interests are interesting."

Mrs. Peepgrass rushed at Gwendolyn and tried to grab the frogs but Gwendolyn darted down the aisle. The kids laughed. Homer rested his chin in his hand. It was going to be a long morning. Gwendolyn wasn't the kind of person to give up an argument. He rubbed the sore spot in his leg where Earl had jabbed the pencil. Wouldn't Earl feel stupid when an entire museum was named the Homer Winslow Pudding Museum of Treasure? He set the English composition book upright on his desk, then stuck his hand into his jean pocket and clutched the gold coin.

That's when a shadow passed over Homer's desk.

The sun, which had been shining through the row of windows, suddenly disappeared. Homer peered over his English composition book. Outside the center window, a small cloud hung much lower than a cloud is supposed to hang. Homer stared at it.

And something in the middle of the cloud stared back at Homer.

7

Weird Cloud

A cloud with eyeballs is perfectly acceptable in a fairy tale. And if the reader finds the cloud confusing, he or she can reread the chapter as many times as he or she wants until it makes sense. There might even be a glossary in the back of the book with a definition:

Cloud with Eyeballs—A distant cousin to Tree with Ears.

But in the real world, clouds with eyeballs are not supposed to exist. Even Homer, who believed in all sorts of things that weren't supposed to exist, like the Lost City of Atlantis and King Arthur's Camelot, felt dumbfounded. But a treasure hunter knows to listen to his gut, and Homer's gut insisted that this was not a mirage. So he crept to the window to get a better look.

Mrs. Peepgrass stopped chasing Gwendolyn. "Homer Pudding, what are you doing now? Why are you staring out the window?"

"Um, there's a weird cloud."

Mrs. Peepgrass pressed her hand to her bosom as she tried to catch her breath. "I swear, you Pudding children are going to be the death of me. Homer, this is not the time to talk about clouds. Gwendolyn, put those dead frogs away and get on with your presentation."

"Fine!" Gwendolyn set the frogs on the coatroom shelf, then, with her arms folded tightly across her chest, she took her place at the front of the classroom. Homer, however, stayed at the window.

The cloud moved closer. The pair of eyes blinked. They were normal-size eyes, the kind you'd find on most people's faces. When Homer tilted his head, the cloud tilted. When he tilted his head the other way, the cloud tilted the other way. It was the creepiest thing he'd ever seen.

"Homer!" Mrs. Peepgrass screeched.

Gwendolyn stomped her foot. "Homer!"

Homer wasn't trying to be rude. He didn't know that his sister had spent ten hours in front of the mirror practicing her presentation. He didn't know that she'd changed her clothes four times that morning or that she'd brushed her hair with one hundred strokes to make it extra smooth. What he did know was that a cloud with eyeballs was staring at him and that is why he said, loud enough for the entire class to hear, "That cloud has eyeballs and it's staring at me."

As soon as those words left his mouth he regretted saying them, of course. But words, once they float out of someone's mouth, are forever. If you could figure out a way to retrieve words, you'd become a very rich person indeed.

All the students jumped from their chairs and ran to the window. "What cloud?" Carlotta asked, pressing so close that Homer could smell her bubblegum lip gloss.

"I don't see a cloud," Beatrice said.

"That's because there is no cloud," Melvin said. "Homer's a liar."

Indeed, the cloud had gone. Homer leaned on the windowsill, craning his neck to look up at the sky. How could it have disappeared so quickly? Had it evaporated? Could eyeballs evaporate?

Earl punched Homer's arm. "Maybe the cloud's lost. Maybe you should let it borrow your compass."

Mrs. Peepgrass clapped her hands three times. "Back to your desks everyone. Homer, where do you think you're going?"

"I'm going outside to look..."

"This is not the time for games. Back to your desk, young man."

"Homer!" Gwendolyn curled both her hands into fists. Her face got all blotchy. "Stop being so weird. You're ruining my presentation."

Homer shuffled back to his desk. He didn't want to ruin his sister's presentation, but he couldn't shake off the image of those unnatural eyes. Maybe he'd eaten one too many huckleberry pancakes for breakfast. His body was so busy digesting the big lump of dough that his brain had gone all fuzzy.

He slid low in his seat and pulled his English composition book closer to his face. While Gwendolyn explained what the inside of a frog looked like, Homer hid from the stares and snickers of the other students. Great, another reason for the kids to make fun of him. He tried to distract himself by reading a paragraph about incomplete sentences. Totally boring. That, by the way, was an incomplete sentence.

At the end of the school day, Homer waited for the

schoolhouse to clear, then he collected his coin book from the shelf and stepped onto the porch. Soft light filtered through the school yard's grand oak tree. Gwendolyn and Carlotta had already passed the feed store and none of the other kids had stuck around to tease him. A group headed into the mercantile to buy nickel candy. Homer searched the sky, happy to see only normal clouds. He hoped that Gwendolyn wouldn't say anything to their parents, because Mrs. Pudding would probably get all worried and make him go to the doctor for an eye exam.

Homer checked to make sure his coin was still in his pocket. Then he stuck his nose into his coin book and resumed his search. By the time he reached his driveway, he had come to the last page, but the coin's identity remained unsolved. Uncle Drake would have told him not to be discouraged. "There are no unsolvable mysteries, only mysterious solutions." Homer decided that tomorrow he'd go to the library and look through the coin books. Maybe Mr. Silverstein, Milkydale's librarian, could special order some from The City. He tucked the book under his arm and reached into the mailbox.

When the Pudding children arrived home from school they immediately began their afternoon chores. Farms cannot work efficiently unless all family members do chores. If you are a city dweller, your chores are probably very different from country chores. Perhaps you have to sweep your elevator, or pick garbage off your sidewalk, or get your doorman a nice cup of coffee. If your family is rich, you might not even know what the word *chore* means. Lucky you.

Homer's first chore was to collect the mail. On that day, the mail included a catalog for farm machinery, the latest issue of *Goat World*, and some letters. The front cover of *Goat World* had a picture of two border collies. MEET THE AWARD-WINNING COLLIES OF THE CRESCENT GOAT FARM. Uh-oh. Mr. Pudding wouldn't like that.

"He's sick!" Squeak ran down the driveway, his boots kicking up bits of gravel. "He's sick. Real sick!" He grabbed Homer's hand, pulling with all his might.

"Who's sick?" Homer asked.

"Dog. He's real sick."

"Dog?"

Squeak turned his little dirt-smudged face up at Homer. "The new one. I named him Dog."

"Uncle Drake's dog is sick?"

"No, Homer. *Your* dog is sick. Come on."

8

Paint Milkshake

Dr. Huckle's white truck was parked next to Mr. Pudding's red truck. Dr. Huckle was Milkydale's only veterinarian. She specialized in the treatment of goat ailments. Since every family in Milkydale owned goats, her old truck sputtered up and down the long farm driveways most every day.

"Over there," Squeak said, pulling Homer's hand.

Dr. Huckle knelt beside a white picket fence. The new dog lay on his side, panting. The farm dogs had gathered around, as had Mr. and Mrs. Pudding and Gwendolyn.

The goats stuck their heads between the fence boards for a better view. Dr. Huckle picked up one of Dog's long ears and peered into it with a skinny flashlight. "Are you sure he drank paint?" she asked.

Mr. Pudding stuck his hands into his overall pockets. "Saw it with my own eyes. I was getting ready to white-wash the fence and I went into the barn to get my paint-brush. When I came back, that dog had its face right in the bucket, lapping away."

A splat of white paint had dried on Dog's nose. His tongue, streaked white, hung out the corner of his mouth. He moaned as his belly rumbled. Homer remembered the time at the Milkydale County Fair when he'd eaten five corn dogs. Late that night, his stomach had puffed out like a basketball and had rumbled like a thundercloud.

Poor Dog.

Homer fiddled with the mail, wondering what to do. It was *his* dog, after all. He knelt and patted Dog's head. "Will he be okay?" he asked.

"That depends." Dr. Huckle poked her flashlight into Dog's mouth. "Has he eaten anything else that he's not supposed to eat?"

"He ate some sticks and a beetle," Homer said.

"Sticks and a beetle?" Mr. Pudding rubbed the back of his neck. "What kind of dog eats sticks and beetles?"

"And cherry blossoms," Homer added.

"That's very odd." Dr. Huckle removed a stethoscope from her black bag. "Very odd."

"I'm sure he'll be right fine," Mrs. Pudding said, kissing the top of Homer's head. "Not to worry. He's just confused, being in a new place and all."

Dr. Huckle pressed the stethoscope against Dog's chest.

"Is he gonna die?" Squeak asked.

"He isn't going to die," Mrs. Pudding said, taking Squeak's hand. Then she leaned close to the doctor. "He isn't? Is he?"

"What dog in its right mind would drink whitewash?" Mr. Pudding asked. "I don't think that dog's got a right mind."

"Whitewash looks like milk," Mrs. Pudding said. "Maybe he thought it was milk."

Mr. Pudding shook his head. "That dog's got something wrong with its brain if it thinks paint is milk. I couldn't get it to help herd the goats. It slept most of the day."

"Basset hounds aren't bred to herd," Dr. Huckle replied. "But they can smell a rabbit ten miles away. Rabbit hunters love bassets."

"We don't hunt rabbit," Mr. Pudding said.

"Urrrr." Dog's back legs went stiff and he closed his eyes.

"Did he die?" Squeak cried, clutching Mrs. Pudding's arm.

"No. He's still alive," Dr. Huckle said. "I'd better take his temperature."

Homer grimaced. *Poor Dog.*

But as Dr. Huckle reached for her bag, Squeak, trying to help, accidentally knocked it over. A little glass bottle rolled out and broke against a rock. A pungent odor rose into the air. Max, Gus, and Lulu tucked their tails between their legs and ran off. The Pudding family stepped away, as did the goats. "That stinks," Gwendolyn said.

"It's aromatic spirits of ammonia," Dr. Huckle said, fanning the air with her hand. "Nothing to worry about." But then she rubbed her chin in puzzlement. "Hmmm. That's interesting. Your new dog's not reacting."

While the Pudding family members were pinching their noses, Dog just lay there.

"I wonder." Dr. Huckle took a cotton ball from her bag, dabbed it in the spilled liquid, then held it to Dog's nose. He didn't wince or move. He just kept panting. "Amazing," Dr. Huckle said. "Why, I do believe that this basset hound can't smell."

"Can't smell?" Mr. and Mrs. Pudding said.

Dr. Huckle nodded. "That explains why he's been eating strange things. He's got no sense of smell to tell him what he's supposed to eat."

Mr. Pudding folded his arms. "I told you there was something wrong with that dog. I knew it the moment I saw it. Leave it to my brother to find a useless dog."

"Maybe he's not useless," Homer said hopefully.

"This is quite a tragedy," the doctor said. "The sense of smell is the most important sense for a dog. They greet one another through smell, they mark their territories with their individual scents. They choose mates, hunt, herd, and track all based on a keen sense of smell. This poor guy is shut off from the ordinary day-to-day things that dogs do. He's at a terrible disadvantage." She collected her instruments and closed her black bag. "I don't think there's any kind of treatment. He's going to require a lot of looking after. You can't leave him alone. He'll need to be closely watched."

Mr. Pudding snorted. "What? We don't have time to watch a dog."

"Well then, I suggest you find a new home for him, maybe with a nice retired person who has nothing to do. Without supervision, that dog's certain to eat something poisonous and the next time it might kill him."

"I'm not watching him," Gwendolyn said. "I'm way too busy."

"I'll watch him," Squeak said.

Mrs. Pudding gave her youngest son a hug. "That's

very helpful of you, Squeak, but it's Homer's dog. Homer will watch him."

"Homer?" Gwendolyn said. "How's he gonna watch a dog? He doesn't pay attention to anything but his maps."

"I didn't know how to take care of a baby until I had one," Mrs. Pudding said. "But I figured it out and I'm sure Homer can learn how to take care of this dog." She tousled Homer's curly locks. "Why don't you come inside, Dr. Huckle, and I'll make us a nice pitcher of lemonade. I've got some molasses cookies just out of the oven."

"Make sure your dog drinks plenty of water," Dr. Huckle told Homer. "He should be feeling better by morning."

"You'd best get a bucket, Homer, and clean up that broken glass before one of the goats steps in it," Mr. Pudding said.

The ammonia's sharp stench drifted away as Homer cleared the glass. While everyone else enjoyed molasses cookies in the Pudding kitchen, Homer sat next to Dog. They stared into each other's eyes—one pair bright blue, the other pair brown and watery. Homer had been so focused on the gold coin, he hadn't thought much about the dog. Had Uncle Drake known that he couldn't smell? Maybe Dog wouldn't be much use on an expedition, but he'd proven useful as a delivery boy. An immediate fondness filled Homer as he realized that this dog, with its long ears and loose skin, with its big head and short legs, was different from all other dogs.

And as it has happened throughout history, and as it will continue to happen, two outsiders found one another.

"I'll watch over you," Homer said.

"Urrrr."

The Unexpected Invitation

In an attempt to cheer up her husband, who was still reeling from the news of his only brother's untimely passing, Mrs. Pudding made chicken and dumplings for supper, which was the Pudding family's favorite meal. Mr. Pudding sat at the head of the table, a pile of mail at his elbow. His gaze darted to his brother's loafers, which sat in a corner. Homer, at the other end of the table, tried not to look at the shoes.

"How did things go at school today?" Mrs. Pudding

asked as she set bowls on the table. "Did everyone enjoy your frog presentation?"

Gwendolyn sat extra slumped. "*Someone* ruined my presentation by acting weird." She narrowed her eyes at Homer. He shifted nervously. Maybe his sister would be nice for once and not tell on him.

"Gwendolyn Maybel Pudding, it's not polite to call another person weird," Mrs. Pudding said.

"What would you call a person who saw a cloud with eyeballs? 'Cause I know what I'd call that person." Gwendolyn tapped her spoon against the table, waiting for a response. Homer held his breath. Squeak giggled.

"I'd call that person not right in the head," Mr. Pudding said.

Gwendolyn sat up straight and jabbed her spoon in Homer's direction. "Well guess what? That person was Homer, and he announced it to the entire class right when I was about to give my presentation. I almost died."

Mrs. Pudding gasped. Mr. Pudding looked down the table and scowled. "Homer? You told the entire class that you saw a cloud with eyeballs? What's the matter with you?"

What's the matter with you? Homer had been asked that question many times in his life, but he'd never come up with an answer. *What's the matter with you?* is easy to answer if your nose is bleeding or your foot has suddenly fallen off. "There's nothing the matter with me," he said. "I'm sorry. I didn't mean to ruin Gwendolyn's presentation."

"Of course there's nothing the matter with you," Mrs. Pudding said.

"I want to see a cloud with eyeballs," Squeak said, tucking his napkin into his shirt.

"Well you can't because there's no such thing," Mr. Pudding said. "Cloud with eyeballs." He poured himself a glass of goat milk. "I don't know where I went wrong."

FRRRRT!

Mr. Pudding nearly tipped over the milk pitcher. "What in the name of goat cheese was that?" He lifted the edge of the tablecloth and glared at the source of the sound.

Dog, who lay at Homer's feet, was having a terrible time with his digestive system. The whitewash had begun to work its way through his intestines, along with all the other things he had eaten that day, which included a slug, half of Squeak's grilled cheese sandwich, and some goat poop.

"Put that dog outside," Mr. Pudding grumbled.

"We can't put him outside, dear." Mrs. Pudding walked around the table, ladling chicken and dumplings into everyone's bowl. "If we put him outside he might eat something he's not supposed to eat."

"He might die," Squeak said.

Mr. Pudding took a bite of supper.

FRRRRT!

"How's a man supposed to enjoy his meal with a dog like that under the table?"

"Dear, you're spraying bits of carrot all over your son."

Mr. Pudding stabbed a dumpling. "Dr. Huckle charged me thirty dollars just to tell me that the dog can't smell." He shook his head. "I don't think keeping that dog is a good idea. How's it gonna fit in around here?"

Homer reached down and patted Dog's head. "But I'll watch him, I promise."

Squeak slid under the table. "Don't make him go away," he cried.

Mrs. Pudding looked long and hard at her husband. No words were necessary with a look like that. Mr. and Mrs. Pudding might not have thought that Homer was up to the task of watching the new dog, but as long as Squeak put up a fuss, then the dog would stay.

Mr. Pudding sighed, ate the dumpling, then shuffled through the day's mail. "What have we here?" He held up a silver envelope.

Gwendolyn dropped her spoon and squealed. "That's

from the Museum of Natural History!" She threw herself across the table and yanked the envelope from her father's hand. Homer grabbed Squeak's milk glass to keep it from falling over as the table lurched. Squeak climbed back onto the bench.

"Look, look. They finally wrote back." Gwendolyn bounced on her chair. "I can't believe it, I can't believe it." She stuck her butter knife under the envelope's flap and ripped it open.

"Just a minute," Mrs. Pudding said, leaning over Gwendolyn's shoulder. "That envelope isn't addressed to you."

"Of course it is," Gwendolyn said. "I've written eighty letters to the museum's director. Of course it's addressed to me."

"No, it's not. It's addressed to Homer."

"To me?" Homer swallowed a soft lump of potato. Except for his subscription to the Map of the Month Club and the letters from his uncle, he never got anything in the mail.

Gwendolyn stared at the silver envelope, her lips slowly forming the words, "Mr. Homer W. Pudding." Color drained from her face. She didn't move, didn't take a breath. She looked as if someone had stuffed her.

"Sweetie?" Mrs. Pudding whispered.

Gwendolyn's fingers turned white as she clutched

the envelope. Then she opened her mouth so wide that everyone at the table could see the little wobbly thing in the back of her throat. She screamed so loud that, out in the yard, the farm dogs began to howl. From beneath the table, Dog howled, too.

"Howooo!"

"What's this nonsense?" Mr. Pudding said. "Mind your temper, young lady."

Gwendolyn's mouth snapped shut. "Homer W. Pudding?" she read again. "HOMER W. PUDDING?"

Mrs. Pudding pulled the letter from Gwendolyn's sweaty grip. "Calm down, Gwendolyn."

But Gwendolyn didn't calm down. "WHY IS THAT LETTER FOR HOMER?" She pounded her fist on the table. The dumpling bowls rattled. "WHY? WHY? WHY?"

Homer had no idea why the letter would be for him. He'd never written to the Museum of Natural History. He'd never even visited the place.

"This is so unfair. Homer ruined my presentation and you aren't even punishing him, and now he gets a letter from the Museum of Natural History." Tears of frustration filled Gwendolyn's eyes.

"I'm sorry, Gwendolyn," Homer said.

"Now Gwendolyn, let's see what the letter says before you work yourself into a huff." Mrs. Pudding handed the letter to Homer. "Honestly, I don't know why there always has to be so much commotion around here. I'm sure most families don't act like this at the supper table. Go on, Homer. Read it. Out loud, please."

This was the second letter Homer had received in as many days and it wasn't even his birthday. He pulled out a silver card, cleared his throat, then read the fancy engraved lettering.

> *Dear Mr. Homer W. Pudding,*
> *You are cordially invited to attend a VIP gala event tomorrow night at the Museum of Natural History. Please arrive promptly at ten o'clock in the evening. You will find the VIP entrance on the south side of the building.*
>
> *Yours truly,*
> *Madame la Directeur*
> P.S. **Do not** *bring your parents.*

"What nonsense is that?" Mr. Pudding asked. "Do they really think we're the kind of parents who'd send our son to a party all by himself?"

"What's a VIP?" Homer asked.

"It means, 'very important person,'" Mrs. Pudding explained.

Color returned to Gwendolyn's face like a volcanic eruption. "Homer's not *important*."

"Everyone's important," Mrs. Pudding said, kissing Homer's cheek. Then she took her place at the table.

Homer would never, in a million years, consider himself important. Important people did important things, and all Homer did was read maps and books about treasure hunting. He slipped his bare feet under Dog's warm belly. "It must be a mistake," he said. It had to be a mistake. Gwendolyn's dream was to work at the Museum of Natural History as a Royal Taxidermist. The invitation should have gone to her. "You can go instead," he told her, holding out the card. Gwendolyn's eyes widened.

"No one's going," Mr. Pudding said. "That museum's in The City and no member of the Pudding family is going to step foot in The City. Not after what happened to my brother."

"But, Dad…" Gwendolyn gripped the edge of the table.

"I don't want to hear another word about it. And that's final." Mr. Pudding wiped the back of his neck with his handkerchief. "Now all I want is some peace and quiet so I can eat my supper."

FRRRRT!

"Oh, for the love of…"

"Homer," Mrs. Pudding said. "Why don't you take

your dog outside so he can do his business before bed-time. And close up the barn while you're at it."

"Okay. Come on, Dog." Homer was glad to get away from Gwendolyn's angry glare and his father's ornery mood. And further discussions about clouds with eye-balls. As he walked to the door, Dog followed, leaving a trail of noxious fumes.

Outside, Homer stepped into his boots. Max, Gus, and Lulu greeted him, their tails wagging. They sniffed Dog, then spread out across the yard, their noses on the alert for predators. The full spring moon floated above a horizon of rolling hills. While Dog piddled, Homer put Max, Gus, and Lulu into the barn. Then he reached into his jean pocket and pulled out the gold coin. The last time he'd seen his uncle was over two months ago when he'd come to the farm for a visit. He'd brought a tube of pink lip gloss for Gwendolyn, some fancy perfume for Mrs. Pudding, a pigskin football for Squeak, a bottle of imported brandy for Mr. Pudding, and a pocket tele-scope for Homer. "Very soon I'll be setting out to search for Rumpold Smeller's treasure," he'd told Homer as they'd sat in Homer's room. Homer remembered the excitement dancing in his uncle's brown eyes.

"Rumpold Smeller's treasure?" Homer had barely been able to believe it. "Did you find the map?"

"I can't discuss the map's whereabouts. Not yet. But

I can tell you that I found something else. Something *amazing*." A boyish grin had spread beneath Uncle Drake's scruffy mustache. "Something that will definitely help me find the treasure."

"Something amazing? And it's not the map?"

"Even more amazing."

"What is it?"

"I'll tell you soon. When the time is right. You see..." He had paused, then he'd gripped Homer's shoulder. "Even the most noble treasure hunter can go bad. The lure of limitless wealth can eat at the soul the way cancer eats at the body. You must be very careful about trusting others in this business. Always remember that."

Homer had nodded. He'd read enough treasure-hunting biographies to know that trusted friends had turned on one another on many occasions. "Can I come with you?" he'd asked.

"When you're older. Right now it's too dangerous for a young'un. There are forces that will stop at nothing to get Rumpold Smeller's treasure. Besides, I've still got to get funding for the expedition." He'd run his hand over his square jaw, his voice turning serious. "Listen to me, Homer. I know you're not happy here in Milkydale. Your ma says you've been having a hard time with the kids at school. But don't let their teasing turn you away from what you love. It doesn't matter what other people think. Treasure hunting's in your blood as much as it's in mine." He'd put an arm around Homer's shoulder. "I want you to promise that if anything should happen to me, you won't give up your dreams. Because if I don't find Rumpold Smeller's treasure, then I want you to be the one to find it. Promise?"

"I won't give up my dreams," Homer had vowed. "I promise."

That last visit seemed so far away. It had ended with a promise, one that Homer was determined to keep. He held up the gold coin. Could the coin be the something amazing that his uncle had spoken of? Could it be the answer to finding Rumpold Smeller's treasure? What did those letters stand for? Land of Strange Things? Land of Secret Things? Land of Secret Treasures? Oh, that sounded good.

"Pssst."

"Huh?" Homer's heart skipped a beat. He looked up.

A small puffy cloud hovered above one of the gnarled cherry trees. But instead of eyeballs peering out, a man hung upside down from the bottom of the cloud like a trapeze artist.

10

Ajitabh the Cloud Man

If ever you think you might be seeing something strange, like a man hanging upside down from the bottom of a cloud, you should probably give your eyes a good rub. It could be a piece of dust or a stray eyelash that's causing the disturbance. This is often the reason why people think they see UFOs. A fruit fly stuck on the cornea looks exactly like a flying saucer.

But even though Homer rubbed and rubbed, the man just kept hanging there.

"Hello?" the man called, waving his arms. "I say, can you hear me?"

Dog whimpered and hid behind Homer's legs. Homer's heart banged against his chest as if it were trying to get out. He rubbed his eyes again. It took a few moments for his vision to clear and when it did, the man had moved closer.

"Are you Drake's nephew?" The man's shiny black hair swung in the air. The hem of his white shirt began to inch down his torso, toward his armpits. He reached up and tucked it into his pants, which disappeared into the cloud.

"Uh-huh," Homer said, frozen in place. Dog squeezed his head between Homer's shins, a quiet growl rising in his throat as he looked at the upside-down stranger.

The man stroked his pencil-thin mustache, which curved around his mouth until it met up with a pointy black beard. "You don't look one flamin' bit like Drake."

The shock wore off as Homer realized that these were the eyeballs he'd seen earlier. It hadn't been a mirage. He tilted his head, trying to get a better view of the cloud's belly. "How do you do that?" he asked. "Clouds are just water vapors."

"Actually, a cloud is a collection of tiny water droplets or ice crystals that are so light they can float in air." The man spoke with an odd accent. The cloud whirred, then lowered a few feet. The man held out a hand. "Allow me to introduce myself. My name is Ajitabh. I was born in New Delhi but schooled in Britain. I have heard a great deal about you, Homer."

Homer reached up and shook Ajitabh's hand. "How do you know who I am?"

"Your uncle Drake was my dearest chum. Terrible way to go. How in the blazes did he let himself get eaten by a tortoise, that's what I'd like to know?" He paused, a sad look spreading across his face. At least Homer thought it was a sad look—it's difficult to tell on an upside-down face. "My deepest sympathies to your family and all that."

"You knew my uncle?"

"We used to hunt for treasure together."

"You did?" For a brief moment, Homer felt giddy. What luck to meet a friend of his uncle's just when he was trying to solve a mystery that his uncle had left him. "What kind of treasure? Where did you go? What did you find?"

A whirring sounded again and the cloud lowered until Ajitabh and Homer were face to upside-down face. "This is not a social visit, I'm sorry to say. I must know if your uncle left you anything—anything at all after his death. You must tell me." A reddish tinge had spread across his cheeks and neck.

Homer wanted to trust this supposed friend of his

uncle's. Ajitabh might know what *L.O.S.T.* stood for. He might know if Uncle Drake had found Rumpold Smeller's map. But something didn't feel right. Maybe it was the serious tone of the man's voice, or the way the moonlight created sinister shadows on his face. Homer's gut told him not to say anything about the coin. "Sometimes gut instinct is the only thing a treasure hunter can rely upon," Uncle Drake had often said.

Homer stuck his hand in his pocket and gripped the coin protectively. "He didn't leave me anything."

The man raised his eyebrows. "I say, have you something in your pocket?"

"No." Homer took a step away, nearly tripping on Dog who was still wedged between his shins.

"Why the devil are you backing away?"

"No reason," Homer said, his suspicion growing.

The cloud floated closer. "I know Drake left you that hound." Ajitabh pointed at Dog. "But you must tell me if he left you anything else. He would want you to tell me. Your life could be in danger."

A tingling sensation crept up Homer's spine as he remembered his uncle's words. "Even the most noble treasure hunter can go bad."

"Homer!" Mr. Pudding called from the kitchen door.

Homer turned toward the farmhouse but the cherry trees blocked his view.

"Homer, don't go." Ajitabh reached out and grabbed Homer by the front of his shirt. Homer squirmed. "You must tell me. What did Drake leave you?" The cloud whirred and Homer rose into the air, his boots dangling a couple of feet off the ground. "Tell me."

"Let go," Homer said, kicking his legs. He tried to loosen Ajitabh's grip.

"Grrrrr." Dog clamped his teeth around the heel of Homer's boot and pulled.

"Tell me," Ajitabh demanded, tightening his grip so that the seams under Homer's armpits began to rip. "Don't be a bloomin' fool. You can trust me." He grimaced, straining to hold Homer's weight. His face turned purple.

"He gave me the dog. Nothing else," Homer said. "Let me go." He kicked with all his might. Two buttons popped off his shirt. The seams ripped further. Dog pulled the boot loose, then clamped his teeth around the other boot.

"Homer!" Mr. Pudding called again. "Where are you?"

"Dad!" Homer cried.

Ajitabh glanced over at the farmhouse, then looked Homer right in the eyes. "I'll come back for you," he whispered. "Until then, be careful. Remember, your life could be in danger." He let go of Homer's shirt.

"Ouch," Homer said as he tumbled onto the grass.

Dog stuck his nose into Homer's scared face. Expecting Ajitabh to grab him again, Homer scrambled to his feet and ran. "Dad!"

"Homer?" Mrs. Pudding stepped onto the porch and held out her arms as Homer barreled into them. "Whatever's the matter? What happened to your shirt? Where is your other boot?"

"There's...there's...there's..."

"Is it a coyote?" Mr. Pudding started down the stairs.

"No." Homer pointed frantically toward the cherry trees. "A man. A man in a cloud."

"What?" Mr. Pudding stopped in his tracks. He and Mrs. Pudding looked toward the trees. But there was no cloud. And no man. Only a dog chewing on a boot.

"Homer," Mrs. Pudding scolded. "You're supposed to make sure your dog doesn't eat anything bad. Go get that boot away from him."

"But Mom, there was a man hanging from a cloud. He grabbed me." Homer raised his arms to reveal the ripped shirt seams.

Mr. and Mrs. Pudding shared a worried look. Then Mrs. Pudding sat on the porch swing and pulled Homer next to her. Squeak peeked outside but she waved him back into the house. "Your teacher just telephoned," she told Homer as she tucked one of his curls behind his ear. "You didn't do your subtraction problems today and you didn't turn in your Milkydale history essay last week or your solar system diorama. Mrs. Peepgrass said that even though we've talked about this over and over, you still spend most of your time daydreaming. And today you made up a story about a cloud just to get attention."

"I didn't make it up. There *was* a cloud at school today and I just saw it right over there," Homer insisted, pointing again. "And there *was* a man hanging upside down from the cloud. He said he was a friend of Uncle Drake's and that they used to hunt for treasure together."

"Hunt for treasure?" Mr. Pudding walked back onto the porch. He folded his arms, took a deep breath, then gave Homer a long, serious look. "Now look here, Homer, I've had just about enough of this. Treasure hunting destroyed my brother's life and I'll be hog-tied if I'm gonna let it destroy yours."

"Now, dear…"

"No. Enough is enough." Mr. Pudding tucked his thumbs into his overall straps. "There's no use in having the boy believe that he can do something he can't. He's not one bit like my brother. He's not cut out for mountain climbing, or deep-sea diving, or any of that crazy stuff my brother was always doing. Homer's future is here, on this farm, and I'll have no more talk of treasure hunting in this house. And no more books about treasure hunting or magazines or maps or anything that has to do with treasure hunting."

Mrs. Pudding and Homer's mouths fell open but they sat in silence. Though Mr. Pudding hadn't raised his voice, his tone left no room for argument.

"The only books he'll be reading are the ones that Mrs. Peepgrass tells him to read. And don't think he can sneak in some treasure reading at the library. Tomorrow morning I'm calling Mr. Silverstein and telling him that Homer's not allowed to step foot in there unless it's on official school business. And that's my final word." Then, having finished his declaration, Mr. Pudding stomped off toward the barn.

Homer slid to the far end of the porch swing, away from his mother's hugs and kisses. No more books or magazines about treasure hunting.

No more maps.

He shivered as if he'd been dunked in an ice bath.

And so, on that very night, Mr. Pudding hauled all of Homer's treasure hunting things into the attic. Homer ran his hand along his empty bookshelf. His first edition of *The Biography of Rumpold Smeller*, his worn copies of *Long Lost Ships* and *X Marks the Spot: An Encyclopedia of Buried Treasure* were gone. Thumbtack holes and faded rectangles were the only evidence that his beloved maps had once covered the now bare bedroom walls.

The room echoed with emptiness, for Homer, unlike other boys his age, did not collect rocks, or slingshots, or trophies. No kite hung from the curtain rod, no skateboard stood in the corner, no squirt gun sat on the windowsill, ready in case an unsuspecting sister walked by. Everything he cherished had something to do with treasure hunting—his rusty trowel, his collection of plastic mummies, his Holy Grail replica—and now they were gone. Only his bed, his clothes, and a desk covered in boring schoolbooks remained. Oh, and two items Homer had managed to hide—the Galileo Compass that hung beneath his shirt and the gold coin tucked in his pocket.

Mrs. Pudding cracked open the bedroom door. "I thought you might like some company." She opened the door wider and Dog ambled in. He circled a few times, then stretched across a pile of dirty clothes. Mrs. Pudding laid a half-eaten boot on Homer's desk. "You'll have to wear your old sneakers until we can get to Walker's Department Store."

Homer turned away. He didn't care about the stupid boot.

"I know you think this is unfair," his mother said softly. "But try to understand, Homer. Your father just wants you to stop spending so much time with your maps and books and instead, spend more time with everyone here in Milkydale."

"I don't like Milkydale." Homer folded his arms as tight as he could. "And no one in Milkydale likes me."

"I like you, Homer. I love you. And Squeak loves you, and your whole family loves you. But we worry about you." She turned his swivel chair around and looked into his blue eyes. "Milkydale is your home. You must try to be a part of it."

"But Uncle Drake would want me to…"

"Drake was a good uncle but he had some wild ideas. He wasn't quite right in the head. Do you understand?"

"Dad's afraid that I'm not quite right in the head, isn't he?"

"He's just trying to protect you. When you're all grown up you can make your own choices. And maybe you'll follow in your uncle's footsteps." She smiled tenderly. "But for now you must pay attention in school and help on the farm. And stop making up stories. Now get into your pajamas and go to sleep. You'll feel better in the morning." Then she left, closing the door behind her.

Homer didn't feel like changing into his pajamas. He didn't feel like paying attention in school or helping on the farm. There was only one thing he wanted to do, but there were no more coin books to search through.

Moonlight drifted through the bedroom window, casting a soft glow about the room. Dog got up from the laundry pile and scratched at the side of the bed. With a heave, Homer lifted him onto the quilt. Then they lay side by side. Dog's stretched-out body reached to Homer's knees. He pressed his wet nose against Homer's cheek. His warm breath smelled like rubber boot but Homer didn't mind. Dog knew what it felt like to be misunderstood. People thought he was stupid because he ate strange things, but it had nothing to do with lack of intelligence. People thought Homer was weird because he dreamed about strange things. But it had nothing to do with being "not right in the head."

Homer and Dog turned their sad faces toward the map-less ceiling. "They think I'm crazy," Homer whispered, giving Dog a good scratch. "I know the cloud man was real and I think he wanted Uncle Drake's coin. Tomorrow, Dad's gonna call Mr. Silverstein at the library and then I won't be able to do any research. How will I find out what *L.O.S.T.* stands for?"

With a groan, Dog got up and ambled to the end of the bed. Then he slid off and stood in front of Homer's bedroom door. "Urrrr."

"It's too late to go out," Homer said.

Dog scratched at the door. "Urrrr."

"I said it's too…" Homer sat up. "Hey, that's a good idea. I could go right now." Half-excited, half-terrified, he tiptoed to the window. There was plenty of moonlight to see by. If he kept to the side of the road, the overhanging tree branches would hide him should anyone in a cloud fly by. Uncle Drake had said that nighttime was the very best time for a treasure hunter to move about.

"You'd better stay here," he told Dog. "They don't let dogs in the library."

Dog cocked his head and watched as Homer put on a green corduroy jacket. Then Homer grabbed a flashlight from his desk drawer and his Swiss army knife, which his dad hadn't confiscated because Mr. Pudding believed that every boy needs a Swiss army knife.

"Stay," Homer said, opening the door.

"URRRR."

"I'll be right back. Stay."

Dog threw back his head. "HOWOO—"

Homer clamped his hands around Dog's muzzle. "Okay, okay, you can come."

11

The Library at Midnight

Sneaking out of an old farmhouse is not an easy feat, what with creaking floorboards and squeaking stairs lying in wait. Add Dog's *click-clack*ing toenails and it was some kind of a miracle that they managed to get out without waking the rest of the family.

Homer hesitated on the front porch. He'd never done anything like this before. His dad would explode if he found out. But something deeper than fear tugged at Homer—the need to be validated, to be understood. He'd prove to everyone that he had what it took to be a treasure hunter. *Take away my maps, take away my books, but I'm going to find out why Uncle Drake sent me this coin!* With a deep breath he started down the driveway, Dog at his heels. "Keep a lookout for clouds," he whispered to Dog.

A moonlit sky, freckled with stars, stretched over the rolling hills. Despite the moonlight, most people would have stumbled, for night's shadows can camouflage holes and ditches. But Homer was an expert at walking while reading, so it really didn't matter whether he walked to town by sun or moon. Once down the driveway he clung to the edge of the road, listening for trucks. Except for rustling leaves and branches, the night was silent.

Homer nearly jumped out of his skin when Carlotta Crescent peeked out from behind her mailbox. "Whatcha doing, Homer?"

"Nothing," he replied.

"What's that?"

"My new dog."

"What's his name?"

"Dog."

"What kind of name is that?"

"I dunno." *Darn it.* Carlotta would probably tell Gwendolyn about his sneaking out, and Gwendolyn would most assuredly tell their parents.

"I bet you're wondering what I'm doing out here in

the middle of the night," Carlotta said. Her long hair was pulled back in a yellow ribbon that matched her yellow bathrobe and slippers. "Don't you want to know what I'm doing?" She held up a pair of binoculars.

Homer shrugged. "I guess so." He wanted to tell her that she was holding a pair of Extra Strong Borington Binoculars, designed by Sir Richard Borington, a famous treasure hunter who had preferred to conduct most of his quests from the comfort of his elephant's velvet saddle. But that was the sort of information that always got him labeled *weird*.

"I'm doing a report on screech owls and my mom and dad said I can sit out here and watch for them, but only this one time since it's a school night." She yawned. "I haven't seen any. Whatcha writing your report on?"

Had Mrs. Peepgrass assigned a report? "I gotta go," he said, continuing down Grinning Goat Road.

"I'm bored," Carlotta called after him. "Can I come with you?"

Other than Gwendolyn, Carlotta was the only kid at school who actually talked to Homer. For a second, he thought about inviting her along. It would be less scary to have someone to walk with, but Ajitabh had said he'd be back and that might put Carlotta in danger. Besides, Homer didn't want anyone to know about the coin. Not yet.

"Can I come with you?" she asked again.

"No." Homer kept walking.

"Why can't I come with you?"

"Just because. Sorry."

"Oh. Okay. Bye, Homer. See ya tomorrow."

Homer turned onto Peashoot Lane, hurried over the wooden bridge, then stopped at the edge of town. He'd never been there in the middle of the night and the stillness surprised him. No trucks chugging along, no old men complaining about the price of grain, no school kids screaming from the playground. Dark and shut up tight, Milkydale seemed like a ghost town.

Rather than cutting across the road, Homer kept close to the buildings, in case the cloud drifted by. The Milkydale Public Library stood next to the schoolhouse. The old wooden building had gotten a new coat of white paint last year and a new brass sign for the entrance. Moonlight tumbled off the library's roof but each of the windows was pitch black. Homer hurried up its front steps. He tugged on the door handle. Even in a town like Milkydale, where no one ever stole anything except maybe a piece of nickel candy now and then, library doors were locked at night. He'd brought the Swiss army knife for lock-picking—something he'd never done but had read about. But fortunately, just around back, Homer spied a window that was cracked open. He found a wheelbarrow in the library's garden and rolled it beneath the window. Then he collected some garden bricks and stacked them inside the wheelbarrow, until, when standing on the top brick, his stomach reached the window's sill. For a moment he wondered if he'd forgotten something. Flashlight, check. Swiss army knife, check. Compass and coin, check. Everything seemed in order. He slid the window open and climbed in.

Losing his balance, Homer landed face-first in the stairwell that connected the library's main floor to its upper floor. No one yelled, "Who's there?", which was a huge relief. His face throbbed, but his nose didn't seem broken. Cautiously, he stood. Then he pulled the flashlight from his pocket and clicked it on.

The moment Homer entered the main room of the Milkydale Public Library, his fear faded. You see, the library was one of the few places where Homer felt completely at ease, where he was supposed to do the exact thing that he loved doing best of all. In a library, people who *don't* read are considered to be the weird ones.

Anyone who loves books the way Homer does, loves libraries, too. It doesn't matter if the library has fancy red leather chairs and gold-plated shelves that reach to a vaulted ceiling, or if the library has splintery wooden benches and shelves made of old milk crates. It's the scent that sets the book lover at ease. It's better than grandma's perfume, or freshly baked chocolate chip cookies, or even toast. It's a scent derived from paper, mildew, dust, and human endeavors. The oldest books smell best of all, ripened by time like expensive goat cheese.

But there was no time to stand around enjoying the aroma. The coin mystery needed to be solved!

Homer knew exactly where to find books about coins but just as he started across the worn carpet, someone knocked on the front door. He whipped the flashlight around. Carlotta pressed her face against the door's oval window.

"What are you doing here?" Homer asked after unlocking and opening the door.

"You forgot your dog," she said, squeezing her way in. Dog followed, his velvety ears swaying with each step. "I was petting him and then you disappeared into the shadows. He started walking around in circles. He looked so sad. What's the matter with him?"

"He can't smell. I guess if he can't see me, he doesn't know how to find me," Homer realized. He felt real bad about forgetting Dog. He still wasn't used to having something to look after. He reached down and patted Dog's head. Next time they went for a walk, he'd be sure to bring a leash. "Sorry, boy." Dog wagged his short tail.

"Say, whatcha doing in here?" Carlotta closed the

front door. "I don't think you're supposed to be in here at night. You might get in trouble."

"Thanks for bringing me my dog. You can go home now."

"But I want to know what you're doing." She raised her eyebrows. "Besides, I don't want to walk home by myself."

Homer sighed. It looked like he was stuck with her. "I've got some work to do so you'll have to wait until I'm done. Then I'll walk you home."

"Are you working on your report?"

"Uh, yeah," Homer lied.

He wandered over to the reference section and ran his flashlight's beam along the shelves. Then he tucked the flashlight under his arm and pulled out an oversize book called *Coins of the World* by I. M. Flump. He sat on the floor, set the heavy book in his lap, and opened to the last section, called "Rare and Unusual," which seemed like a good place to begin.

"The library's creepy at night," Carlotta said, sitting next to him. "I don't like it. Let's go home."

"I gotta find something," Homer said. Dog pushed his way under the coin book, draping his long body across Homer's legs. Homer balanced the book on Dog's back. His gaze flew across page after page, searching for anything that resembled the coin in his pocket.

Something on the upper floor made a creaking noise.

"Do you think this place has ghosts?" Carlotta pressed closer to Homer. A soapy scent drifted from her hair.

"Ghosts?" Homer looked up. Treasures often came with ghostly companions—previous owners who refused to leave their worldly goods behind. Maybe books came with ghosts, too. A tree branch rapped against the window. Both Homer and Carlotta held their breaths. Then, Homer's flashlight went dark. Carlotta grabbed his arm.

"What happened?" she whispered.

Homer shook the flashlight. "The battery's dead." Even though moonlight trickled in through the library windows, it wasn't enough for Homer to read by. And he needed to read, as quickly as possible, before his parents noticed that he was gone. After sliding Dog off his lap, he hurried to Mr. Silverstein's desk. The power went out all the time in Milkydale, especially during winter storms, so everyone kept a stash of candles. Sure enough, he found some in the middle drawer, along with a book of matches.

"Homer, are you almost done? My dad's gonna get real mad if he finds out I'm not looking for screech owls."

"I've got to find something, Carlotta. It's real important."

"Okay." She smiled as Homer sat next to her. "You

know, everyone thinks you're weird but I think you're smart."

"Uh, thanks."

And so, with Dog repositioned on his lap, and Carlotta Crescent holding the candle by his side, Homer continued his search for the coin. Carlotta talked about her new puppies and her upcoming birthday party and a million other things while Homer focused on the task at hand. Page after page, illustration after illustration, minute after minute, hour after...

It smelled like smoke.

Homer opened his eyes. Not used to staying up so late, he had fallen asleep against the bookcase. Dog was asleep on his lap, snoring loudly. Carlotta was asleep, too, her head on Homer's shoulder. Why did it smell like smoke and what was that glow?

"Carlotta!" Homer shook her. "It's on fire. The library's on fire!"

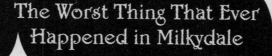

12

The Worst Thing That Ever Happened in Milkydale

"O n fire? Oh no!" Carlotta cried. "I must have dropped the candle."

Sure enough, that's exactly what had happened. Just after Carlotta had dozed off, the candle had slipped from her hand, rolled across the floor, and found the edge of a dictionary. The flame had climbed the dictionary, then had made its way down the shelf, growing like a fiery serpent as it had fed upon book after book.

It was the most horrific sight Homer had ever seen.

"We have to get out," Carlotta said. "Mrs. Peepgrass

told us that if we're ever in a fire, we're supposed to get out right away."

"But the books…"

"Homer! Mrs. Peepgrass said that *things* aren't as important as *lives*."

Homer, who only heard about one percent of the things Mrs. Peepgrass said, remembered the story of Millicent Smith, an American treasure hunter who died after going back into her blazing house to try to save her bungee cords. "She was the world's best volcano jumper," Uncle Drake had told him. "The treasure-hunting community lost her expertise forever. Fire shows no mercy. Remember that."

Smoke stung Homer's eyes as he helped Carlotta to her feet. He tucked the coin book under his arm. "Come on, Dog." They headed toward the front door but didn't get far as flames leaped off the bookshelf, blocking the way. Carlotta started coughing. Dog barked at the flames.

"The stairs," Homer said. He grabbed Carlotta's hand and pulled her toward the stairwell. "Dog!" he called. But Dog stood his ground. The room was quickly filling with smoke. Homer rushed back and tugged on Dog's collar. "Come on, will ya?" But Dog shook off Homer's grip and kept barking. Homer couldn't get a full breath. He dropped the coin book, wrapped his arms under

Dog's belly, and picked him up. Wobbling beneath Dog's weight, he carried him into the stairwell.

With a groan, Homer collapsed. Dog tumbled onto the floor. The window was still wide open but too high to reach. Scrambling to his feet, Homer put his hands under one of Carlotta's slippers and pushed her up the wall. "Help!" Carlotta cried, sticking her head out the window. "HELP!"

Out in the main room, the library's front windows buckled and shattered. A wailing siren approached. Luckily, the fire truck didn't have far to go because the fire station stood in the center of town. Headlights lit up the night as members of the Milkydale Volunteer Fire Brigade arrived, most in their pajamas.

"HELP!" Carlotta yelled again and again.

"HELP!" Homer yelled, struggling to push her higher up the wall. Smoke trailed into the stairwell. Dog started barking again.

A pair of big hands reached through the window and pulled Carlotta to safety. Then a ladder slid through and the fire chief landed next to Homer. "Anyone else inside?" he asked.

"No," Homer said, breathless. The fire chief slung Dog over his shoulder like a sack of potatoes and they all made their escape.

Sitting on the grass across from the library, Homer

held tight to Dog and watched as flames shot up the roof. It was the worst thing he'd ever seen and he fought the urge to vomit. Despite the brigade's valiant efforts, the library could not be saved. Mr. Pudding pulled up in his truck, as did Mr. Crescent and every other farmer within earshot of the siren. As the last timber fell, attention turned to the boy, girl, and dog, each smudged with soot, sitting in the grass.

"It's my fault," Carlotta said, teary-eyed. "I dropped the candle."

"No," Homer said. "It's my fault. I—"

"Of course it's your fault," Mr. Crescent interrupted. "My Carlotta would never have gone into the library at night on her own."

"Hold on there, Crescent," Mr. Pudding said. "Don't you go blamin' my boy."

The fire chief took off his hard hat. "What were you doing in there?" he asked.

Homer looked at his father, whose face had turned as pale as the moon. How could he tell him? The library was supposed to be off limits. Treasure-hunting books were off limits. He'd be so disappointed.

"He burned it down on purpose," someone yelled. "He's always been weird."

"He's a juvenile delinquent."

"No," Carlotta cried. "It's not Homer's fault. We fell

asleep and I dropped the candle. And his dog can't smell so it couldn't warn us about the smoke."

"Can't smell?" Mr. Crescent puffed out his chest. "The Pudding farm's got a dog that can't smell? That sounds about right."

"This is the worst thing that's ever happened in Milkydale," someone said.

As people crowded closer, pointing their fingers and shouting accusations, Homer hung his head and closed his eyes, desperately wishing for a book to hide behind. Burning down the best place in Milkydale hadn't been part of his plan. He'd failed miserably. Maybe his dad was right—maybe he wasn't cut out for treasure hunting. Maybe his future was back on the farm after all.

"What are you going to do, Pudding?" Mr. Crescent asked. "Your boy burned down the only library in the county."

"What am I going to do?" Mr. Pudding hollered. "Your girl's the one who dropped the candle."

"Yeah? Well your dog's the one that can't smell. If it had been one of my champion border collies, there'd have been no fire."

Then everybody started yelling. Blame and insults were thrown around. Poor Mr. Silverstein, the librarian, arrived in his blue pajamas and started to cry. Homer's whole body trembled as he sat in the grass, smoke filling the night sky. He couldn't bear the pain on Mr. Silverstein's face. He felt cold all over.

Carlotta jumped to her feet, her yellow bathrobe stained with grass. "Homer saved my life," she said, but no one paid any attention.

"You'll have to build a new library," Mr. Crescent said. "You hear me, Pudding? You'll have to build us a new one."

Mr. Pudding shook his cap right in Mr. Crescent's face. "I'll build a new one. Don't you worry, Crescent. I'll build a right fine library. That's my promise."

"Everyone clear out," the fire chief ordered. "There's nothing more to see. Take your kids home. We'll deal with this in the morning."

Mr. Pudding didn't say anything on the drive home. Nor did Homer. What could he say? *Sorry* seemed too small a word.

The red truck's headlights cut through the lingering smoke, which hung foglike along the road. Dog sat in the truck's bed, his jowls wiggling with each bump in the road. Homer stole a sideways glance at his father, who gripped the steering wheel as if he were afraid it might fly out of his hands. How was he going to build a new library? Where would he get the money or the time?

Everyone hates me, Homer thought. *Even my own father.*

When they got home, Mrs. Pudding, Squeak, and Gwendolyn were waiting on the front porch, brimming with questions. Homer watched from the truck. "Homer burned down the library," Mr. Pudding said. "I promised to build a new one."

"Homer did *what*? You're gonna *what*?" Mrs. Pudding wrung her hands. "How can we afford that?"

"I gave my word and a man's only as good as his word."

That's when Dog, once again forgotten, threw back his head and howled from the truck bed.

Mr. Pudding spun around. "Crescent's right," he said angrily. "A normal dog would have smelled the smoke. Tomorrow morning I'm calling that lawyer's office and telling them to come and take it away. And that's my final word!" He stormed into the house, with Squeak and Mrs. Pudding at his heels.

Homer didn't want to go inside and face the endless string of questions. His mother's face would be heavy with disappointment and worry. Squeak would cry because Dog was going to be returned. Gwendolyn would tell him that he'd ruined her life. Truth was, he'd ruined all their lives. At least that's what he told himself as he sat in the truck, trembling.

Homer felt his dreams drifting away like smoke in the wind. Why fight it? Goat farming was his destiny. He'd get a pair of overalls from the Husky Boys section at Walker's Department Store and start learning to run the family business.

"Urrrr." Dog scratched at the back window. Homer slid out of the passenger seat and climbed into the truck's bed. He wrapped his arms around Dog. "He's gonna send you away," he whispered. "I don't want you to go. It's all my fault." He'd ruined Dog's life, too. Dog was supposed to have a happy life on the farm, but now he'd be sent back to Snooty and Snooty's law office. What had the letter said? That if the item was returned, it would be . . . *destroyed*?

Gwendolyn stepped onto the truck's back bumper. "Come on. Get out of the truck," she said in her bossy voice.

"Leave me alone." Dog's fur was soft against Homer's face.

His sister leaned over the tailgate. "Listen. We're gonna pretend that we're going to bed. Then as soon as Mom and Dad fall asleep, we're gonna run away." She jumped off the bumper and opened the tailgate.

"What?" Homer looked up.

"I'm going to that VIP party, no matter what Dad says. But your stupid name is on the invitation so I need you to go with me."

"Gwendolyn, you don't understand. I just burned

down the library. I broke Dad's rule about not going there and now you want me to run away? Don't you think I'm in enough trouble?"

"Exactly my point. You're already in huge trouble. How much worse can it get?" She put her hands on her hips. "I'm figuring you can stay here and go to school and get made fun of because you burned down the library, or you can come to The City with me." She scowled real hard. "Well?"

"The City?"

For a few crazy moments, Homer Winslow Pudding had tried to cast his dreams aside. But as much as a goat can't stop being a goat, Homer couldn't stop being a treasure hunter.

And so, a tiny spark of an idea fluttered through his mind. Surely The City had a library, probably much larger than the one he'd burned down—probably with a huge collection of coin books. The mysterious gold coin had to be valuable, otherwise why would his uncle have hidden it? Maybe it was worth enough money to build a new library! And while he was there, maybe he could find out more about his uncle. Find out where he had been living. Find out why all his stuff had disappeared. There might be a clue amid his uncle's belongings that would give Homer a better chance of completing his uncle's quest to find Rumpold Smeller's map.

But Mr. Pudding had forbidden them to go to The City.

On the other hand, Mr. Pudding had said that a man's only as good as his word. Homer had promised his uncle that he'd never give up his dreams.

Dog poked Homer with his wet nose. There was one more reason to go. If Dog was sent back to Snooty and Snooty, he'd be destroyed. Surely Homer could find a nice, new home for Dog along the way. A happy, safe home.

"Okay," he told his sister. "We'll go with you."

PART THREE

THE CITY

13

The Runaways

Running away from home is not a good idea. Unless, of course, you happen to be forty years old, and then your parents will probably shout, "Hurrah!" and change the locks the minute you've stepped off the front stoop. But in the case of Gwendolyn and Homer, ages fifteen and twelve, setting off in the middle of the night would only bring their parents immense heartache and worry.

Perhaps they had good reasons for running away— Gwendolyn, to pursue her dream of becoming a Royal

Taxidermist at the Museum of Natural History, and Homer, to honor his promise to his uncle, to help his father rebuild the Milkydale library, and to hopefully find Dog a safe, new home. But what they didn't understand, as they tiptoed past their parents' bedroom, was that children who travel alone often become the targets of evil-minded scoundrels. And because their decision to run away had been impromptu, which means that they hadn't thought it out, neither of them had packed an extra pair of underwear, or a toothbrush, or a first-aid kit, or a tin of cookies so they wouldn't starve to death.

However, they did bring the things that were most important to them. For Gwendolyn, a duffel bag filled to the brim with her stuffed creatures and her copy of *The Official Guidebook to the Museum of Natural History.* For Homer, his Swiss army knife, his Galileo Compass, a flashlight, and the mysterious coin.

Homer's legs ached because he'd never walked from his house to town twice in one night. "Hurry up!" Gwendolyn yelled about a million times as she galloped down the road. Dog's little legs could barely keep up, while Homer's didn't fare much better. His thighs started to chafe.

At 12:46 a.m., Homer, Gwendolyn, and Dog arrived at the Milkydale train depot. It wasn't much of a train depot, just a water fountain with a rusted-shut pump and a bench sitting under a tin roof. The Pudding children had taken the train a few times, when they'd gone to the coast to visit their grandparents. But never at night. And never alone.

Fortunately, the depot sat at the edge of the fairgrounds, so Homer didn't have to look at the pile of smoldering ashes that had once been the town's beloved library. Gwendolyn sniffed the air. "It still smells like smoke. Even way over here."

Shame heated Homer's face. He wondered if burned books made a special kind of smoke that clung to the world forever, in the same way that a book, once read, clings to its reader forever.

As he untied the makeshift leash from Dog's collar, a rope he had grabbed on the way out of the house, Gwendolyn dumped her duffel on the bench, then read the train schedule. "We've got ten minutes till the next one. How much money did you bring?"

Dog settled under the bench for a nap. Homer tucked his flashlight into his jacket pocket, then turned his pants' pockets inside out. "I've got a ten-dollar bill, a five-dollar bill, three one-dollar bills, and some change." He'd been saving his birthday money so he could buy a new protractor and some large sheets of paper for map drawing. "How much do you have?"

"Two dollars," Gwendolyn said.

"That's it?"

"Taxidermy supplies are expensive, Homer. Do you have any idea how much formaldehyde costs?" She snatched Homer's money from his hand. "I hope it's enough for our tickets." Then she plopped herself beside the duffel and pulled out the mysterious invitation. "Don't you just love her name? Madame la Directeur. I bet she's smart *and* beautiful." As Gwendolyn rambled on and on about the invitation, the moon disappeared behind a cloud.

A cloud? Could it be *the* cloud? There was no place to hide. The tin roof offered no camouflage. Was the cloud moving closer? Homer crawled under the bench.

"Homer? What are you doing?"

"Nothing."

"You're soooo weird." She opened her museum guidebook. "I wonder where the party will be. I hope it's in the Hall of African Mammals. How long do you think it takes to stuff a giraffe?"

Homer wished she'd be quiet. Back in the cherry orchard, when he'd met Ajitabh, the cloud had made a whirring sound. If Homer could hear above Gwendolyn's jabbering, he'd know if Ajitabh was trying to sneak up on him. But on and on she spoke, about things of absolutely no interest to Homer.

There wasn't much room under the bench, and the

cement felt cold and rough against his palms. He laid his head on Dog's warm side. Terrifying images marched through his mind in a sort of nightmare parade—the gaping mouth of a man-eating tortoise, hands reaching from a cloud, row after row of flaming books. *Think of something nice*, he told himself. He tried desperately to conjure a pleasant image but the flames kept shooting across the library. Closing his eyes tightly, he let Uncle Drake's face fill his mind.

Homer knew every inch of his uncle's face because he had stared at it during countless hours of storytelling—the scruffy mustache, the long nose, the jagged scar at the base of the chin. But what Homer most remembered was how Uncle Drake's brown eyes would dart excitedly when he got to a dangerous part of a story.

"I wish you could have seen it, Homer. That chasm was bottomless, I swear it. If the rope had broken one second earlier, I'd be a goner for sure."

A train whistle scattered Homer's memories. Startled, he bumped his head on the underside of the bench. Dog rolled onto his belly and peered out. The *chug chug* of the engine grew louder and a white light illuminated the little depot. Gwendolyn jumped to her feet. "Come on, Homer," she called, waving at the approaching train.

Homer crawled out from under the bench as the black train pulled up in a swirling dance of steam. The conductor stepped out. "Where're you two headed?" he asked.

"To The City," Gwendolyn said.

He looked around, then pushed his black hat off his forehead. "Don't usually see children traveling alone at this hour. You got someone meeting you in The City?"

"Uh, yeah," Gwendolyn said. "We're going to stay with...our aunt."

"You got money for your tickets?"

"Yeah."

"Well, get on board then. Got a schedule to keep."

Without a moment's hesitation, Gwendolyn picked up her duffel and climbed up the metal stairs. Homer's legs froze as doubt overcame him. Was he doing the right thing? The City was very far from Milkydale. Maybe he should go home. He was just a kid, after all. Couldn't his promise to never give up his dreams wait until he had grown up? Mrs. Peepgrass would get real mad if he missed school for any reason other than a contagious rash or a fever. And his mother and father would worry even though he'd left a note on his pillow: DON'T WORRY. I'M GOING TO MAKE EVERYTHING RIGHT.

"Urrrr." Dog pressed his front paws on the train's first stair and tried to pull himself up. "Ur, ur, ur, ur, ur." He bounced on his little back legs and wiggled his rump.

"Looks like your dog wants to go for a ride," the conductor said.

"Ur, ur, ur, ur, ur."

Dog was trying awfully hard to get up those steps. Did he know that he needed to find a new home? "You're right, Dog," Homer said, pushing away his doubts. "We've come this far, we might as well keep going." He wrapped his arms around Dog's fat belly, took a deep breath, and heaved him up the steps. Then they followed Gwendolyn into a dimly lit car. The conductor blew a whistle and the train chugged out of the station.

"That dog will cost extra," the conductor said, his voice booming through the car. It was dark in there, and there appeared to be no other passengers.

"What?" Gwendolyn cried, sliding into a window seat. "But he's just gonna sit on the floor."

"Doesn't matter if he sits on the ceiling."

Gwendolyn folded her arms. "But he's just a stupid dog. He can't even smell."

"Doesn't matter what he can or can't do. Those'll cost extra, too." The conductor pointed to her duffel from which three pairs of glass eyes peeked out.

"But they're dead," Gwendolyn said. "All of them are dead."

"Oh." The conductor fiddled with his whistle. "Well, I guess I won't charge you if they're all dead. But the dog's not dead so he'll still cost extra." He held out three tickets. "Two minors and one dog, round-trip from Milkydale to The City. That'll be thirty dollars."

Homer stepped forward. "But we only have twenty dollars."

The conductor tapped his black shoe. "You mean to tell me that your parents sent you to the train station without an adequate amount of money to pay your fare?" He leaned close to Homer. "You wouldn't be running away now, would you?"

Homer held his breath, trying to remember Gwendolyn's lie. "We're going to see our . . ."

"Our aunt," Gwendolyn said.

"Well, you're still ten dollars short," the conductor said.

"Wait. We haven't counted the change." Gwendolyn reached into her pocket and pulled out the coins that Homer had handed over. "Five, thirty, fifty-five, hey, what's this? It looks like gold. It's got some letters on it." Homer gasped as his sister waved the coin at the conductor. "Will this pay for the rest of our fare?"

"That's mine!" he cried, jumping over Dog. "I didn't mean to give it to you. Give it back!" He lunged at Gwendolyn's hand but she moved it out of reach. "Gwendolyn!" He threw himself at her, knocking her against the window. The coin flew out of her hand, over the seat, and landed somewhere in the train car.

Pling.

"Get off, Homer!" Gwendolyn pushed him aside. "You almost flattened me."

Homer fell to the floor, frantically searching for the coin. "Where is it? Where'd it go?" He looked under the seats and up and down the aisle. "Where is it?" His hands and knees turned black with dust and grime. "I've got to find it." He stuck his head under each seat. Gum wrappers, potato chip bags, and spilled mints lay about, but no gold coin.

"If you can't pay the fare, I'll have to let you off at the next stop," the conductor said snippily.

Homer's eyes filled with angry tears. "It's lost. You lost it, Gwendolyn! Uncle Drake gave it to me and you lost it." That piece of information slipped out, unintended. "YOU LOST IT!"

"Urrrr?" Dog cocked his head. Then he stuck his nose to the floor and started sniffing. The sniffing turned to snuffling as he ambled down the aisle to the last row, which was hidden in darkness.

"Dog?"

"Careful, kid," the conductor said. "The light's not working back there."

"Dog?" Homer pulled out his flashlight and hurried to the back of the car. In the last row of seats he found Dog lying on his back, rolling from side to side on the floor. Then Dog flipped onto his feet and started pawing at something.

Homer crouched and aimed his flashlight at Dog's paws. "Hey, you found it," he said as the light bounced off the edge of the coin. But no matter how desperately Dog dug, he couldn't free it.

For the coin was trapped beneath the largest black boot Homer had ever seen.

14

An Elongated Lady

It's not nice to make fun of people just because they have big feet. There are many smart, nice, talented people who happen to have feet like dinosaurs. And it causes them great embarrassment when their feet keep elevator doors from closing, or when they have to stand sideways on the escalator, or stick their legs out the sunroof.

Dog whimpered and scratched at the massive boot. Flakes of dried mud fell onto the floor. Homer, still crouching, thought that he might be able to slide the coin free with his Swiss army knife, before the boot's owner even noticed. But just when he reached into his pocket, a hissing noise issued from somewhere overhead. He squinted as a lantern lit up the row of seats.

"Do you like sitting on the floor?" a baritone voice asked. "I sit on the floor when I'm feeling too sad to sit on the couch. When I'm extra sad I take long walks. Nighttime is the best time for a long sad walk."

Homer tilted all the way back to get a full view of the speaker. Up, up, up she went—an expanse of black cape that ended near the ceiling where her head happened to be. Homer cleared his throat and said loudly, so that she could hear him all the way up there, "I'm sorry to bother you but that's mine." He pointed.

The woman set the lantern on the seat beside her. Then she leaned forward. Her long silver hair tickled Homer's face. "This?" Dog stopped scratching as she lifted her boot and picked up the coin with fingers the size of hotdogs. She looked at one side, then the other. Without any sort of expression, she returned the coin to Homer.

"Thank you." He clutched it in his sweaty palm, silently swearing to never lose it again.

The woman stared at Homer. Homer stared at the woman. Dog stared at a cockroach as it scurried past. Then he ate it.

"Hey, you still owe ten dollars," the conductor said, walking to the back row. "If you don't pay, I'll have to deposit you at the next station."

The woman titled her head, studying Homer as if he were a brine shrimp in a petri dish. "Do you wish to be deposited at the next station?" She raised her oversize eyebrows.

Homer shook his head. He'd never met a woman with such a low voice. She sounded like Mr. Fitzwaller, who sang in the very back row of the Milkydale Community Choir.

"The next station is a dreary place, indeed." The woman sat up straight and reached into a black purse. "Conductor, this boy does not wish to be deposited at the next station so I shall pay the amount due." She handed a ten-dollar bill to the conductor. In return he handed three tickets to Homer, then walked to the next car.

Homer peered down the aisle. Gwendolyn, who was busy sorting through her duffel bag, trying to figure out which of her animals would most impress Madame la Directeur, had forgotten all about her brother.

Homer shoved the tickets into a pocket. "Thanks again." Then a question slipped out of his mouth. "Are you from Iceland?" He had every reason to believe the woman was Icelandic because, on his eighth birthday, Uncle Drake had given him a book called *Long Forgotten*

Lands. The inset maps were gloriously painted in rich sepia tones. His favorite was titled "The Land of Giants." According to that chapter, a race of very tall people had once inhabited Iceland. There, deep beneath the volcanoes, they had mined for emeralds, sapphires, and rubies.

The woman folded her gargantuan hands. "I am not from Iceland. Are you from Iceland?"

Homer's neck had started to cramp so he moved into the seat across from the woman. "I'm from Milkydale. I thought you were from Iceland because you're…" He hesitated, not wanting to insult her.

"Ah, I see where you're going with this." She pulled her cape around her shoulders. "You believe that I am a giant. Well, I am, but not the kind to which you refer. I was born with a condition that made me grow very fast. In the same way that your dog was born with a condition that kept him from growing."

"He's got a *condition*?"

"His breed has a form of dwarfism. That's why his legs are disproportionate to his body."

Dog walked in a circle, then lay at Homer's feet. "His legs *are* kind of short," Homer said. "Hey, do you like dogs? This one's real nice and he needs a home. My dad won't let me keep him."

She frowned. "I do not keep animals. I tend to sit on

them. Not on purpose, of course. That dog is a fine-looking hound. I'm sure someone will want him."

"I hope so." Homer reached down and patted Dog's head. "I might have trouble finding him a place. He can't smell."

"We all have things we cannot do." She gazed out the top of the window. Darkness whooshed past. "I cannot ride a Ferris wheel. I do not fit, you see." A tear sparkled in her right eye.

Homer imagined the Ferris wheel at the Milkydale County Fair, with its bright lights and tin-can music. Sitting at the very top of the wheel was the closest he'd ever come to flying.

"Ferris wheels aren't that great," he lied.

"Thank you for attempting to make me feel better, but I still feel as sad as always." The tear wiggled, then fell onto her wide cheek. "There are so many things I cannot do. I cannot ride a horse. I cannot thread a needle or fit into an elevator. I cannot sneak up on anyone."

Homer felt very sorry for this woman. Her sadness reached across the space between their seats and tugged at him. "I can't play football," he said. "I'm not fast enough, so I always get tackled. And I can't do oral reports because my heart starts pounding so loud that I can't hear my own voice. And I can't go to the library because I got in trouble and Dad said I couldn't go." He bit his lower lip. He was about to confide something to a total stranger, but he felt as if she'd understand. "The library burned down." His stomach lurched as the blaze ignited, fresh and furious in his mind. "It was an accident but it was my fault."

"That's a terrible thing, burning down a library." The tall woman continued to stare out the window. "I, too, have done terrible things. Unspeakable things. But I cannot call them *accidents*." She whipped her head around so quickly that Homer jumped in his seat. "You should keep that coin in a safe place. The City is full of thieves." She reached into her bag again and pulled out a matchbook. "If you tuck your coin into this, it will be safe. No thief would want to steal a matchbook."

Homer smiled nervously, then took the matchbook. It read: ZELDA'S TRINKET SHOP. As the lady watched, he tucked the coin into the matchbook, then stuck it in his pocket. It seemed like a good idea. Not as brilliant as hiding it beneath a fold of sagging basset hound skin, but good nonetheless. A whistle blew and the train slowed.

"Gloomy Moor," the conductor announced from the doorway. "All off for Gloomy Moor." Brakes squealed as the train came to a full stop.

"This is my destination." The tall woman collected her bag and lantern, then raised herself from the seat, bending to keep from bumping her head. "It was nice to meet you, Homer Pudding."

"It was nice to meet you, too," he said.

Once the woman had departed, Homer returned to his sister's row. Dog followed, eating a piece of discarded bubble gum along the way. "Did you find your coin?" Gwendolyn asked, dusting off one of her stuffed rats.

"Yeah."

"Did you give it to the conductor?"

"No. But the tickets are paid for, so don't worry." Homer shuffled his feet. "Hey, Gwendolyn. Could you not tell anyone about the coin? I mean, that it was from Uncle Drake?"

Gwendolyn shrugged. "I don't care about your stupid coin."

Homer took the window seat opposite his sister. Outside, at the edge of the Gloomy Moor station, the woman raised her lantern and looked back at Homer. Then she waved. He politely waved back. With a swirl of her black cape, she disappeared into a cloud of steam. It had been nice of her to pay the fare. But he wondered, as the train pulled away, what kind of terrible, unspeakable things she had done. And then a shiver darted down his backside.

She'd called him Homer Pudding.

He didn't recall mentioning his name.

15

Tomato Soup Girl

"H omer."

Homer rubbed his eyes. A bad dream evaporated until only its edges could be remembered—flames, sirens wailing, more flames. Dog lay across Homer's lap. With the armrest pushed out of the way, Dog took up two seats. His drool had seeped through Homer's jacket sleeve. "What's going on?" Homer asked.

"We're here," Gwendolyn said.

Homer pressed his sleepy face to the window. Tall

buildings whizzed past, illuminated by streetlights and the first rays of morning. Block after block of bricks and cement, iron and steel, colorless, cold and rigid. Home, with its dappled hills and shady trees, seemed a world away.

The conductor hurried through the car. "Next stop The City. All off for The City." A nervous flutter tickled Homer's stomach. He had a lot to accomplish, but wasn't sure where exactly to begin.

The train screeched to a stop. After tying Dog to the rope leash, Homer followed Gwendolyn into the station. Frantic people swarmed every inch of the building. Coming and going, lugging suitcases and backpacks, they pushed around Homer, while a few tripped over Dog. The front of the station proved louder, with honking trucks, shouting vendors, and roaring engines. The noise hit Homer square on, like a box to the ears. A blast of stink collided with his face, thanks to a row of taxicabs that sat idling at the curb, their tailpipes spitting out snakes of exhaust. "Yuck," Gwendolyn said, plugging her nose.

Because Milkydale's air was always sweet with fruit blossoms and freshly mowed grass at this time of the year, taking a deep breath was an enjoyable activity. Homer didn't realize that if you took a deep breath in The City at this time of year, or at any time of year for that matter, you stood a good chance of inhaling one of those exhaust snakes and dying from a fit of coughing.

"Homer, stop coughing, you're embarrassing me." Gwendolyn slung her duffel bag over her shoulder. "Excuse me," she said to a passing man in a checkered suit. "Which way is it to the Museum of Natural History?"

"Twenty-seven blocks that way," he replied with a tilt of his head.

Twenty-seven blocks? Homer had no idea The City was so vast. A delivery truck drove past. Homer's eyes watered as he broke into another coughing fit. By the time his vision cleared, Gwendolyn was a half block ahead.

"Come on," he urged, tugging on the rope. But the going was slow because Dog decided that it was absolutely necessary to stop and pee on *everything*. He lifted his short leg on an iron fence, a fire hydrant, and a garbage can. "Gwendolyn!" Homer cried. "GWENDOLYN!" She stopped and waited. "I don't want to go to the museum yet," he said when they finally reached her. "I need to find a library."

"Too bad." She wrapped her arms around her duffel. As they crossed a busy intersection, a bunch of cars honked.

"But I need to do some research," Homer insisted.

"Whatever. Do it later."

"I need to do it now, before..." *Before the man named Ajitabh finds me.* "Before Mom and Dad come to get us."

"Dad won't come to get us. He'll never set foot in The City. And Mom has to stay home and take care of Squeak."

"But I need to..."

Gwendolyn's hair soared as she whipped around. "This is the most important day of my life, Homer, and you're trying to ruin it. I'm not missing that party. Do you hear me? I'm not missing it just so you can go to the library."

Homer was used to Gwendolyn getting her way. He usually didn't care when she got the bathroom first or when she got to choose which movie they were going to watch. Trying to win an argument with Gwendolyn was like trying to find treasure in your backyard. But more was at stake than a full bladder or a boring time at the theater. "The party's not until ten o'clock tonight."

"So?"

"So we have lots of time."

"And what if we get lost? Or what if we get caught by a policeman who wants to know why we're not in school?" Gwendolyn set the duffel on the sidewalk, then put her hands on her hips. "It's too risky. We'll go straight to the museum and wait for the party."

Homer clenched his fists. "I'll be there. Don't worry. I promise."

She bit her lip. What could she do? She needed him. His name was on the VIP invitation. "FINE! Go do your stupid research, but you'd better meet me at the museum before ten o'clock or..." She leaned real close and lowered her voice. "Or I'll tell Dad that you went into another library."

"I said I'll be there!"

"You'd better." Gwendolyn heaved the duffel bag over her shoulder and stomped off.

Homer watched as his sister walked away, her footsteps feisty and determined. The Pudding kids had different interests, no doubt about that, but they shared the same passion for their dreams. Nothing was going to get in Gwendolyn's way. Homer admired that. He raised his hand to wave, hoping she'd turn around, but she disappeared into the crowd. The towering shapes of the endless buildings made him feel small, as if he might also disappear and no one would notice. He almost ran after her, suddenly afraid to be left on his own in such a loud, stinky place.

"Solitude is the treasure hunter's destiny," Uncle Drake had once told him. "While you might begin your quest in a large group, as Sir Richard did with his elephant wranglers and veterinarians, you will face the final test of endurance and intellect on your own."

I can do this, Homer thought, but he didn't feel convinced so he said it out loud. "I can do this."

"Do what?" A girl knelt next to Dog and scratched his rump so that Dog's back legs did a little dance. "What can you do?"

Homer didn't know what to say. He hadn't meant for anyone to hear.

"Hey, how come your dog looks so sad?"

"He just does." Dog kept dancing while the girl scratched. They seemed to be getting along very nicely. "He needs a home," Homer said. "Do you know someone who wants a dog?"

The girl stood. He and the girl were about the same height and were both wearing denim jeans. But while Homer wore a green corduroy farm jacket, she wore a red apron with a little nametag: LORELEI. Her hair was real short and dyed pink. No one in Milkydale had pink hair. "Why don't you keep him? He's a cute dog."

"I'd like to keep him but my dad won't let me."

"That's too bad." She looked Homer up and down. "You a tourist?"

"I dunno." He didn't want to tell her that he was a runaway.

"Whaddaya mean you don't know?" She circled around, looking Homer up and down. "You're either from here or you're not from here."

Her questions were leaning a bit on the snoopy side. "I'm not from here."

"What's your name?"

"Homer."

She stopped circling and smiled. "Like the writer?"

"No. Like my grandpa."

"Well, Homer, my name's Lorelei. Want some tomato soup?" She pointed to a cart that stood at the edge of the sidewalk. The cart had a red umbrella with big letters: SCALDING HOT TOMATO SOUP. "You look like you need to eat. Do you like to eat?"

"I guess so." Homer's stomach rumbled as he followed her to the cart. Steam rose as she removed a metal lid. "You got money?"

"No."

"No matter. I got lots of this stuff." She ladled red liquid into a Styrofoam bowl. Homer sat on a bench next to the cart, balancing the bowl in his lap. "Here's a spoon."

"Thanks." Homer blew on the soup. Across the street, a bunch of ladies sat at little painted tables outside a bakery. They wore fancy hats and sipped small cups of tea. Homer suddenly missed his mother. He blew on the soup again, then took a few sips. "It's good," he said. Mrs. Pudding never served soup for breakfast.

Lorelei sat next to him and opened a packet of saltine crackers, which she fed to Dog, one at a time. Crumbs flew out the sides of his mouth. "Scalding hot soup!" she hollered a couple of times. No one came to buy soup. "Most people want hotdogs with all the fixin's, you know? The City's full of hotdog carts."

Homer wished they had a hotdog cart in Milkydale. He ate two more bowls of soup while Dog ate six more packets of crackers. Lorelei curled her legs onto the bench. "Homer's one of my favorite writers," she said. "I love *The Odyssey*, don't you? I've read it nine times. Odysseus got to go to all those places and meet all those weird people like that Cyclops and that witch. Have you read *The Odyssey*?"

"Yeah. Mrs. Peepgrass assigned it last year." Mrs. Peepgrass usually chose love stories about people named Heathcliff and Scarlett O'Hara, the kind of stories Homer wasn't much interested in. But *The Odyssey* had been different. "It was pretty good."

"Pretty good?" Lorelei swung her legs off the bench. "It's the best story ever written. Odysseus was a hero. He left his home and family to go fight in the Trojan War. But when he tried to get back home, he had to face peril after peril. He thought he'd only be gone for a short while but he was gone for twenty years. Twenty years."

Homer stopped eating as a powerful homesickness fell across him like a shadow.

"Just goes to show you that you never know what might

happen." Lorelei slid onto the sidewalk and scratched Dog's head. "So, whatcha doing in The City?"

He pushed the feeling away. "I'm looking for a library. Do you know where one is?"

"Sure. I go there all the time. Want me to show you?"

Homer reached under his collar and pulled out his compass. "If you tell me what direction to go, then I can find it."

Lorelei's eyes got real wide and she leaped to her feet. "Hey, that's a Galileo Compass. How'd you get one of those? Are your parents rich?"

A huge grin broke across Homer's face. "You know about Galileo Compasses?"

"Of course I do. I had one once but I lost it. They're the best compasses in the world." She stuck her face right up to the dial. "Sure wish I could find mine. I retraced my steps a million times. If I could find it I'd never lose it again." She sighed. Then she grabbed the empty soup bowls and tossed them into a garbage can. "You know, it's pretty easy to get lost in The City, even with a fancy compass like that. I'd better take you to the library." She set the lid back onto the soup canister and started pushing the cart down the sidewalk. Homer and Dog followed.

Homer didn't feel as nervous talking to Lorelei as he always did when he talked to Carlotta. Lorelei didn't seem to care that her face was smudged with dirt or that her short hair was kind of stringy. Or that she took big clomping steps like a boy. But she liked to read and she knew about compassess, so Homer thought she might possibly be the greatest girl ever. "Whatcha going to the library for?" she asked.

"I need to do some research." Homer wasn't sure how much to tell and how much not to tell. "I inherited something because my uncle died."

"That's too bad," she said. The cart's wheels rumbled. "My parents died. So did my grandparents."

"That's terrible. I'm sorry." Homer pulled Dog away from a fire hydrant. "Who do you live with?"

"Just me."

How was that possible? How could a kid live all alone in The City? He was about to ask that question when Dog tugged hard at the end of the leash. "Urrrr." He pulled Homer off the sidewalk and into a little flower bed. Lorelei stopped pushing the cart as Dog sniffed the dirt. "I don't know why he's doing that," Homer said, trying to pull Dog out of the bed. "He can't smell. He can't smell anything."

"You're gonna get a ticket if he messes up those flowers," Lorelei said. "I got a ticket once for spitting on the sidewalk."

But there was no pulling Dog from the flower bed

because he'd walked around a rosebush and had tangled his leash in the thorny branches. As Homer tried to untangle the leash, a door slammed and a tall man stomped down the front stairs, right next to the flower bed. "Well I never!" he exclaimed angrily. Then he shook his fist at one of the upper story windows. "I'll never do business with Snooty and Snooty again. Do you hear me? NEVER AGAIN!"

"You want some scalding soup?" Lorelei asked. The man snorted at her, then hurried down the sidewalk.

As Dog continued to sniff, Homer remembered the letter. *The law office of Snooty and Snooty regrets to inform you that your relative, Mr. Drake Pudding, has been declared dead due to the carnivorous appetite of a reptilian beast.* He was just outside the office of his uncle's lawyers. Surely they'd know what had happened to his uncle's belongings.

"Uh, Lorelei," he said. "I need to do something here before I go to the library."

"Suit yourself," she said with a shrug. "The library's eight blocks northeast. Well, see ya around. Bye, Dog!" And off she went, just like that.

"Thank you," Homer called as her red apron disappeared around the corner. He wished he could spend more time talking to her. She'd been so nice. But the rope went taut again as Dog rolled in the dirt. "Hey, stop that." Then Dog scrambled onto his paws. Dirt and pansies flew in all directions as he began digging a hole.

"We're gonna get a ticket," Homer said. The rose-bush toppled over as the hole grew. Passersby shot dirty looks at Homer. A clump of bluebells landed on a lady's head. A tulip flew into the road. He pulled the leash as hard as he could, lost his balance, and fell onto the side-walk. That dog was as stubborn as Gwendolyn!

"Urrrr." Dog stopped digging and trotted out of the flower bed. He stood over Homer, wagging his tail. Then he dropped something into Homer's lap.

16

Misters T. and C. Snooty

Homer got to his feet, brushed dirt from his jacket and pants, then examined the heart-shaped brooch, careful not to prick himself on its rusty pin. Dirt was jammed into every crevice, but once polished up it might be pretty. "You sure know how to find things," he told Dog as he tucked the brooch into his jacket pocket.

Dog wagged his little tail, then sneezed. Soil sprayed from his nostrils.

Homer set the rosebush into the hole, then packed

dirt tightly around it. He collected the other upturned plants and tidied up as best he could. He started to lead Dog into the building, but Dog hesitated on the stairs. "Urrrr."

"Don't worry," Homer told him. "I'm not returning you. I promise. I would never do that. I just need to ask the Snootys a question."

No one else stood in the building's cold, shiny lobby. Homer skimmed the sign on the far wall. LAW OFFICES OF TOE AND JAM, FLOOR 3. LAW OFFICES OF PICKLE AND DILL, FLOOR 18. LAW OFFICES OF LIVINGSTON, SWINDLE, AND LEMONGRASS, FLOOR 25. LAW OFFICES OF SNOOTY AND SNOOTY, FLOOR 32.

Dog was having trouble keeping upright on the slick marble floor. His little nails scratched desperately as he tried to get some traction. He slid past the water fountain. Then slid over to an empty shoe-shine stand. Homer had to reach down and grab Dog's collar to keep him from sliding right back out the front door.

Homer pushed the elevator button. A grinding noise sounded from the upper regions of the building as the elevator made its slow descent. Homer fidgeted nervously, for he'd never been to a law office or even to a thirty-second floor. There were no elevators in Milkydale. They had one at Walker's Department Store, in the next village over, but it only went to the second floor.

Homer pushed the button again. Surely Snooty and Snooty would know where his uncle's belongings had gone. Books and treasure hunting equipment can't just vanish into thin air.

The double doors slid open. "Come on," Homer said, stepping into the empty elevator. Pumping his back legs like an ice skater, Dog slid inside. Homer pushed button number thirty-two. Odd music floated from the ceiling—a toe-tapping melody without words.

Wa wa la la la la twing twing.

The doors began to close. "Hold that elevator!" a voice boomed.

Homer and Dog backed into the corner as a beefy man stopped the doors with his briefcase, then stepped inside. He took up so much space that Homer could only see a horizon of blue pinstripes. The man jabbed at a button. "Better hold tight," he warned. "This elevator's got a temper." Right on cue, the elevator lifted a few feet, then dropped back to the lobby. Dog's ears flew above his head. Homer bounced off the man's backside.

The man jabbed the button again. "Prepare yourself. Feels like it's going to be a doozy of a ride."

The elevator lurched, rising higher this time. Then, with an exhausted groan, fell back to the lobby. Tomato soup sloshed as Homer's stomach did a somersault. The man punched the button again and again. "Hope it doesn't dash us to our deaths like it did to poor Mr. Lovelord."

"Uh, excuse me," Homer said, trying to squeeze his way past the expanse of pinstripes. "I think we'll take the stairs."

"There aren't any stairs." The elevator lurched again and started its slow climb, the cable complaining the entire way. Homer braced himself against the wall. Dog whimpered and wedged between Homer's shins.

Creak. Groan. Grind.

"Going to the thirty-second floor I see." The man looked over his shoulder. "Got business with Snotty and Snotty?"

"Snooty and Snooty." The cable made a sound that reminded Homer of a brooding chicken.

"Well, you'd better take my card in case you suffer injuries on the way back down. Snotty doesn't handle that sort of thing." He handed Homer a white business card. MR. DILL, ATTORNEY-AT-LAW, SPECIALIZING IN PER-SONAL INJURY AND UNWANTED PARTY GUESTS. "Why don't you take this, too." He pulled a catalog from his brief-case and handed it to Homer: STOUT AND HEFTY: DAPPER CLOTHING FOR DAPPER FELLOWS. "First impressions are everything, young man. Just because you come from the country doesn't mean you have to look like you come from the country."

The elevator lurched to a stop. Button eighteen lit up. Fluorescent light bled across the elevator ceiling as the doors slid open. "Remember my card," Mr. Dill said. "If you should need it." He stepped out but before Homer could escape, the doors smacked shut.

"Wait!" Homer cried. The elevator shook violently. Homer dropped the catalog and slid to the floor. He wrapped his arms around Dog's trembling middle. His mouth said, "We'll be okay," but his brain said, *We're going to die!*

Treasure hunters die all the time—it's one of the job's main hazards. Other hazards include losing a limb, catching an exotic rash, and being rejected by your family and friends because they think you're weird. But dying is the biggest hazard because if you're dead, well, then you're dead.

It's a well-known fact that treasure hunters rarely die in normal ways, say from a long illness or old age. Millicent Smith died in a fire. Sir Richard got sat on by his elephant. Rumpold Smeller walked the plank. Drake Pudding was eaten by a giant tortoise. But no treasure hunter, as far as Homer knew, had been killed by an elevator. It seemed unfair that his death would come on the very first day of his quest. Before he'd found a single piece of treasure.

He tightened his grip around Dog as the elevator rose

higher. All the grinding, lurching, and jolting made him feel like he might throw up. Dog panted miserably. The cable shrieked. "Hold on," Homer said, squeezing his eyes shut. "We're almost there." The elevator rocked back and forth, convulsed a few times, then stopped moving. All was still. The music paused. Button thirty-two lit up. Then the elevator made a pleasant *ding* sound, as if it were the nicest, most civilized elevator in the world, and the doors slid open.

Stumbling over each other, Homer and Dog made their escape.

Never in his twelve years had Homer Winslow Pudding been so happy to stand on solid ground. As his stomach settled he took a long look around the thirty-second floor's reception room. The door at the far end had a sign: NO ENTRY. PRIVATE OFFICE. Two massive gold-framed portraits hung on each side of the door. The first was of an old man in a powdered wig and black robe. CONSTANTINE SNOOTY. The other was of the same old man in the same powdered wig and black robe. THERMOPOLIE SNOOTY.

On the other side of the room sat a vacant desk with a sign: RING BUZZER FOR ASSISTANCE. So he rang.

No one came to assist. Homer shuffled nervously in front of the desk. He picked up a plaque: MR. TWADDLE, LEGAL SECRETARY. It was the same man who had delivered the letters to the Pudding farm. Homer picked up a framed photograph of Mr. Twaddle in flowered swim trunks, holding a coconut drink. "Remember this guy?" Homer asked, showing Dog the photo.

Dog stood on his hind legs and scratched at Homer's jacket pocket. "Urrrr." He scratched again.

"You want this?" Homer took out the heart-shaped brooch. Dog dropped to the floor and wagged his tail. "Well, I guess you can have it. You're the one who found it." Homer tucked the end of the rusty pin safely into its clamp, then gave the brooch to Dog. Dog carried it to the other side of the room, dropped it in front of the door marked NO ENTRY. PRIVATE OFFICE. Then he sat and stared at the door.

That dog definitely does some weird things, Homer thought as he rang the bell again. Mr. Twaddle apparently liked going on holiday because there was a photo of him in ski gear and another of him on horseback at a place called the Dude Ranch and another of him on a cruise ship. Homer picked up a photo in which Mr. Twaddle, wearing a pinstriped suit, was posing in front of a bookcase. Something about the photo struck Homer as familiar. He looked closer, his gaze traveling across the bookcase. He gasped. All the books were about treasure hunting!

He reached over and rang the bell. And rang it and rang it and rang it.

"My turn!"

The office door flew open. Dog barked. Startled, Homer dropped the picture. An old man in a powdered wig and black robe pumped his arms madly as he wheeled his wooden wheelchair toward the doorway. Dog barked again, then scrambled to get out of the way.

"It's not your turn. It's my turn!" Another old man, also in a powdered wig and black robe, also sitting in a wooden wheelchair, tried to pass the first old man. They looked exactly like their portraits.

"You've gone senile. Get out of the way," said the first old man.

For a moment, the two chairs got stuck in the doorway. Then one of the Snootys hit the other Snooty on the head with an umbrella, gaining a momentary lead. "Ha, ha! I'm going to be first."

"Oh no you won't."

Wigs askew, they rolled across the reception room, beating one another with umbrellas until they came to a screeching stop at Homer's feet.

"May I help you?" they asked in unison.

The scent of old age, a smell similar to the buttermilk his mom kept on the kitchen counter, crept toward Homer, along with the minty scent of arthritis lotion. He stepped back. "Uh, I'm Homer Pudding. You sent me a letter."

The first Snooty scowled. "We don't know anything about letters. Our secretary handles letters."

"You also sent me this dog."

The other Snooty stuck out his lower lip. "We don't know anything about dogs. Our secretary handles dogs."

"Would you like to sue someone?" the first Snooty asked, his eyes widening.

The other Snooty inched forward. "You could sue the person who made your jacket. It's quite ugly."

"Or you could sue my brother for insulting your taste in clothing."

They turned and glared at each other. "I hate you."

"I hate you more."

"Excuse me," Homer said as the Snootys tried to poke each other's eyes out. "My uncle Drake died and you sent me a letter saying he had left me this dog."

They stopped poking and glared at Dog. "That's the droopiest dog I've ever seen."

"I've seen droopier."

"Are you returning the dog? There's a five-day limit on returns."

"No, I'm not returning him." Homer gave Dog a reassuring look. "I'm not here about the dog. I'm trying to find out where all my uncle's stuff went. He had lots of equipment and books and maps."

"Stuff is handled by our secretary, Mr. Twaddle," they said in unison.

"Where is Mr. Twaddle?"

"On holiday."

Homer fidgeted. Mr. Twaddle had told Mrs. Pudding that he didn't know anything about Uncle Drake's stuff. He'd said all that was left was a pair of shoes and the dog. But all those treasure hunting books in the photo seemed mighty suspicious. "Do you know where my uncle lived? Before he died? He never gave us an address. I could go there and look for myself."

"Who are you again?" they asked.

"Urrrr." Carrying the brooch in his mouth, Dog wandered up to the wheelchairs. With a toss of his head, the brooch flew out of his mouth and hit the first Snooty on the nose.

"Ouch!"

The second Snooty pointed his umbrella at Homer. "Your dog has injured my brother, Constantine. Call the courthouse. I'm going to sue your dog."

They're crazy, Homer thought, which was probably why Mr. Twaddle took so many holidays.

"Wait." Constantine plucked the brooch from his lap and held it in his bony hand. "I can't believe my eyes. Why, it's my long-lost brooch. I bought it on the very day she proclaimed her love. But then it was lost. How I've longed for its return."

"Hmmmph," snorted his brother. "What a load of nonsense. She never actually proclaimed her love."

Constantine's face turned red. "She certainly did. She chose me, not you. And I was going to give her this brooch that very night and tell her that I loved her in return but then it *mysteriously disappeared*." He leaned over the side of his wheelchair until he was nose to nose with Dog. "Where did you find this?"

"Urrrr."

"He found it in the flower bed," Homer said. "Outside the building."

"In the flower bed?" Constantine Snooty wheeled his chair to the room's only window. "Young man, open this." He rapped the windowsill with his umbrella. Homer opened the window. "Now look down and tell me what you see."

Homer stuck his head out the window. Thirty-two floors was a dizzyingly long distance from the ground. Even the Milkydale Ferris wheel didn't reach that high. "I see a street, and people, and the flower bed where Dog dug up that brooch."

"Exactly!" Constantine spun his wheelchair and pointed a trembling finger at his brother. "You threw it out the window, didn't you, Thermopolie?"

Thermopolie adjusted his powdered wig. "No comment. I have the right to remain silent."

"I knew it!" Constantine hollered. "You threw it out the window because you were jealous. You wanted her but she wanted me. And we were going to meet that night at Chez Bill's and I was going to give her the brooch and ask her to marry me. But when I went to get the brooch from my desk it had disappeared. Then I had to fill out the police report and then the elevator broke down and by the time I got to the restaurant she had gone. I never saw her again." He stomped his feet against the footrest. "I'm going to sue you for ruining my life!"

The Snootys wheeled their chairs, circling each other like wild roosters, their wigs bobbing like head feathers. "I saved your life," Thermopolie said. "What kind of future would you have with a woman who can't fit into an elevator or ride on a Ferris wheel?"

Can't fit into an elevator or ride on a Ferris wheel? Could it be? Had the brooch been meant for the sad woman on the train? As the Snootys raised their umbrellas and took aim at each other's heads, Homer tried to figure out what to do. Clearly they didn't care about *his* predicament. If only he could talk to their secretary, Mr. Twaddle. "Excuse me but..."

"I'm going to kill you!"

"Not if I kill you first!"

They charged, umbrellas swinging, eyes bulging, but it was a sudden tremor beneath Homer's feet that caught his attention. A man had leaped through the open window and landed beside the secretary's desk. At first Homer didn't recognize the man's face because it wasn't upside down. Black hair hung to his shoulders and a black mustache dipped to his pointed beard. Ajitabh, the cloud man, waved a sword at Homer. "We must talk."

Homer's heart jumped into his throat. Though death by sword would look better than death by elevator in the *Encyclopedia of Treasure Hunters*, Homer still clung fiercely to the conviction that he was too young to die.

The Snooty brothers, so busy trying to strangle each other, didn't notice the intruder. Dog growled. Homer, his legs gone wobbly, backed up until he reached the elevator.

"Homer, there's no time to waste," Ajitabh said. "You must come with me."

Dog circled Ajitabh, barking, but keeping a good distance. Homer punched the elevator button. *Ding.* He couldn't believe his luck. It hadn't been called back to the lobby. The doors slid open.

Wa wa la la la la twing twing.

"Dog!" Homer yelled. Ajitabh tried to grab Dog but just as he reached out, the Snooty brothers crashed into him. As Ajitabh struggled to untangle himself from wheelchairs, flailing limbs, and umbrellas, Homer dove into the elevator and slid across its floor on the Stout and Hefty catalog. He crashed into the back wall, then scrambled to his feet. "DOG!" he cried. Dog barreled in. Homer punched the LOBBY button. "Come on, close, close, close!"

"I admit it!" Thermopolie cried. "I threw the brooch out the window."

"I knew it!" Constantine hollered. "Prepare to die!"

"Homer, wait!" Ajitabh pushed the wheelchairs aside. "I need to talk to you."

Please close, please close, please close. Homer punched LOBBY again.

"Homer, I know about the coin. Homer…" Ajitabh called, reaching out.

The elevator doors closed.

17

The Soup Warehouse

Homer and Dog ran down the crowded side-walk, confused and frightened, bouncing off pedestrians like pinballs. There'd been no time to put on Dog's leash. No time to stop and ask for directions. That cloud man could swoop down at any moment. How did he know about the coin? Would he keep trying to kill Homer unless Homer handed it over? Which way was the Museum of Natural History?

"Look where you're going," a lady snapped.

"Watch out," a man said as Dog galloped between his legs.

"Sorry," Homer called out for the hundredth time. He had to find Gwendolyn. She'd never believe him. She'd roll her eyes and say, *I don't want to hear one of your stupid stories, Homer*. But she had to believe him. Ajitabh was dead serious about getting his hands on the coin.

Dog groaned. He slowed to a trot, his tongue hanging out the side of his mouth. Homer was tired, too, but that sword had looked really sharp. Gustav Gustavson, the Swedish treasure hunter made famous by his discovery of Aphrodite's toothbrush, had lost the end of his nose in a sword fight. Homer put a hand over his nose. That must have really hurt.

Dog started to stagger as if he were about to tip over.

"Hey, put that dog on a leash."

"Get that dog out of the way."

"Sorry." Homer couldn't run much farther. His muscles ached and blisters threatened his heels. His lungs burned with each breath. He looked over his shoulder. No sign of any clouds, just a sheen of polluted air. Maybe they could take a short rest.

And that's when he saw a familiar red umbrella.

"Scalding hot soup!" Lorelei yelled. "Get some scalding hot tomato soup!" Homer must have looked as freaked out as he felt because Lorelei dropped her ladle. "What's the matter? You look like someone's trying to kill you."

"Someone is trying to kill me," he said, gasping for breath. Dog collapsed beside the cart, wheezing like Mr. Pudding's old truck. "A man tried to kill me with a sword."

Lorelei grabbed Homer's arm. "Why would someone try to kill you?"

"He wants something." Homer checked his pocket to make sure the matchbook hadn't flown out. "He can't have it."

Lorelei's gaze darted to Homer's pocket. Then she let go of his arm. "Well, Homer, I've learned that if somebody wants something real bad, then that person will do *anything* to get it. You'd better come with me. I know where you can hide." She closed her soup lid. "Your dog doesn't look too good." Dog, still on his side, still panting, had gone cross-eyed. "We'd better give him a ride."

Lorelei took Dog's front end, Homer took the back end, and with a heave, they lifted him off the sidewalk. "He's so heavy," Lorelei groaned as they set him on top of the cart. Dog, his tongue still hanging out, didn't seem to notice that he'd been moved.

"Guess he's not much good at running," Homer said, not wanting to admit that he wasn't so good at it, either.

With Dog in place, both kids gripped the handle and started pushing the wheeled cart down the sidewalk. Lorelei directed the way. Homer looked over his shoulder so many times that when Lorelei announced, "We're here," he had no idea how they had gotten there.

They stood in a brick-paved alley between two cement buildings. Dampness hung in the air, along with a menagerie of unpleasant odors that seeped from an overflowing garbage can. "Where are we?" Homer whispered, afraid to disturb the rats that were building a nest in a discarded sofa. Homer didn't like rats. Farmers have to deal with them all the time because rats love living on farms. Barns provide lots of good animal droppings to eat and straw for nest building. But Homer knew that rats carried diseases and could gnaw their way through anything. A shiver of disgust ran down his spine as one of the rats scurried across the alley, its claws clicking against the bricks. Dog opened one eye, then sat up. A snarl vibrated behind his upper lip.

Lorelei took out a key and opened a metal gate. The door behind the gate had a sign: SOUP WAREHOUSE. "Help me push the cart in," she said after opening the door. Once inside, she closed the gate and the door, then flicked on a light switch. Homer and Dog looked around.

Towers of boxes filled the cold cement room. Each

box had a label: SPLIT PEA, ITALIAN MEATBALL, CLAM CHOW-DER—every kind of soup imaginable. Lorelei led Homer past a stack of CHICKEN AND NOODLE and CHICKEN AND RICE, into another room of box towers. LIMA BEAN, LEN-TIL BEAN, BACON AND BEAN. "Park the cart here," she said. Together, they lifted Dog off the top and set him on the cement floor. His wheezing had settled and his tongue was back where it belonged. He started sniffing along the ground, then disappeared behind a tower of VEG-ETABLE BROTH.

"I thought you said he couldn't smell?"

"He can't. Dog?" Homer found him scratching at a narrow space between two towers. "Whatcha got there?" Homer reached his hand into the space and found something round and cold.

"My Galileo Compass!" Lorelei cried. Sure enough, it looked just like Homer's, only it wasn't as shiny and it weighed a bit less. And it didn't have a personal engraving on the back. "I can't believe you found it. I'm so happy. Thanks, Dog." She slid the compass around her neck, then gave Dog a hug.

Homer patted Dog's head. "Good boy." He'd sure feel bad if he'd lost his Galileo Compass.

"Come on. I'll show you my place."

"Your place?"

Homer and Dog followed Lorelei behind a stack of

CHICKEN AND STARS to a smaller door with a sign: UTIL-ITY CLOSET. She opened the door, then got on her knees. "You have to crawl through." Then she pushed against the closet's back wall. A panel swung open. "Follow me."

No way would Ajitabh think of looking for me in a soup warehouse utility closet, Homer thought. "Go on," he said, giving Dog a little push. But Dog locked his legs, refusing to go first, so Homer crawled around him, scraping his sides as he squeezed through. Dog followed.

With a flick of a matchstick, Lorelei lit two candles. "Well? What do you think?" she asked proudly. "This is my place."

While most people would think that the room was nothing much, just an old sleeping bag and pillow, and some milk crates filled with clothes and knickknacks, Homer sat in awe. How he longed for a place of his own, where he could keep all his maps and books and no one—NO ONE—could ever take them away.

"I found the warehouse last year when they accidentally left the door open. The workers only come here at night to load and unload boxes. And that little cart was just sitting there. It never got used so I helped myself. No one even knows I'm here. And I can eat anything I want." She took off her apron and tossed it into one of the crates. Then she grabbed a can opener and opened

a can. "Want some? They all taste pretty good cold."
Homer frowned. "Go on. It's not stealing or anything.
I keep the rats out of the warehouse and in exchange, I
eat a bit of soup."

That sounded like a fair deal. Mr. Pudding had spent
a lot of money on rat traps over the years.

Homer accepted the can and a plastic spoon, then
plunged the spoon into the soup. Minestrone was definitely better warm but he didn't much care because his
near-death experience had left him famished. He watched
as Lorelei opened a can for herself. He might have felt
sorry for her because she didn't have a mother to make
her pancakes, or an uncle to tell her stories, or a little
brother to push on the rope swing. On the other hand,
she didn't have a dad who forbade her to talk about treasure hunting, she didn't have a big sister who bossed her
around, and she didn't have to go to school. "You're so
lucky. You can do whatever you want."

"Yeah. I can." She smiled. "When I want to read I go
to the public library. When I want to use a fancy bathroom, I go to Froodle's on Fifth Avenue. When I want to
take a bath, I go to the public pool. When I want to eat, I
just take a can from the warehouse. It's super great."

"Yeah. I bet it is." Dog groaned. "I think he's hungry,"
Homer said.

"What flavor do you think he'll like?"

"How about chicken and stars?"

Lorelei opened a can for Dog and poured it into a bowl. Dog took a few laps, then his head shot up and the short hairs on his back stiffened. "Grrrr." A rat had stuck its head through a hole in the wall.

Homer pointed. "Uh, there's a rat."

"It's okay," Lorelei said. "It's just Daisy."

The rat named Daisy glared back at Dog, her long nose and black whiskers twitching, her beady eyes never blinking. Dog started barking like crazy. Homer grabbed his collar and pulled him close. "I thought you said you kept the rats out," he shouted over the barking.

"I do. Well, Daisy keeps them out. She hates other rats. But she's my pet." Lorelei held out her hand. The rat leaped onto her palm, then onto her lap. "She lives here with me."

"Oh," Homer said. He clamped his hands around Dog's muzzle and grimaced as Lorelei stroked the rat's back. He wanted to tell her that rats were filthy and dangerous, but that seemed a rude thing to say, even if it were true. "Shhh," he told Dog. Then he unclamped his hands.

Dog settled down. He watched Lorelei cuddle her rat, then went back to eating his soup.

"So, why was some guy trying to kill you?" Lorelei asked.

"Because of the coin." Homer almost choked on a green bean. Why had he blurted that out?

His uncle had warned him about trusting others. But Homer desperately wanted to trust someone. He wouldn't even be allowed to say the words *treasure hunting* once he got back home. Without Uncle Drake he had no one to talk to. Sitting cross-legged, her pink hair standing in spikes all over her head, a pet rat nestled in the crook of her arm, Lorelei looked as though she'd know how to handle a guy with a sword. And she'd been nothing but nice to Homer and to Dog.

So, ignoring everything his uncle had taught him about not confiding in strangers, because sometimes loneliness clouds a person's judgment, Homer laid out the story at Lorelei's sneakered feet.

He told her everything.

That's right. *Everything*.

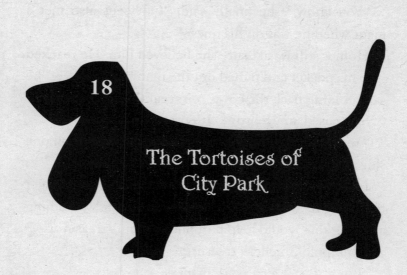

18

The Tortoises of
City Park

"And now I'm sitting in this warehouse eating soup," Homer said after telling Lorelei everything. Shoulders hunched and arms wrapped around his knees, he waited, expecting the reaction he always got—*You're so weird, Homer Pudding.*

At first Lorelei didn't say anything. While Dog licked his bowl clean, she sat in silent thought, her hands folded over the sleeping rat. Homer fidgeted nervously. How could he possibly expect her to believe? But he wanted her to believe. He wanted someone to understand.

"You know," she finally said, "Odysseus also met a giant when he was on his quest."

Homer still wasn't sure she believed him. He reached into his pocket and pulled out the matchbook. "See," he said, folding back the cover to reveal the coin.

She raised an eyebrow. "It's pretty."

"Yeah," Homer said. "There's a treasure chest on one side and the initials *L.O.S.T.* on the other side."

Lorelei ran her hand down the rat's tail. "Let me get this straight. Your uncle told you that he found something amazing that would help him find a pirate's treasure..."

"Rumpold Smeller's treasure."

"But it wasn't a treasure map?"

"Yeah."

"And he never told you what the something was?"

"He said I could be in danger if I knew."

"Do you think that coin is the something?"

"Maybe." Homer brushed his curls from his eyes. "I don't really know. He said he needed to get funding for the quest. Maybe this coin is worth a lot of money and he was going to sell it to a museum."

Dog climbed onto Homer's lap. While it's uncomfortable to sit beneath a dog who weighs more than a bag of cement, not to mention the drooling and gas, Homer didn't mind. They'd only known each other for a couple of days but already they'd almost been killed by an elevator and a man with a sword. Near-death experiences create deep bonds.

Besides, the thought of giving Dog to another home was starting to feel plain wrong.

Lorelei scratched her rat's head. "And you think somebody stole the rest of your uncle's stuff?"

"Yeah. Stuff doesn't just disappear. I'm thinking that the Snootys' secretary knows something about it. He had all those books about treasure hunting in that one photo. He might be trying to find Rumpold Smeller's treasure. Maybe he took my uncle's stuff."

She nodded her head slowly. "Maybe he was looking for the coin, just like the man in the cloud. You're in serious danger."

She understood!

"I need to go to the library," Homer said. "I need to find out what kind of coin this is."

"That's a good place to start. But then I think we should go to the Museum of Natural History. There's a coin collection in the same room where they keep all the gemstones and minerals. It's on the third floor. I know a secret way to get into the museum without having to pay."

And so, at high noon that Tuesday, Lorelei, Homer, and Dog left the soup warehouse and headed into the heart of The City. Daisy the rat stayed behind to guard her turf.

Some people get paid to give tours because they know all sorts of trivia about buildings and monuments. Captain Warp, the famous astronaut, lived here; Ms. Dreary, the famous poet, lived there. But no tour could have compared to the one that Lorelei gave Homer. She called it Lorelei's Favorite Places.

They began in the reading room at The City Public Library. A floor-to-ceiling stained-glass window cast the room in soft blue light, which was so relaxing that everyone in the room was sound asleep, even the librarians. So no one complained when a droopy dog wandered in.

Soft snoring floated through the air as Lorelei stacked coin books on a reading table. "Let me see the coin again," she whispered. He showed it to her. Once it was safely tucked back into his pocket, they each picked up a book and began what turned out to be a very long search. Lorelei never complained. She flipped the pages eagerly and nudged Homer when his eyelids grew heavy and his head started to droop.

"That was the last book," Homer said two hours later, his voice thick with disappointment. A librarian raised her head, mumbled something about library cards, then fell back asleep.

"Let's get out of here," Lorelei said. "Before we fall asleep, too."

They found Dog in the periodical section, sleeping on a half-eaten issue of *World of Water Bugs*. "Bad boy," Homer whispered as he stuffed the remains of the magazine under the shelf. Then he noticed half-eaten issues of *Beautiful Balconies* and *Pork Monthly*. "Oh no." He peered around the shelf. A trail of torn magazine pages covered the aisle. "Bad, bad boy."

Every time they went to a library, something terrible happened.

Dog woke up and wagged his tail. "Urrrr."

Lorelei picked a shred of paper off Dog's nose. "Does he always eat magazines?"

"You've no idea." Homer felt terrible about the magazines, but what could he do? He didn't have any money to pay the library for the damages, and he didn't have time to go to jail. One day, when he'd found his first treasure, he'd buy as many magazines as their shelves could hold. He wrote a note on one of the torn pages, "I promise to pay you back," and slid it beneath a sleeping librarian's arm.

"I'm hungry," Lorelei said as they walked out of the soothing blue light and back into the hazy city air. "I know where we can get something to eat." She led Homer and Dog to the next stop on her tour—a homeless shelter. Groups of people sat around tables, reading newspapers and playing cards. Some reached out to pet Dog. "They always have free doughnuts," Lorelei said. Sure enough, boxes of day-old pastries sat on a counter. "I like the ones with pink sprinkles."

Homer and Dog ate three each. "How come these people don't have homes?" Homer whispered.

Lorelei shrugged. "Different reasons. But mostly because they don't have anyone to take care of them."

Homer didn't say anything, suddenly aware that if Lorelei didn't have the soup warehouse, she'd be homeless, too. What would happen to her if she lost the room at the warehouse? Where would she go? He'd been thinking about asking her if she'd like to take Dog, and be his new owner, but that didn't feel right. Even though she seemed to like Dog, he needed a lot of looking after and she already had that pet rat to take care of.

Next, she showed him how to sneak into a movie theater through the exit door. They caught the last half of an alien invasion film while Dog ate popcorn off the floor. Caught up in the excitement and a little giddy from the sugary doughnuts, Homer forgot about the coin, still safely tucked into his pocket. "I've seen this four times," Lorelei said, warning him before the gory parts.

After the movie, Lorelei showed Homer how to catch a free ride on the back of a trolley, how to nab coins from a wishing fountain, and how to turn those coins into the best chili-smothered hotdog Homer had ever tasted. And as dusk covered The City in a hazy blanket,

Lorelei led Homer to City Park. "The tortoise area is over there. I thought you might want to see it."

He swallowed the last bit of hotdog. Did he want to see the place where his uncle had died? Not really, but he'd come to The City for answers, and so far he hadn't found any.

As his mood changed from carefree playfulness to downright dread, the terrain changed, too. Just down the gravel path, the trees took on a sickly look, their leaves crinkled like candy wrappers, their trunks black with grime. Homer wouldn't have been surprised to hear them cough. "The park used to be pretty," Lorelei said. "I don't know what happened to it."

The path wound around a murky lake. A chain-link fence separated casual strollers and bikers from the lake's dangerous inhabitants. "They put up the fence after your uncle..." She didn't finish the sentence. She didn't need to. She stood directly beneath a big sign: DANGER. DO NOT FEED THE GIANT TORTOISES.

"There they are," Lorelei said.

Park lights, perched high up in the trees, shone upon the lake. Dog pressed his nose against the fence and started barking. Homer had never seen a giant tortoise. A dozen lay on big boulders at the edge of the lake. They turned their green faces toward Dog as he tried to squeeze under the fence. Homer grabbed his collar.

"I don't see how one of those could eat an entire person," Lorelei said, gripping a few of the links. "Their mouths don't look so big."

Homer agreed. While the largest tortoise was the size of a wheelbarrow, its head was only the size of a small cantaloupe. One of the tortoises looked at Homer. Homer shuddered and turned away. Reptilian eyes had been the last thing his uncle had seen.

"The killer tortoise escaped," Lorelei said. "I read about it in the paper. The zookeeper was going to take it away but it mysteriously disappeared."

"Disappeared?"

"Yeah. It could be out there, right now, wandering around, eating more people."

Homer wanted to pull his jacket over his head. He suddenly missed his parents. He missed his bedroom, with its four solid walls. Darkness was settling and he imagined reptilian eyes searching hungrily for the next victim. Then he remembered Gwendolyn. He'd been having so much fun, he'd forgotten all about her. What had she done all day? All alone. He reached down and grabbed Dog's leash. "I need to find my sister."

"Oh, right. You've supposed to go to that party." Lorelei kicked the dirt.

"You can come, too."

"Really?" She smiled. "I've never been to a VIP party

before." Then she looked at her ragged sweater and jeans. "I'm not dressed for a party."

"So?" Homer smiled. "I'm the VIP and I'll tell them that you're my guest. And after we get in, we can go look at that coin collection."

They hurried from the park. Night had fallen and The City had changed dramatically. The crowds had gone. Buses and taxis had disappeared. Rats scurried across sidewalks and roads. Dog barked at each rat until he made himself hoarse. The soles of Homer's feet ached as he kept pace with Lorelei's clomping steps, but he didn't mind. He felt lucky to have made such a good friend. The day had been a blast. Surely poor Gwendolyn's day had been long and boring.

"We're here," Lorelei announced.

They stood in front of a massive stone building. MUSEUM OF NATURAL HISTORY was carved into a stone arch. Ivy-covered pillars flanked wide stone steps. Dog tried to eat a piece of ivy but Homer pulled him away. He looked around for Gwendolyn but the place appeared to be deserted. He walked up the stone steps and peered through the windows at the ticket booth. CLOSED. Not even a security guard stood on duty. A clock above the ticket booth read 9:50.

"We're not late," he said with relief. "The party starts at ten. The VIP entrance is supposed to be on the south side of the building." Lorelei and Homer reached for their compasses. Then they followed a garden path to the museum's southern wall. Floodlights perched along the museum's roof cast the grounds in soft white light. "Here it is," Homer said. He stopped in front of a door with a handwritten sign taped to it: VIP ENTRANCE.

"Gwendolyn," Homer called. He tried to open the door but it was locked. He knocked. "Gwendolyn?"

"You sure she wanted to meet you here?"

"Yes. This is why she came to The City. She's got to be here." Homer nervously looked around. Then he knocked on the door again. Dog piddled on a shrub. "And she couldn't get in without me. My name's on the invitation."

"What's this?" Lorelei picked up a squirrel. "I think it's stuffed."

Homer's heart skipped a beat as he took the squirrel from Lorelei. "This belongs to Gwendolyn. She'd never leave one of her animals behind." Not only had Homer left home without permission, he had also managed to lose track of his sister. Surely his father would punish him for the rest of his life. He pounded on the door again. "What could have happened to her? Gwendolyn!"

PART FOUR

THE MUSEUM
OF
NATURAL HISTORY

19

A Party for Very Important People

And that's when the door opened. "Mr. Pudding?" A woman stood in the open doorway, her top half much skinnier than her bottom half. Her short black hair was cut in a perfectly straight line.

Mr. Pudding? Homer looked over his shoulder. Was his father standing behind him?

The woman cleared her throat. "Mr. Homer W. Pudding?"

Homer scratched his ear. "Oh, you mean me."

Holding out a gloved hand, the woman stepped

forward. "I am pleased to meet you. It's not every day that I get to meet a...VIP. May I call you Homer?"

"Sure." Homer shook her hand. She had a painfully firm grip.

"I am Madame la Directeur, Executive Director by Royal Decree of the Museum of Natural History. You received my invitation?" Homer nodded. His hand throbbed. "And you followed my instructions?" She raised her eyebrows. "You came *without* your parents?"

"They're..." Homer fiddled with Dog's leash. "They're back in Milkydale."

"Excellent. If you'll follow me."

"Have you seen my sister, Gwendolyn? She told me to meet her here."

"Your sister is already inside."

"She is?" Immense relief flooded Homer like a cool glass of water. "That's great. Um, this is my friend Lorelei. She'd like to come to the party, too."

"Hi," Lorelei said with a little wave.

Madame pursed her cherry-red lips. She cast a searing look at Lorelei, taking her in from head to toe. Then she ran a gloved finger along a strand of perfect white pearls that encircled her neck. "This is an *exclusive* party. Invitees only."

"Oh," Homer said. "But I thought..."

"Exclusive."

"Whatever," Lorelei told Madame. "I don't need your stupid exclusive party." She turned to Homer. "I've got to go home, anyway, before the warehouse workers show up. Come find me tomorrow, okay?"

"I'm sorry, Lorelei," Homer said. "I didn't think there'd be a problem."

She shrugged. "No biggie. I'll see you tomorrow, okay? I'll be selling soup in the same place." Then she whispered, "The coin collection is on the third floor." Before he could stop her, she ran off into the night.

Homer knew exactly how Lorelei felt because he had run off many times when he'd come face to face with something "exclusive." *You can't join our club, Homer. You can't be on our team, Homer. No weirdos or wimps allowed, Homer.* He knew that behind Lorelei's shrug and declaration of "whatever" lay hurt feelings. He would have run off with her but he wanted to see the museum's coin collection. He needed to see it.

"Leave that creature outside," Madame la Directeur said, pointing to the squirrel that Homer still held.

"But it's my sister's."

"Leave it outside." Her eyes narrowed. Homer set the squirrel on the ground. Then he stepped through the doorway. Madame's voice turned prickly. "Dogs are not allowed in the museum. You will have to leave that creature outside, too."

"My dog?" Homer clutched the rope. "But what if someone takes him?"

"Who would take that? That's the droopiest dog I've ever seen."

A dribble of drool dangled from Dog's lower lip. He raised his ears and looked at Homer. "Urrrr?"

"But I'm supposed to take care of him. He can't smell and if I don't watch him, he might eat something poisonous. Or he might get lost."

"There's nothing poisonous out there. You can tie him to a tree." She tapped her fingers on her round hips. "Do you wish to attend the party or not?"

Homer hung his head. Other than family birthdays, he'd never been to a real party. And a party for VIPs sounded very exciting. "It's just for a little while," he whispered, kneeling next to Dog. "You'll be okay. Just a little while and then I'll come back and get you." Being left alone behind a museum at night didn't sound okay to Homer but what was he supposed to do? Sit out there with Dog and miss the opportunity to see that coin collection? He stood and walked back out the door. The rope went taut as Dog stiffened his legs, refusing to budge.

"Come on," Homer urged.

Dog sat. Homer tugged. Dog slid a few inches forward, then clamped his teeth around the rope and scooted a few inches backward. Homer tugged. Dog pulled. Tug, pull, tug, pull. Madame tapped her pointy shoe. "I'm waiting."

"Ugh," Homer said, dropping the rope. "He's too heavy. Can't he just come with me? I promise he'll be good." He wasn't so sure he could keep that promise but he had to give it a try. "And he won't pee on anything." Again, no guarantees.

Madame smoothed her skirt, then took a long breath. "Well, because it's past closing time I will make an exception. But do not allow him to wander about." Clearly the museum's director was not a dog person. No chance she'd give Dog a new home.

"Thanks." Homer picked up the rope. Then he leaned over and whispered, "You'd better be good." Dog wagged his tail.

Madame la Directeur's high heels clicked as she led Homer and Dog down a hallway. They passed lots of rooms with desks and filing cabinets. Then they passed a door with a sign: GARBAGE ROOM. The door stood half-open and something familiar caught Homer's eye. He stopped walking and peered in. Gwendolyn's duffel bag was crammed into a garbage can. A stuffed field mouse and stuffed raccoon peeked out. Gwendolyn would never have thrown away her work. *Never.* "Excuse me," Homer said. "But why is—?"

"No time for questions. Do keep up." Madame quickened her pace. When she reached the end of the hall, she walked under an archway and disappeared into a haze of blinding light. Homer and Dog hurried to catch up. They both squinted as they passed beneath the archway. "Welcome to the museum's Grand Hall," Madame called from the center of the gigantic room.

As his eyes adjusted, Homer took a big breath. He was standing between the legs of a dinosaur skeleton—a *Tyrannosaurus rex*, to be exact. Its bleached bones reached halfway to a vaulted ceiling. Dog started to growl but Homer clamped a hand over his muzzle. "I promised that you'd be good," he whispered. When the growl subsided, Homer let go. "Good boy."

Everything in the Grand Hall was massive in scale. A pterodactyl with a six-foot wingspan hung in a corner, its claws posed to snag some prey. A mammoth stood at the base of a central stairway, its trunk raised to the sky. A glass-encased giant squid spanned the length of a wall. Even the golden clock, set above the entrance to the gift shop, was the size of a wagon wheel.

Homer rushed to a bin marked MAPS. He hesitated.

"You may have one," Madame said as she started up the red carpeted stairs.

"Thanks." Homer unfolded the glossy paper, then unfolded again and again until it was flat. It was a tourist map, easy to read, full color, mass-produced by the thousands. There'd be no secret clues waiting in such a map, only clear, easy directions so visitors wouldn't get lost. Hall of Prehistoric Man, Hall of African Mammals, The Ocean Dome, World of Birds. A color-coded legend highlighted services such as the bathrooms, coatroom, gift shop, and cafeteria. And a standard north-south arrow sat in the top right corner, which every compass-wearer appreciates.

"The party is this way," Madame called from the top of the stairway. She walked along a balcony railing, then disappeared from view. Homer refolded the map, perfectly and precisely, then tucked it into his jacket pocket.

Have you ever tried to refold a map? Most people will never master the feat. It's an accordion-pleated conundrum that boggles the mind. Actually, it's best to never unfold a map in the first place, unless you have nothing else planned for the day.

Dog stood at Homer's feet, holding a bone in his mouth. "Oh no. Where'd you get that?" After a struggle, Homer pulled the bone free. Then he looked over at the T. rex, who just happened to be missing one of its toes. Homer ran back and shoved the toe into place. Dog tried to take another toe but Homer pushed him away. "Maybe I should have left you outside."

"Homer!" Madame called from the upper floor.

Homer knelt and lifted Dog's chin so he could look right into those red-rimmed eyes. "Listen," he whispered. "I don't know if you can understand me, but please don't do anything to get us kicked out. I really need to see that coin collection."

"Urrrr." Dog licked Homer's face.

"Yuck," Homer said, wiping his face with his jacket sleeve. But then he smiled and he was pretty sure, as the corners of Dog's mouth twitched, that Dog smiled, too.

At the top of the stairs, Madame ushered Homer and Dog into an exhibit called Life on the Edge, which turned out to be a long, narrow room filled with displays of North and South Pole critters. The floor was transparent like ice, the exhibit walls were painted arctic blue, and the room's thermostat was set on extra chilly, all to create the illusion that one had just stepped into an arctic world. Homer shivered.

"Homer!" Gwendolyn waved happily. She sat on a bench in front of a penguin display. A package of mint cookies lay on her lap. A single balloon, tied to the bench, floated beside her.

Homer waved back. His sister was actually smiling—a big, happy grin flecked with bits of cookie.

"Would you like a cookie?" Madame asked. She took a small package from her suit pocket and handed it to

Homer. They were dinosaur-shaped sugar cookies from the museum's gift shop. Dinookies.

"Thanks."

Madame looked at Gwendolyn. "Are you enjoying the party?"

"It's great," Gwendolyn said. "It's the best party ever."

The best party ever? Homer furrowed his brow. How could this be the best party ever? There were no streamers, just that single balloon. No party hats or music. No punch bowls or chocolate fountains. No piñatas or cakes.

"Make yourself comfortable, Homer. We have much to discuss." Madame pointed to an empty spot next to Gwendolyn.

Discuss? Yes, Homer had a ton of questions, like *Why did you invite me here?* and *Why aren't there any more guests?* Two people did not add up to a party, in his opinion. Especially if those two people spent every single day together.

But a buzzer sounded overhead and a man's voice burst from a speaker in the wall. "Madame?"

"What is it?" she asked curtly.

"We have a disturbance outside."

"Can't you handle it?"

"You know I can't be seen here. I'm supposed to be on holiday."

"Fine!" Madame pursed her lips real tight and clenched her fists. "The things I have to put up with." Then she gave the Pudding kids a stern look. "Under no circumstances are you to leave this room." Her high heels clicked and her blunt hair swayed as she hurried from the room.

"Isn't she beautiful?" Gwendolyn asked. "And this place is a million times bigger than it looks in the guide-book. I've been here all day. When I told them who I was at the ticket booth, Madame let me in for free. I ate macaroni and cheese in the cafeteria—not goat cheese, by the way. They don't serve goat cheese here, isn't that great? I showed Madame all my animals and she liked them. She said I was destined to become a Royal Taxi-dermist. Maybe one of the greatest Royal Taxidermists ever." Gwendolyn smiled dreamily. "*Ever.*"

Homer sat next to his sister. He pushed the bag of Dinookies behind his back, hiding it from Dog because he'd already eaten popcorn, magazines, and pink sprin-kle doughnuts, none of which was proper dog food. At some point he'd need to get some proper dog food. "Did you say that Madame liked your animals?"

"Of course she liked them, Homer. Why wouldn't she like them? She took the entire duffel bag and promised she'd put my animals on exhibit. I'm going to get my own wing. Can you believe it? The Gwendolyn Maybel Pudding Wing!"

But Homer had seen the duffel bag crammed into the garbage can.

Madame la Directeur had lied to Gwendolyn, but why? "Gwendolyn, I think you should know…"

"She's so nice." Gwendolyn leaned against the penguin's glass window. "I want to be just like her when I grow up. She specialized in herpetology at university, which, in case you don't know, and you probably don't, is the science of reptiles and amphibians. Then she became a Royal Taxidermist and worked her way up to running the entire museum. We talked for a really long time."

Dog pressed his black nose against one of the display windows. A low growl vibrated in his throat as he stared into the glass eyes of a stuffed polar bear, lounging on the edge of a fake glacier.

Homer punched the single balloon. "It's not much of a party. Did Madame tell you why she invited me here?"

"Oh, I asked that right away. I told her that it must have been a mistake because I'm the one who wrote all those letters and she told me that it had definitely been a mistake. She said I was the VIP, not you." Gwendolyn flipped her hair behind her shoulders. "She said that treasure hunting isn't as important as taxidermy."

As Dog waddled around the exhibit, leaving a nose smudge on every glass window, something nipped at the back of Homer's mind. "You told her I was a treasure hunter?"

"No," Gwendolyn said, folding her arms. "Because you're *not* a treasure hunter, Homer. Reading about treasure hunting isn't the same as actually doing it."

"But then how did she know...?"

"She knows all about you. She's very smart. She said she even knew Uncle Drake. She asked if he'd left you anything special. I told her about your droopy dog. She asked if he'd left you anything else. And then I remembered that coin."

The room felt chillier. Homer jumped to his feet. "You told her about the coin?"

"Is there a problem?"

The situation was like a map with missing pieces. What he now knew was that the invitation had not been wrongly addressed. Madame had sent the invitation to Homer because she had wanted to talk to *him*. If she had cared one ounce about Gwendolyn, she wouldn't have thrown away the duffel. Would she try to take the coin? Like Ajitabh, would she do anything to get it? And if Homer refused to give her the coin, would his parents ever see him again? Would he become a part of the prehistoric man exhibit? *Look Agnes, that's the fattest stuffed cave boy I've ever seen.*

"Gwendolyn, I think we're in trouble." Homer grabbed his sister's arm. "We need to get out of here."

She pulled her arm free. "Are you crazy? I'm not leaving."

Homer tiptoed out of Life on the Edge, then peered over the second-floor railing. The Grand Hall stood empty. Except for Dog, who was growling at a stuffed walrus, all was quiet.

"You're not supposed to leave the room," Gwendolyn whispered from behind Homer. She stood in the entry to Life on the Edge.

"No one's down there," Homer told her. "We can make a run for it. Come on."

Gwendolyn put her hands on her hips. "And why would I want to make a run for it?"

Homer didn't get the chance to explain because a siren wailed outside. A blue light shone through the Grand Hall's windows and pulsed across T. rex's legs. Homer ran down the grand staircase and across the hall to the row of windows that faced the street. He pressed his nose against a pane of cold glass.

A police car had pulled up to the sidewalk. Madame la Directeur stood talking to a police officer. Next to her, under a streetlight, stood a man in a cap and overalls.

"It's Dad!" Homer cried.

20

The Cave of Brilliance

Though Homer couldn't hear what was being said, he could tell his dad was hollering by the way he was shaking his fist. Madame stood very still, her gloved hands clasped behind her wide hips.

"What did you say?" Gwendolyn called from the balcony.

"Dad's outside."

"Oh, crud!" Gwendolyn ran down the stairs and pressed her face next to Homer's. "He's going to take us back home. I don't want to go home. He can't make me.

I'm staying!" The glass fogged up, so Homer wiped it with his jacket sleeve.

Homer wanted to run outside, for surely Madame wouldn't try to take the coin in Mr. Pudding's presence. But hiding behind his father's broad back wouldn't solve anything and it wouldn't be something a true treasure hunter would do. He still hadn't solved the mystery of the coin and he still hadn't found his uncle's belongings. And Ajitabh was out there, somewhere, probably sharpening his sword. Madame knew Homer's address, and Ajitabh had visited the farm, so they would easily find Homer once he returned to Milkydale. And if he ran outside, his father would take him home for sure.

Home. Back to that black smoky hole where the library had once stood. Back to the empty bedroom. Back to everybody telling him he was weird and that he'd never be a real treasure hunter.

But worse than all those things, Dog would be returned to the Snootys.

"I'm going to tell Dad to stop yelling at Madame la Directeur," Gwendolyn said. "It's so embarrassing!"

"Gwendolyn, wait!"

But there was no stopping his sister once she set her mind. She ran past the ticket booth and pushed open the entry door. Homer wiped the window again and watched as she rushed down the museum stairs, past a pair of lion statues, and down the walkway. Just as she reached Mr. Pudding, another car pulled up and a large man in a blue pinstriped suit stepped out. Homer recognized him from the elevator ride. Fishing through his crowded pockets, he found the business card. MR. DILL, ATTORNEY-AT-LAW, SPECIALIZING IN PERSONAL INJURY AND UNWANTED PARTY GUESTS. Madame spoke to Mr. Dill, who then spoke to the police officer. She pointed at Mr. Pudding.

Was it really against the law to be an unwanted party guest?

Mr. Pudding didn't notice Gwendolyn because he was hollering at the police officer. Gwendolyn tugged on her father's sleeve. He swept her into a hug, then held her at arm's length, hollering some more. Homer grimaced. He and Gwendolyn were in big trouble, no doubt about it. Their punishment would be the longest chore list in history. News reporters would travel to Milkydale to interview the children who never stopped doing chores.

But before Homer could imagine all the horrid things his father would add to the chore list, the scene outside turned ugly. The officer pulled out a billy club and waved it at Mr. Pudding. Mr. Pudding shook both his fists and his cap flew off his head. The officer grabbed Mr. Pudding's arm and shoved him into the patrol car.

Gwendolyn kicked the officer, who then shoved Gwendolyn into the patrol car and closed the door.

And all the while, Madame la Directeur calmly stood by, not moving a finger.

"Stop! Wait!" Homer ran to the ticket booth and was about to push open the museum door when he remembered something. "Dog?" he called. Where was he? "DOG!"

The patrol car sped away. Madame shook Mr. Dill's hand. Then she picked up Mr. Pudding's cap and threw it into the bushes. As she headed back toward the museum, a sinister smile spread across her face. Homer knew, without an inkling of doubt, that danger was heading his way—a high-heeled force that would come between him and his quest. No way was he going to hand over the coin.

He ran back through the Grand Hall. Frantically, he opened his museum map. Lorelei had said that the coin collection was on the third floor. His eyes scanned the index. Cave of Brilliance, third floor. Clutching the map, he charged back up the carpeted stairs. "Come on!" he yelled as he ran past Life on the Edge.

Dog, who'd been engaged in a staring contest with a stuffed narwhal, slid across the glassy floor and followed Homer down the hall. Far below, a door slammed shut and heels clicked across the Grand Hall's marble floor.

Homer found the door to the stairwell. Not in a million years would he take another elevator. Halfway up, Dog started huffing and puffing so Homer looped his arms under Dog's middle and heaved him up the last steps. "You gotta stop eating so much," he grumbled. Then, grabbing Dog's leash, he stumbled onto the third floor. Homer froze, holding his breath. The elevator stood silent. No clicking heels approached. "Come on," he whispered.

Charging down the hall, they passed a giant stuffed praying mantis that guarded the entry to World of Insects. Dog whimpered and picked up his pace. A stuffed ostrich stood outside World of Birds. "There it is," Homer whispered. At the end of the hall, twinkling light beckoned from the mouth of a gigantic cave. Just inside the cave, Homer and Dog skidded to a stop.

It was the stuff of stories and dreams. Row after row of little treasures, each set neatly on black velvet, each protected beneath a lighted glass case. Rubies, sapphires, diamonds, turquoise, amber, and jade. What pirates set sail for, what treasure hunters left home for—glittering, shiny miracles, grown deep in the earth. But there was no time to ogle. A tingling feeling shot up Homer's legs as he spotted the display at the back of the cave. He led Dog past a wall of geodes and pressed his hands against the back case, his eyes skimming each section—Roman coins, Egyptian coins, and Celtic coins. *Come on, come on. Where is it?* Greek, Persian, and Mayan coins. Dis-appointment swept over him. Not a single coin was engraved with a treasure chest or the letters *L.O.S.T.* "It's got to be here."

Dog growled. Homer spun around.

Madame la Directeur stood in the cave's entry. "You won't find it in there," she said coldly, gemstone light bouncing off her dark eyes.

"Uh, find what?" Homer asked, moving away from the coins. "I don't know what you're talking about." His heart skipped a beat as he realized that there was no other way out of the cave.

"You don't need to pretend, Homer. I know about the coin."

"What coin?" Homer felt as trapped as a fossil in a rock.

Madame took a step into the cave. "The coin that your uncle cleverly sent to you. I don't suppose you'd like to give it to me, as a thank-you for inviting you to our little party?"

Homer pressed his lips real tight, not saying a word. Was she insane? Even if the party had been an *actual* party, he wouldn't give her the coin. No way.

"I can show you where the coin came from." She raised her eyebrows and took another step. "Isn't that why you're here? Wouldn't you like me to show you?"

Homer thought hard and furious about his choices. He could try to escape but where would he go? He'd come to The City to solve this mystery and so far he'd found a great big nothing. This woman could clearly not be trusted. She'd lied to Gwendolyn, she'd had his father and sister arrested, but she knew what he wanted to know.

He tightened his grip on Dog's leash. "Okay. Show me."

21

The Realm of Reptiles

*G*wendolyn was right, Homer thought as he followed Madame from the Cave of Brilliance. Madame la Directeur was beautiful. But it wasn't a warm kind of beauty like Mrs. Pudding's—the kind that flows from a smiling face and covers everyone like a warm quilt. Madame's beauty came from an awful lot of makeup and from fancy clothes and jewelry. It was the kind of beauty that is meant to impress upon first glance. Homer wasn't impressed.

"All that sparkles is not splendid," Uncle Drake had

often said. "Remember that fool's gold might look like treasure, but it's just a worthless chunk of rock."

At the end of the hall, Madame pushed the elevator button. Homer shook his head and Dog backed away. "We don't like elevators."

"We're going to the first floor," she said. "So get in."

"No." Homer held his chin up and looked her straight in the eye. "We'll take the stairs."

Madame clenched her jaw. Her neck and cheeks flushed. "Fine! We'll take the stairs."

Upon reaching the first floor, Homer and Dog followed Madame into the Realm of Reptiles. Hot, heavy air greeted them with a smothering hug. A path of Astroturf wound between fake tropical trees. Stuffed pythons, boa constrictors, and cobras dangled from branches, their glass slit eyes watching hungrily. Dog's coarse back hairs stiffened and a low growl rose in the depths of his throat. "Keep that mongrel away from the exhibits," Madame said as she led them into the heart of the jungle. "This room is my pride and joy." She stopped in front of a wall of glass.

Keeping a safe distance between himself and Madame, Homer looked past his own reflection into the frozen eyes of a man dressed in safari gear. *That's the kind of outfit I need*, he thought, admiring the multipocketed khaki shorts and the crisp khaki shirt. *Uncle Drake used to dress like that*. Homer ran a hand over his corduroy jacket. Too bad they didn't carry safari clothes at Walker's Department Store.

He continued to gaze with envy. The man's hat was waterproof with a wide brim for sun protection. His trekking boots and extra-thick wool socks provided leech and snake protection. He clutched a pair of Extra Strong Borington Binoculars. Behind the man, a shotgun and rucksack leaned against a field tent. Books and maps were scattered on a small field desk, along with a camera. "Who is he?" Homer asked.

"That is a replica of Dr. Lionel Wortworthy," Madame said. "The greatest herpetologist who ever lived."

"Oh. You mean he studied reptiles and amphibians?"

"Precisely. Dr. Wortworthy caught and stuffed every specimen in this room."

"All of them?" There had to be hundreds of creatures in there, from the tiniest neon red frog to a tree trunk–size yellow anaconda.

"Do you mind?" Madame pointed to the window where Homer had pressed his fingers. Then she removed a handkerchief from her suit pocket and wiped away his fingerprints. From the corner of his eye, Homer saw Dog lift his leg on a stuffed iguana. "I have spent a great deal of time on this exhibit. Everything you see is authentic. Those are Dr. Wortworthy's actual clothes, that's his actual tent, and that was his favorite camera.

It's all real. Except for Dr. Wortworthy, of course. But it's his true likeness."

"Who are those guys?" Homer asked, pointing to two faces, half-hidden behind some shrubs at the back of Wortworthy's exhibit. While pointing, he accidentally dropped Dog's leash. Dog took off to explore the room.

"Those *guys* are cannibals. That's how Dr. Wortworthy met his unfortunate demise."

"Oh." A terrible image of the doctor sitting in a stewpot filled Homer's mind.

Madame tossed the handkerchief at a corner garbage can, but missed. Grumbling, she picked it up and stuffed it into the can. Then she gave the can a kick. Then another kick. After a deep breath, she turned back to Homer. "Where was I? Oh yes. Dr. Wortworthy was my father. He spent his life searching for rare and unknown species of reptiles and amphibians. Between expeditions, he'd stop here at the museum and drop off his specimens. Because he was such a prolific collector, his wife, Wilma von Weiner, had a special present made for him."

"Wilma von Weiner?" Homer said. "She's one of the most famous treasure hunters ever. She discovered the Lost Temple of the Reptile King."

Madame curled her upper lip. "If you're going to interrupt me, then at least tell me something I don't already know." She began to pace. "As I was saying, the special present that Wilma, my mother, presented to my father was a coin—a commemorative coin with the letters *L.O.S.T.* on it."

"*L.O.S.T.?*" Homer cried. Then he tried to hide his excitement by examining his jacket buttons. "Um, you wouldn't happen to know what those letters stand for? Not that I really care."

"Of course I know what they stand for." Madame stopped pacing. "They stand for...uh...they stand for...um...'Lots of Stuffed Things.' Yes, that's it. 'Lots of Stuffed Things.' Because, of course, Dr. Wortworthy stuffed so many things over the years."

That sure didn't sound right. And the way she'd hesitated reminded Homer of all the times he'd hesitated, just before lying to Mrs. Peepgrass about paying attention. "No, Mrs. Peepgrass, I wasn't daydreaming about treasure hunting. I was...um...I was...er...thinking about...fractions and decimals."

Madame's story made no sense. If the coin commemorated the stuffing of many things, why would it have a treasure chest on its flip side?

"The coin that my mother gave to my father is the very same coin that you have in your pocket." Madame stepped closer to Homer. "It belongs to the museum. So if you'll just turn it over to me, then I can put it back in the exhibit where it belongs."

"But I don't..."

She stomped her high heel. "DO NOT lie to me. Drake stole the coin from this museum and then gave it to you. I know it's in your pocket, inside a matchbook, and I want it now." She held out her gloved hand.

Homer nearly fell over a stuffed leatherback turtle as he stepped away from Madame's searing gaze. Why would his uncle steal from a museum when he had spent his entire life trying to find things to donate to museums? And how could Madame know about the matchbook? Gwendolyn knew about the coin but not about the matchbook.

"Is that why you invited me here? Because you think I have your coin?"

"Of course. You don't really think you're some sort of VIP, do you?" She snickered. "I was actually hoping that Drake had given you something else, something we'd both been looking for. But I'll take the coin as a consolation prize."

Homer fought the instinct to shove his hand in his pocket to protect the coin. He sidestepped around the turtle. "I think I'd better be going." Where was Dog?

"You're not going anywhere. Do you want me to call the police and tell them that you are in possession of a stolen object?" Madame strode toward him. "Possessing a stolen object is a crime in The City—a crime that carries a prison term."

"Prison?" Beads of sweat broke out on Homer's forehead. The room's sweltering temperature and the glowing reptilian eyes were starting to make him feel dizzy. He looked past Madame to the room's distant corner. Dog had sunk his teeth into a stuffed alligator.

"No one has to know that your uncle was a thief. That can be our little secret." Madame held out her hand again and wiggled her fingers. "You can come and look at the coin anytime you'd like. You wouldn't want to deny the public a chance to see it, would you?"

"Uncle Drake would never steal from a museum. He always told me that the purpose of treasure hunting is for the greater good." Homer whistled, trying to get Dog's attention. If he made a run for it, he could reach the hallway before Madame. Surely she couldn't run very fast in those high heels. "Dog," Homer called. "Come here, Dog."

"Grrrr." Dog wrestled the alligator, tipping it over.

Madame la Directeur's gaze burned into Homer. "Freedom or jail. Take your pick."

"Um, I need to use the bathroom. I'll be right back." Homer turned to leave. "Dog?"

"Grrrr." An alligator leg flew across the room.

Madame clenched her hands into fists. "Listen, you stupid country bumpkin, that coin is rightfully mine. Hand it over or..."

Dog waddled across the room, a second alligator leg clamped in his mouth. Madame reached down and grabbed Dog's leash.

"Or you'll never see your ugly dog again."

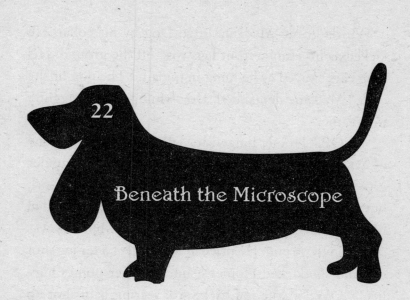

Beneath the Microscope

Madame la Directeur yanked the leash. Dog yelped and dropped the alligator leg. She yanked harder. Dog yelped louder.

"Stop it," Homer said. "You're hurting him."

Madame leaned over, slid her fingers beneath Dog's collar, and pulled it into a chokehold. Dog whimpered and looked at Homer. *Why is she doing this to me?* his watery eyes asked.

"Stop. Oh, please stop," Homer cried. "That's my dog. Please don't hurt him."

With a grunt, Madame lifted Dog by his collar. He kicked as his stubby front legs rose off the ground. His long ears swayed as he hung in midair. "The dog or the coin," Madame demanded. Dog whimpered, struggling to breathe.

"STOP!" Homer lunged at Madame and grabbed one of her arms. His mother had always told him that under NO circumstances was he ever allowed to hit a girl, but what if that girl was choking your dog? He pulled Madame's arm, trying to loosen her grip, but she was surprisingly strong. He pried at her fingers. Her leg shot out and she kicked Homer's shin with her pointy high heel. "OW!" As he fell backward, searing pain shot up his leg but it was nothing compared to the agony he felt watching Dog suffocate. Homer shoved his hand into his pocket and held out the matchbook. "TAKE IT!" he cried. "Take it. Just take it." He threw it at her. She let go of the collar and caught the matchbook in midair. Dog tumbled onto the Astroturf.

Homer fell to his knees and threw his arms around Dog. "I'm sorry," he whispered in one of the long ears. Dog poked his wet nose against Homer's cheek and wagged his tail. Mr. and Mrs. Pudding had always taught their children that it was a sin to mistreat an animal. In her taxidermy practice, Gwendolyn had never harmed a single creature. Each one had been roadkill or been killed by one of the farm dogs or barn cats. By choking Dog, Madame had proven, without a doubt, that she was the worst kind of person.

"Zelda's Trinket Shop," Madame said with disgust as she read the matchbook's cover. She pulled out the coin and tossed the matchbook aside. "Won't that towering freak be surprised when she finds out that I outsmarted her?"

Towering freak? Homer clenched his jaw. The tall woman on the train had advised him to tuck the coin into the matchbook. And she'd watched while he'd done so, and while he'd put the matchbook into his jacket pocket. *She'd* told the museum director.

"I have done terrible, unspeakable things," she'd said on the train.

Homer's thoughts raced. Zelda and Madame were in this together. Zelda hadn't taken the coin during the train ride because the conductor would have heard Homer scream for help. She'd left the dirty work to Madame.

Anger raged inside Homer as he watched Madame la Directeur gaze at the coin. But as quickly as the anger reached a boil, it was drowned by a rush of shame. He'd failed his uncle. Completely and utterly failed.

Madame pushed a button on the wall. A man's voice blared from an overhead speaker. It was the same voice as earlier. "What?"

"Realm of Reptiles. Now!" she ordered.

"Why?"

"Do I pay you to ask why? There's a dog and a stupid kid I need you to get rid of."

Get rid of? She'd kill them both, no doubt about it. Homer grabbed the end of Dog's leash and ran for the hall. "There's no use running," Madame called, not bothering to follow. "He'll find you. I've got cameras everywhere."

Homer's plan was to run through the Grand Hall and out the door by the ticket booth. That was the plan. But the elevator made a *ding* sound as it arrived from the basement. There'd be no time to get past it. "Come on," he urged, pulling Dog into an exhibit called Beneath the Microscope.

Homer desperately looked for a place to hide. A giant microscope stood in the center of the room. Its lens reflected a protozoan onto a wide screen. Styrofoam bacteria, as tall as Mr. Pudding, stood in a cluster. A nucleus with orbiting electrons hung from the ceiling. Homer and Dog ran to the very back of the room, then squeezed behind something that looked like a giant fried egg but was labeled AMOEBA. "Shhh," Homer whispered, crouching next to Dog. "Don't move." His heart pounded in his ears. Dog stuck his nose in Homer's sleeve.

"Twaddle!" Madame hollered.

"What?"

Homer peered around the amoeba. Madame and Mr. Twaddle, the Snootys' secretary, stood just outside the microscope exhibit. Mr. Twaddle wore the same pin-striped suit and two-toned shoes that he'd worn on the Sunday prior, when he'd delivered Dog to the Pudding Farm. Wasn't he supposed to be on holiday?

"The front door is locked so they can't get out. They're probably somewhere on this floor," Madame said. "Once you've gotten rid of them, meet me in the lair. We need to finish searching through those belongings."

"But I've searched through them already."

She shoved the coin in his face. "Look, you idiot. You see the little hole that's been drilled into this coin? Drake managed to sneak the coin past you by attaching it to the mutt's collar. It doesn't take a brain surgeon to figure that one out." She poked him in the chest. "So don't tell me you've searched all his belongings because you haven't found the map and it's got to be there!" She poked him again, this time he almost fell over.

Homer held his breath. Madame la Directeur had his uncle's belongings and she was looking for a map. It had to be the same map that Uncle Drake had been looking for. The one and only map.

"What's so important about that coin?" Mr. Twaddle asked.

"None of your nosy business. But I've wanted it for a very long time and now it's mine." She kissed the coin. "Well? Why are you just standing there? Go find the kid."

"Yeah, yeah," Mr. Twaddle grumbled.

"Hurry up." She shoved him. "I'll meet you in the lair."

Faint elevator music drifted into the microscope room as the elevator doors opened and closed. Dog pulled his nose out of Homer's sleeve and started to yawn. Homer clamped his hand over Dog's mouth.

"Shhhh."

"Hey, kid!" Mr. Twaddle called. "Where are you? Kid!" His voice faded as he searched a different exhibit.

If Uncle Drake had found Rumpold Smeller's map, Madame had no right to take it. But the last thing Homer wanted to do was to follow her into some sort of lair. Lairs are evil places, owned by evil people—everyone knows that. Lairs have things like poisonous moats, torture chambers, and doomsday weapons. But what were his options? If he went to the police department they'd never believe that Madame, a director by Royal Decree, had stolen his coin and his uncle's belongings. And he had no proof. He couldn't even lead them to the lair. They'd think he'd made the whole thing up.

Still, he could go home and start on that massive chore list. He could try to avoid the vacant lot where the library had once stood. Try to forget that he'd failed to protect his uncle's most treasured possession. Try to forget about treasure hunting altogether. Then watch his dad send Dog away.

Homer massaged the sore spot on Dog's wrinkled neck where Madame had choked him. "I won't let her hurt you again," he whispered. "But we've got to find her lair. It's the only way to get proof." Dog turned his watery eyes up at Homer and whapped his tail against the amoeba.

"There you are!" Mr. Twaddle grabbed Homer's arm and pulled him to his feet. Dog started barking.

"Let me go!" Homer cried, kicking Mr. Twaddle's shin.

"Stop squirming." Though not much taller than Homer, he easily overpowered him and forced him into the hallway. Dog clamped his teeth around Mr. Twaddle's pant leg. "Get off me." Mr. Twaddle shook his leg. Dog tumbled backward, a piece of fabric between his teeth. "Hey, these are my good pants." Homer tried to kick the other shin but Mr. Twaddle shoved him up against the wall. "I said stop squirming. You're making this difficult." Well, that was the point. What did he think? That Homer would quietly follow him to who-knew-where?

Dog scrambled to his feet and sank his teeth into Mr. Twaddle's ankle. "Ahhhh!" Mr. Twaddle let go of Homer and grabbed Dog. With a grunt, he heaved Dog over his shoulder. "Can't believe you still have this stupid dog. Leave it to Drake Pudding to have such a stupid mutt." He started down the hall, Dog bouncing against his shoulder.

"Let him go," Homer cried.

"Come on, kid, I'm not gonna hurt you. I just need to make sure you leave the museum." Then he whipped around and glared at Homer "But if you try to kick me one more time, I might change my mind." Dog whimpered.

Somewhere, deep inside, Homer believed that Mr. Twaddle wasn't going to "get rid" of them. Maybe he shouldn't have felt that way, but he did. Killing a kid was a whole lot more serious than stealing a coin. But that didn't mean he wasn't capable of hurting them. So Homer didn't fight or argue. Instead, he followed Mr. Twaddle down the hall, his mind racing. *Maybe I can get some information from this guy.*

"I saw your photos at Snooty and Snooty's office. I saw the one with all the treasure-hunting books."

Twaddle kept on walking. "This thing weighs a ton. What do you feed it? Doughnuts?"

"I have lots of treasure-hunting books, too," Homer said.

"Good for you."

The hallway ended near the gift shop, just across from

the Grand Hall's wide staircase. A bin of polished rocks stood outside the gift shop. Little kids would think of those colorful rocks as treasures. "Why does Madame la Directeur have my uncle's things?"

"You're swimming up a dangerous river, kid. You keep asking questions like that and the same thing'll happen to you that happened to your uncle. That woman will stop at nothing. Take my advice. Leave the museum while you can. *Alive.*"

The same thing'll happen to you that happened to your uncle.

As Homer followed Mr. Twaddle across the Grand Hall's marble floor, a frightening thought grew in his brain. What if it hadn't been an accident after all? Gwendolyn had said that tortoises don't eat people. Lorelei had pointed out that their mouths were way too small to swallow a person.

That woman will stop at nothing.

A queasy feeling washed over Homer's body. What if Madame la Directeur had been responsible for Drake Pudding's death?

Mr. Twaddle unlocked the ticket door and pushed it open. Then he dumped Dog outside. "Go home, kid. The City's no place for a country boy." Homer wanted to ask more questions but Mr. Twaddle shoved him into the night, then slammed and locked the door. Homer watched through the glass as Mr. Twaddle grabbed a bag of Dinookies from the gift shop, then sauntered away.

Uncle Drake had been murdered. But why? So that Madame la Directeur could get her hands on his belongings and search for Rumpold Smeller's map? The most famous pirate map in the world, searched for by countless treasure hunters and never found. But what if his uncle had truly found it? How could Homer allow his uncle's killer to get away with murder and the map?

"Hi, Homer."

Homer nearly jumped out of his shoes. He turned to find a smiling face and a head of crazy pink hair standing next to him.

"I couldn't get back into the warehouse because all the stock boys had already shown up. So I thought I'd come and see how the party went."

"Lorelei." Homer had never been so happy to see anyone. Even Dog seemed happy as he poked her with his nose. "Lorelei, I need your help. You said you got into the museum for free all the time. Will you show me how?"

She frowned. "Can't you just go back to the VIP entrance? Why do you have to sneak in?"

He had already told her everything. What harm could come from telling her the rest? Words flew out of his mouth. "She killed my uncle. It wasn't an accident. I don't know how she did it but she made it look like a tortoise ate him. Tortoises don't eat people. Gwendolyn knows that kind of stuff. And they never found his body, just his shoes. She could have put the shoes near the tortoise to make it look…"

"Calm down, Homer. Take a breath or you'll faint."

Homer took a breath. "She called him a thief. Then she took the coin. She said it belongs to the museum but if it belonged to the museum then my uncle wouldn't have given it to me. He wasn't a thief. And she took all his stuff because she thinks he has a map. That's why Mr. Twaddle told my parents that Uncle Drake didn't leave any belongings. Because he's working for her and she took everything. She choked Dog." Homer showed Lorelei the welt on Dog's neck.

Lorelei knelt and stroked Dog's back. "Who is *she?*"

"Madame la Directeur, head of the museum. That dark-haired lady with those real pointy high heels. She's got a lair."

Lorelei laughed. "A lair? No way. I've been in that museum a million times. I've never seen a lair."

Homer felt his face go red. She didn't believe him. Why should she? He sounded like a crazy person. Who has a lair? This wasn't a science fiction movie. He braced himself, expecting her to laugh again. But she was real quiet as she scratched Dog's rump. Then she looked up. "Okay. Let's see if we can find this lair."

Homer nodded, so overcome with gratitude that he almost hugged Lorelei. He sure didn't want to look for the thing all by himself.

While Dog nibbled on some blades of neatly mowed grass, Homer unfolded his museum map. He and Lorelei sat against a stone lion. Huddling over the glossy paper, Homer ran his flashlight beam over each illustrated floor. "Sometimes you can find a secret space by comparing the external shape of a building to the internal arrangement of the walls."

Lorelei, her shoulder pressed against Homer's, searched with equal determination. No one in Mrs. Peepgrass's class had ever helped Homer look for anything. They would never even believe him if he told them about an evil lair. *You're such a weirdo, Homer Pudding.* But Lorelei was willing to believe. If she still needed a home when this was all over, he'd ask his parents to adopt her. They could turn the attic into her room. They could walk to school together and eat lunch together. She would never have to eat cold soup from a can again.

They ran their fingers along the map—his followed the external walls, hers followed the internal walls. Nothing appeared out of the ordinary. He moved his finger across the illustrated museum grounds. "Hey, what's that?" He traced a pair of thick blue lines.

Lorelei pointed to the map's legend. "Says 'City Channel.'"

"A channel? Like, water?"

"I guess so." She shrugged. "I've never seen any water around the museum. Except for the birdbaths."

"According to this map, the channel runs up to the museum's western wall and then back out the eastern wall. It must go under the museum." Homer held out his compass. "That's not possible, though, because we're at the eastern wall and there's no channel here."

Homer stood and looked out over the garden. "Look at that flower bed," he said. "Look how wide it is. It runs straight from the wall to the street." He ran over and read a plaque that was stuck in the flower bed: OLD CITY CHANNEL BEDS.

"There's a bed just like it on the other side," Lorelei said. "Oh, I see. The channel was filled in."

"Or..." Homer waved the map. "The channel was covered up. What if it's still down there? What if it still runs under the museum?"

"Then that would be the perfect place for a lair."

Homer smiled. They made a great team. "I need to get back inside and look. Will you show me how you get in?"

"Sure. But you have to promise that you'll never tell

anyone else about it. If other people start using my secret entrance, the museum staff might find out and they'll seal it shut and I'll never get in for free, ever again."

"I promise," Homer said solemnly. They shook hands.

"Okay. Follow me."

Homer switched off his flashlight and folded the map, tucking both into his jacket pocket. Then he picked up Dog's leash and they followed Lorelei around the building. He'd lost track of the time. He guessed it to be around midnight, but the glow of The City's streetlights and the floodlights perched along the museum roof suspended the museum grounds between night and day. They followed the north wall. This side of the museum was thick with underbrush and shrubbery. No parking lots, no gardens, just wild foliage. At the wall's midpoint, Lorelei pushed aside some ivy vines, exposing a large metal grate set in the ground. "I think this is for ventilation, but I really don't know." She reached into her sweater, then shoved something at Homer. The something grabbed and clung to the front of his jacket.

Homer held his breath as Daisy the rat stared up at him with her beady eyes, her brown whiskers twitching with annoyance. She climbed up the jacket's collar until her nose reached his chin. Would she go for his jugular? She sniffed his neck, his mouth, his right ear, then his left ear. He stood frozen and cross-eyed as she sniffed the tip of his nose. "Nice rat," he whispered.

"Grrrr." Dog pawed at Homer's leg.

Lorelei knelt and with a heave, pulled the grate free. She stuck her head into the metal pipe. "It's a long crawl." Her voice echoed off the steel walls. "And there's lots of spiders. I'm just warning you in case you don't like spiders."

Spiders were the least of Homer's worries. He wasn't sure he could fit into the pipe.

"The pipe leads into the basement. There's another grate at the other end but it's easy to remove. I've never explored the basement. Just a bunch of offices, I think."

"Lorelei? Do you mind?" Homer grimaced as Daisy sniffed his face.

"Oh. Sorry." She peeled Daisy from his shirt. He shuddered.

And that's when a whirring sound filled the air and white light flooded Homer's vision. Two hands reached from the sky and lifted him off the ground.

Lorelei screamed.

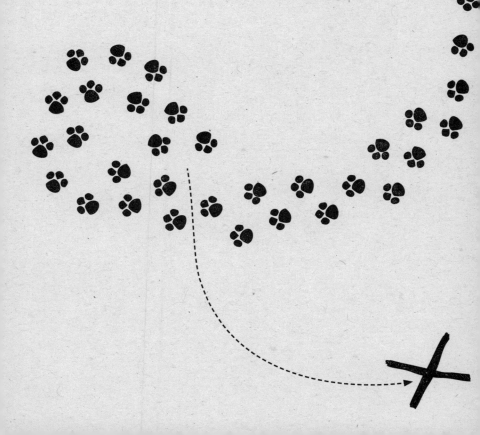

PART FIVE

THE TOWER
IN THE SKY

Clouds, Clouds Everywhere

It took Homer a few moments to realize what had happened. Squinting against the brightness, he reached out a hand. It disappeared into nothingness. Above, below, and all around, whiteness floated.

He was inside a cloud.

Have you ever looked out an airplane window at the very moment when you reach the clouds? It's another world up there, filled with wispy tendrils and frothy fronds. Who hasn't imagined bouncing from billow to billow or sliding down hills of puff? Of course, anyone foolish enough to attempt that would have a very long fall to deal with because clouds aren't one bit solid, just a collection of water vapor.

Which is why Homer felt more confused than ever because he was sitting in a seat. A solid seat. And his feet rested on a solid floor. He reached up and found a roof. He wiped dew from his eyelids, then looked around at his colorless surroundings. "Dog?"

"Urrrr." A paw tapped Homer's shoe.

"There you are," Homer said with relief. He heaved Dog onto his lap. Dog pressed his cold nose into Homer's ear.

"Where are we?" a girl's voice asked.

"Lorelei? Is that you?"

Her pink hair appeared first, then her upturned nose as she stuck her head out of the nothingness. "Someone grabbed me," she said in a shaky voice.

"Me, too." Homer fanned his hands until some of the billows cleared, revealing Lorelei in a seat right next to him. But as soon as he stopped fanning, the whiteness returned.

Lorelei gasped. "We're moving. Can you feel it? We're moving."

"Yeah." Just like on an elevator, a sinking sensation filled Homer's stomach. "I think we're on that cloud I told you about."

"You mean the guy with the sword?" Lorelei took a deep breath and blew until the space between them cleared. Her eyes were wide with fear. "We gotta get off this thing."

"How?"

"I don't know. But I don't like this one bit." Whiteness drifted between them again. "I'm going to jump off."

Homer tightened his grip around Dog. "You can't jump off. We don't know how high we are."

"We've got to do something," Lorelei said, grabbing his shoulder. "We've been kidnapped. Don't you see? People who kidnap kids are *evil*."

Evil seemed to be the theme of the day.

"I'm outta here." She made some shuffling noises and before Homer could say *That's a terrible idea*, his seat tipped.

"What the devil is going on? Stop moving around back there," a man's voice ordered from the void.

Dog's entire body tensed. Homer tensed, too, as he recognized the man's accent. *Ajitabh*.

"It's him," Homer whispered. "Lorelei? Are you okay?"

More shuffling sounds, then his seat leveled. "Yeah," she whispered back. "I...changed my mind."

A pair of goggles thrust out of the whiteness, right into Homer's face. "Best put those on," Ajitabh said.

"Take us back to the museum," Homer demanded.

"Yeah. Right now," Lorelei cried.

"No time to chat. The cloudcopter travels at high altitudes. Unless you wish to freeze your eyeballs and spend the rest of your life as blind as a bloomin' bat, I suggest you wear the goggles." Another pair of goggles appeared. "For the hound."

The temperature had dropped. Homer quickly put on his goggles, then grabbed the second pair and slid them over Dog's head. Dog shook his head, trying to loosen the goggles. "Lorelei, did you get goggles?" Homer asked.

"Yeah." How odd to have her sit so close yet not be able to see her. "Hey, cloud guy, where are you taking us?" she yelled.

The air grew colder still. Homer was glad for his heavy farm jacket. "Unless you wish to fall to your deaths, chaps, I suggest you fasten your seatbelts. There are no doors on this 'copter and I'm taking us into a steep turn."

A *click* sounded as Lorelei fastened her belt. Not wanting to fall to his death on that particular day or on *any* particular day, Homer felt around for his belt. "I can't find it," he said. The heavy feeling in his stomach grew stronger and the cloud tipped. Dog began to slide off Homer's lap. "HELP!" Homer cried. The turn tightened and the cloud tipped further. Homer began to slip out of the seat. "We're gonna fall off!" He held on to the seat's armrest with one hand, his other hand wrapped around Dog.

"Homer!" Lorelei reached out with both hands and grabbed his arm. "Hold on, Homer."

As Lorelei held tight to Homer's jacket sleeve, Homer held tight to the chair and to Dog. Fighting gravity, he pressed his feet against the 'copter's floor and tried to wedge his bottom into the seat. His legs started shaking from the sheer strain. The cloud tipped further. "Help him!" Lorelei called out. "He's not strapped in!"

"What's that?" Ajitabh called from the void. "Can't quite hear you."

Homer squeezed his eyes shut, sending every ounce of strength to his arms and legs. Dog whimpered and slid a bit more. Homer's forearms burned, his shoulders ached. The weight was almost too much to bear. Dog was going to fall to his death and there was nothing he could do.

Dog kicked his stumpy legs, then slid from under Homer's arm. Homer grabbed Dog's collar. "HELP!"

"Hold on!" Ajitabh called. "Pulling out of the turn...now."

The cloud leveled. Dog fell back into Homer's lap. Lorelei, still camouflaged by the cloud, let go of Homer's arm, felt around, then handed him a thick canvas belt. "Here it is."

Homer's heart pounded in his neck as he pulled the belt across Dog and clicked it into place.

Lorelei blew until the space between them cleared. The goggles made her look like she had insect eyes. "You okay?"

"Yeah," he said between deep breaths. He relaxed his legs and rubbed his aching arms. "Thanks. You saved us."

"Yeah, well, maybe you'll save me next time." Cloud crept between them again and Lorelei's scared face disappeared.

Dampness slid inside Homer's collar and he shivered. Ajitabh wanted the coin, no doubt about it. He'd gone to the Pudding Farm looking for it, he'd crashed through Snooty and Snooty's window trying to get it. But Homer no longer had the coin. How would Ajitabh react to that news? Would he let them go or get angry and throw them off the 'copter?

"Let Lorelei go," Homer called out. "She has nothing to do with this."

"Hold on! Turbulence ahead!"

Dog whimpered as the cloud bounced violently.

Lorelei fanned the billows with her hands, then leaned as close to Homer as she could. "We have...to come up...with some...sort of plan," she said, her voice vibrating with each bounce. "As soon...as the tur...bulence stops...we'll both...rush forward...and push...him off."

"Then what?" Homer's legs went numb as Dog bounced on his lap.

"Do I...have to think...of everything?"

The turbulence worsened. Homer thought his head might jar loose and fly off. He considered Lorelei's plan. Even if they did manage to push Ajitabh off the cloud, which would be *murder*, how would they get home? Homer had no idea how to fly a cloudcopter or what a cloudcopter was, for that matter. Or even where they were! "We can't push him off. It's too dangerous. I'll think of something else but for now, use your compass. We'll keep track of the route so we can get home. I'll record the readings."

"Good idea."

Between bounces, Homer searched his pockets until he found his Swiss army knife. He flipped open its miniature pencil. Then he found a blank space on the museum map and wrote Lorelei's readings as she whispered them.

Time passed. Each turbulent minute carried them farther away from The City. Would they have to walk all the way home? Unless Lorelei had her driver's license, then maybe they could steal a truck. "How old are you?" Homer asked.

"Twelve," Lorelei replied. Yep, they'd have to walk. Would this turn out like *The Odyssey?* Would Homer be gone for twenty years?

Finally, the turbulence stopped and the cloudcopter glided smoothly in the night air. An occasional star shone through the cloud's puffy layers. Dog stretched across Homer's lap, his rump hanging off the seat, and fell asleep. Homer used Dog's back as a table and continued to record the compass readings.

One hour passed, then another. Homer's eyelids grew heavy and his head fell forward. He snapped awake. The cloud had stopped moving. Icy air stung his nose.

"Homer, I think we've landed," Lorelei said.

The whirring sound stopped. They took off their goggles. Cloud vapors drifted away and Homer and Lorelei saw the cloudcopter for the first time. It was a small, doorless helicopter, with two passenger seats in the back and a cockpit up front. Shiny metal tubes stuck out all over like needles in a pincushion. A lingering wisp of cloud drifted from the tube closest to Homer. He and Dog peered over the armrest. They had landed on a large, round platform that had no walls, no railing, just an edge that dropped into nothingness. A range of mountains spread out as far as the eye could see, their snow-covered craggy peaks piercing a starry sky.

"I say, why are you two sitting there like a couple of statues?" Ajitabh's head poked out of a hole in the platform. He wore a leather flight jacket. His goggles were perched on his forehead. "Don't dillydally. Who would like a spot of tea?" He sounded rather chipper for a kidnapper.

Lorelei grabbed Homer's arm. Daisy the rat climbed out of Lorelei's sweater and perched on her shoulder. "Don't go. He tried to kill you, remember?"

No one needed to remind Homer of that fact. The gleam of the sword's blade was forever branded in his mind's eye. "Let Lorelei and Dog go. Then I'll give you the coin," Homer said through nearly frozen lips.

"Let Homer go, too," Lorelei cried. "He doesn't have the coin anymore. The museum director has it."

Homer wished she hadn't said that. Pretending to have the coin might have been his only bargaining tool. Would Ajitabh lash out in anger? But their kidnapper stroked his long mustache, then said, "Blasted shame. Not to worry. Membership is still yours to claim even without the coin."

"Membership?" Lorelei lowered her voice. "What's he talking about?"

"I don't know."

"Come come, all of you. The hound and the rat, too.

Mumble will treat us to chickpea curry. He tries his best to bring a bit of India to my lonely mountain home." Ajitabh's head disappeared into the hole.

Homer didn't know what a chickpea was. But he hadn't eaten any of those cookies at the fake VIP party and even though the ride had been rough, his stomach ached with hunger.

"This feels like a trap," Lorelei said. "Remember what Circe did to Odysseus? She offered his men lots of food and then turned them into pigs." She climbed into the cockpit. "Maybe we can fly this thing. We've got the compass readings to guide us home." She ran her hands over the dials. "Do you know how to fly?"

"No." Homer's stomach growled. But more than hunger, curiosity tugged at his body. What membership could he still claim? "I think I should go in there and talk to him. You stay out here." He slid Dog off his lap, then jumped out of the 'copter and onto the platform.

"Howooooo!"

"Don't worry. I know better than to try to leave you." Homer reached up and removed Dog's goggles, then helped him off the 'copter. He attached the leash so Dog wouldn't fall off the platform's edge. Daisy leaped from Lorelei's shoulder onto Homer's arm, then onto the platform where she scurried down the hole.

"Looks like I'm going with you," Lorelei said, jumping onto the platform. "It's too cold out here anyway." She crept to the side and carefully peered over the edge. "We're at the top of some kind of tower," she said. "What a weird place to live."

Vertigo swept over Homer as he stood next to her. A snow-speckled valley lay far below. This was way higher than the thirty-second floor. "I'm sorry I got you into this," he said, stepping away from the edge.

Lorelei shrugged. "I've been in worse places." A breeze rustled the ends of her pink hair. For a long moment they looked into each other's eyes. "I'm scared," she admitted.

"Me, too."

The hole turned out to be an entrance to a steep stairway. Once inside, Homer took off the leash and stuck it into his pocket.

"I'm going to let you eat first," Lorelei said. "And if you turn into a pig, I'm making a run for it. Got it?"

"Got it."

With Dog between them, he and Lorelei descended the stairs, one cautious step at a time.

24

Conqueror of the Sky

Homer, Dog, and Lorelei slowly made their way down the winding staircase. Candles, sitting in small alcoves, sent spidery shadows across the stone walls. They passed eight locked wooden doors but the ninth stood wide open. "In here," Ajitabh called. Warm air beckoned from the doorway. After sharing a look of trepidation, they stepped inside.

Colorful pillows lay scattered across a richly carpeted room. A teakettle hummed on a glowing woodstove. Ajitabh, his flight jacket and goggles shed, lifted the kettle and carried it to a low, round table. He poured steaming brown liquid into three glasses. "Come in," he said, waving his hand. "I hope you like chai."

Homer took a long look at the face of the man who'd tried to kill him—the black mustache and beard, the arched eyebrows, the nearly black eyes—definitely villain features. His clothes, though, didn't look very sinister. A knee-length embroidered white shirt hung over a pair of worn jeans and his feet were bare. But there was the sword, lying on a shelf.

Homer felt a sudden surge of defiance. "What do you want?" he demanded. Dog pushed between Homer's shins. Lorelei peered around Homer's shoulder. "Why have you brought us here?"

Ajitabh set the kettle aside. "I brought you here because I need to speak with you. You kept running from me. Why the blazes did you keep running from me?"

"Why?" Homer's mouth fell open. "Because you were chasing me. And because you tried to kill me with that sword."

"Tried to kill you?" Ajitabh smiled. "The very idea. You are my dearest friend's nephew. I would never hurt you. I always carry my sword when I go to The City. Devil of a place. Been robbed there too many times to count."

Homer narrowed his eyes. "If you didn't want to hurt

me, why'd you jump through that window at Snooty and Snooty's?"

"I couldn't very well land my cloudcopter on the street, could I? Fortunately it has hover mode." He stroked his beard. "You thought I was trying to kill you? A rather unfortunate misunderstanding. My deepest apologies."

"Why'd you grab me in the cherry orchard? You ripped my shirt."

Ajitabh frowned. "Again, my apologies. I desperately wanted to speak to you. I was worried I might not get another chance."

The explanation sort of made sense, but Homer still wasn't sure.

Dog growled as Daisy the rat scurried across the carpet. She settled on a yellow pillow and started grooming her rubbery tail. Lorelei stepped forward. "What about me? How come you grabbed me? I didn't do anything."

Ajitabh picked up one of the glass cups and blew across the tea's surface. "And who are you, exactly?"

Lorelei put her hands on her hips. "What kind of kidnapper are you if you don't even know who you kidnapped? *Who am I?* Who are *you?* That's what I want to know. And why do you live in this tower?"

"Fair questions." He took a sip of tea. "My name is Ajitabh, which means 'Conqueror of the Sky.' I am Indian by birth, but have lived in Britain most of my life. I hold a doctoral degree in inventology from Cambridge University. This tower is my home and workplace. I require...seclusion." He took another sip. "The reason *you* are here, young lady, is because the police were searching the museum grounds for unwanted party guests. If I had left you behind, you might have told them about my cloudcopter. Of course they wouldn't have believed you, but Madame la Directeur would have. She has come very close to finding my tower. I don't wish to give her a new reason to resume her search." He motioned for them to sit.

The room had no chairs. Homer led Dog to a zebra-striped pillow and sat cross-legged as best he could. Lorelei plopped herself on a red-striped pillow. They set their goggles on the table. Dog settled beside Homer and though he closed his eyes, he popped one open now and then to check on Daisy.

"Why would Madame la Directeur want to find your tower?" Homer asked.

"Because she wants to get her greedy hands on my inventions. She would love to peek at my laboratories. All fifteen of them."

"You have fifteen laboratories?" Homer asked.

"I would have built more but the tower was dangerously close to tipping." He pushed aside some newspapers, then sat on a blue velvet pillow. "Where the devil is our food? MUMBLE!"

An old Indian man appeared in the doorway. Bald and hunched over, he wiped his hands on a greasy apron. "Yes?"

"The food?"

"But your lady friend has just landed. Will we be feeding her, too?"

"By all means, but she's not fond of chickpea curry. How about making her favorite pancakes?"

Mumble's face folded into a million crevices as he grimaced. "That lady eats like a whale, nah? I'll be making pancakes all night." He shuffled off.

Homer thought of his mother's huckleberry pancakes, lightly browned and rolled up with strawberry jam. Then he stifled a yawn. Despite his fear that Ajitabh might still hurt them, a wave of sleepiness washed over him. He hadn't slept since the train ride the night before. He wanted to curl up like Daisy.

Ajitabh set his palms on the low table. "Homer, as I've said, you have no need to worry. You are perfectly safe here. I visited City Jail and paid bail. Your father and sister have been released. Fortunately, being an unwanted party guest is only a misdemeanor. I've sent a message to your mother that all is well. I hope you don't mind but I concocted an ingenious story. I couldn't reveal the truth, you see. Not yet. So I wrote in the message that because of your VIP status, the Museum of Natural History had sent you on an all-expense-paid field trip and that you'd return in a few days. I wouldn't want her to worry. By Jove, your uncle was most fond of her." He reached across the table and pushed the cups of tea closer to Homer and Lorelei.

Maybe he'd paid bail. Then again, it could all be a lie. But Ajitabh seemed to have accepted the fact that Homer no longer had the coin. So why was he keeping them around?

Homer picked up his cup of tea and took a sip. It tasted like cinnamon. Lorelei's eyes widened as she watched him swallow. He considered making an *oink* sound, just to freak her out, but the situation was too serious. "How do you know...how *did* you know my uncle?"

Ajitabh raised an eyebrow. "I'm happy to answer that question but the answer is of a *confidential nature*." He looked at Lorelei.

"You want me to leave?" she asked, sitting up straight. "Fine with me. Just take me back to The City."

"Can't do that quite yet. The 'copter needs to recharge. MUMBLE!"

"Yes?" The old man immediately appeared in the doorway, a batter-covered wooden spoon in his hand.

"Please serve pancakes to Miss..."

"Lorelei," Lorelei said.

"Yes, quite right. Please serve pancakes to Miss Lorelei and her rat in the kitchen, then show her to the guest room. I'm certain she could use some sleep."

Lorelei jumped to her feet. Dog also jumped to his feet. "Are you crazy? I'm not leaving Homer. You tried to kill him."

"As I've tried to explain, that was a misunderstanding."

Homer scrambled off the zebra-striped pillow, then led Lorelei over to the window. "Go ahead," he whispered, his back to Ajitabh. "I need to find out what's going on."

"But if he splits us up then we're weaker targets."

Homer rubbed his tired face. "Maybe you can get some information from the cook."

Lorelei nodded. "Okay. Good plan. But neither of us leaves without the other. Agreed?"

"Agreed."

She shot Ajitabh a nasty look, then scooped Daisy off the yellow pillow and followed the old cook out the door.

Homer turned toward Ajitabh. "So, how did you know my uncle?"

But Ajitabh didn't answer because that's when *she* walked in. And Homer knew, to the depths of his being, that he was in trouble.

25

Another Letter

Homer, this is my friend Zelda. Oh, that's right. You two have already met."

The tall lady from the train, the one who had admitted doing terrible, unspeakable things, stooped as she stepped into the room, a lantern swaying in her hand. She took off her goggles and straightened her elongated body. A mere inch of air cushioned her head from the ceiling. Pushing a strand of silver hair from her eyes, she cast a serious look at Homer. "I'm glad to see that you're safe, Homer Pudding." She set the lantern on the shelf next to the sword. "Forgive my muddy shoes, Ajitabh. The night brought sorrowful thoughts. I was out walking along the moors when the 'copter arrived for me." She kicked off her boots. A few of her toes stuck out of her frayed black socks.

"You're the one." Homer took a step back, his face growing hot. "You told Madame la Directeur that the coin was in my pocket, inside a matchbook."

"Now calm down, Homer. Zelda would never give information to Madame."

"But she did." Homer moved closer to Dog. "She's the only one who knew the coin was in the matchbook. She told me to put it there. My uncle gave me that coin. It belongs to me."

"Indeed it does," Zelda said, pushing her black cape behind her shoulders. Her low voice rolled across the room like a foghorn. "Am I to assume that Madame currently has possession of the coin?"

"As if you didn't know that she took it," Homer said.

Ajitabh scowled. "Took it? By force?"

"Well...I gave it to her, but only because she was going to kill Dog." Homer's heart went into overdrive. He felt like running but he didn't know where to go.

"You made the right choice." Zelda crossed the room

in four strides, then bent over to scratch Dog's head. He wagged his tail. "I find droopy dogs to be much more appealing than perky ones."

Homer stepped away, pulling Dog with him.

"Zelda, can I get you a chair?" Ajitabh asked. "We have one around here somewhere."

"For what purpose? I'm used to discomfort. I wouldn't know what to do without it." With much creaking and groaning, she lowered herself onto a pink polka-dotted pillow. Even when seated on the ground, her knees rose higher than the coffee table. She set her black bag next to the pillow, then accepted a glass of chai. "You seem frightened, Homer. Why's he frightened, Ajitabh?"

"He was under the impression that I was trying to kill him." Ajitabh ran his hand through his dark hair. "I told him that was rubbish."

Zelda sighed. "Homer, while you may one day come face to face with someone who wishes to kill you, here, in this room, you are among friends. We both loved your uncle dearly."

Homer folded his arms and scowled. "Why should I believe you?"

"Where the devil is that letter?" Ajitabh asked. "Show him the letter."

Zelda reached into her bag and pulled out a plain envelope. "Drake gave this to me a week ago last Saturday. He came out to my trinket shop on an unexpected visit. He seemed agitated, nervous, kept looking out the window. He told me that he was in danger and that he wanted to make sure you got this letter if…" She wiped a tear from her eye. "If anything happened to him. He didn't want to leave the letter with his lawyer. I don't blame him. Those Snootys are most…*forgetful*." She stifled a sob. "Here. Read it."

Homer took the letter from her outstretched hand. He sat on the zebra pillow and turned the envelope over. A wax seal with Drake's initials, *D.H.P.*, was still intact. As Dog burrowed beneath some pillows, Homer broke the seal and pulled out the letter. A blanket of sadness wrapped around him as he recognized his uncle's handwriting. Only a few days had passed since he'd learned of his uncle's death. It still didn't seem real. He turned his back to Zelda and Ajitabh and read to himself. His uncle's confident voice rose off the page.

Dear Homer,

If you are reading this then I am gone. I'm sorry. I didn't intend to depart this world so early. I hope that I put up a good fight before I died and that you can still be as proud of me as I have always been of you.

You have now met my dearest friends, Ajitabh and Zelda. They are faithful friends and I trust them with my life. I've asked them to look after you and to guide you in your treasure-hunting education. Ajitabh is a brilliant inventor and when you set out on your first quest, he will make certain that you have everything you need. Zelda is a renowned archaeologist and can tell a forgery from an authentic piece of treasure with her eyes closed. Rely on them as I have. They will never fail you.

I trust that by now you have received a delivery from Snooty and Snooty. It is very important that you pay careful attention to the delivery for it is my most treasured possession. I dare not write why you should pay careful attention, in case this letter falls into the wrong hands, but I am confident that you will soon understand why I sent the delivery to you and to no one else. Keep it close. Keep it secret.

But most importantly, my dearest nephew, don't give up your dreams. Great adventures await you. You just have to go out and find them.

Happy hunting!
With all my love, Uncle Drake

Tears fell from Homer's eyes as he read the letter again and again. He hunched his shoulders and wiped his face with his jacket sleeve.

"There's no need to hide your tears," Zelda said. "Sadness is nothing to be ashamed of. Sadness is the truest measure of being alive."

"I thought love was the truest measure," Ajitabh said.

"Do not speak to me of love," she said slowly, as if each word brought her pain.

No one spoke for a while. The woodstove crackled and popped and Dog snored beneath the pillows. Finally, when the tears had subsided, Homer turned around and gazed at his uncle's friends. As his fear melted away, their villainous appearances also melted away. He hadn't before noticed the twinkle in Ajitabh's eyes or the gentleness in Zelda's voice. "Why didn't you tell me who you were on the train?"

"I thought it more appropriate for Ajitabh to speak to you first. He was, after all, your uncle's best friend." She looked away. "And I tend to frighten people."

"Why didn't my uncle ever tell me about you?"

Ajitabh sipped his tea. "He wanted you to finish your schooling before you joined us on a quest."

Homer couldn't believe his ears. He scrambled onto his knees. "Join you?"

"Why certainly. When you came of age."

"When we were on the roof, you said that I could still claim some sort of membership. What membership?" Homer asked.

"Ah yes. That." Ajitabh stood and walked over to the woodstove. He opened its glass door and tossed in a few pieces of kindling. As the fire's warmth drifted throughout the room, Homer peeled off his corduroy jacket, preparing himself for what was sure to be an exciting story. Ajitabh cleared his throat. "The moment I heard that Drake had died, I went to find you, Homer. I needed to know if Drake had given you the coin. But what I discovered was that he had given you that hound."

Dog, his rump sticking out of a pillow pile, snored louder.

"It surprised me to learn of this dog—most likely a stray he had picked up somewhere. Rather nice of you to take care of him."

"I don't mind taking care of him." Homer reached out to scratch Dog but stopped, not wanting to wake him. "But my dad wants to send him back. He can't smell so he eats weird things, but I like him."

"Every boy should have a dog," Ajitabh said, arranging the burning logs with a poker.

"What about every girl?" Zelda asked.

"Girls do well with dogs, certainly, and with cats, horses, rats, and all that. But dogs and boys go together like slugs and rain. It's a simple universal equation. I hope that your father changes his mind." Ajitabh set the poker aside, then returned to his pillow. "Getting back to the issue at hand, after you told me that you had only received the hound, I went to Drake's apartment and found that it had been emptied of everything."

"I know where it all went," Homer said excitedly. "Madame la Directeur stole all his stuff and put it in her lair."

Ajitabh slapped his knee. "By Jove, I suspected as much but I didn't have time to investigate. Zelda called and told me that she had run into you on the train and that you had the coin after all. So I followed you from the train station. I tried to talk to you at the law office but you ran off."

"My sister told Madame la Directeur about the coin. Madame said it belonged to the museum and that Uncle Drake had stolen it."

"Nonsense," Zelda said, her voice rumbling angrily. "Drake Pudding never stole anything. That coin belongs to you, Homer. By giving you the coin, Drake has passed his membership to you. You are to take his place in a secret society."

"A secret society?"

"Yes." She folded her hands. "The Society of L.O.S.T."

26

Secrets and Syrup

H uh?" Homer leaned on the coffee table. "The what?"

"The Society of L.O.S.T.—Legends, Objects, Secrets, and Treasures," Ajitabh said, filling Zelda's glass with tea.

Homer pushed away his bangs. "Madame said that the initials stood for 'Lots of Stuffed Things.' I knew that couldn't be right. But she said the coin belonged to the museum. That it belonged in Dr. Wortworthy's exhibit."

Zelda reached across the table and patted Homer's hand. "Put everything that Madame told you out of your head. She's a liar. She wanted the coin because she desires membership in the Society as much as she desires wealth. Maybe more."

"Madame was kicked out of the Society five years ago," Ajitabh said, "when it was discovered that she had sold stolen treasure for personal gain."

Homer's mind raced as he tried to take in all the information. "She said she knew my uncle. That's how she knew him? Because they both belonged to this… Society?"

"Pancakes are served." Mumble, the old cook, scuttled across the room, a tray perched in his hands. First he set a platter on the table. Homer's stomach went crazy as the scent of steaming pancakes filled the air. "I made them especially *large*," Mumble said, giving Zelda a pitying look. Then, from the pockets of his apron, he pulled out a bottle of maple syrup, a bottle of strawberry syrup, and a bottle of blueberry syrup. "And some chickpea curry." He set a bowl on the table. Then he pulled a meaty bone from his apron pocket. "For the hound."

"Much appreciated, Mumble. How's the girl?" Ajitabh asked.

"She ate five pancakes, then fell asleep in the guest room. But that rat of hers stole my silver spoon. It was a gift from my mother. I treasured that spoon." He shuffled back out the door.

The stack of pancakes was even taller than the one at the Milkydale County Fair's pancake-eating contest. Ajitabh passed out plates, forks, and napkins and everyone dug in. Homer nudged Dog awake and showed him the bone. Dog wagged his tail as he happily gnawed. "These pancakes are great," Homer said after taking his first bite. Although Zelda could probably fit an entire pancake into her mouth, she cut them into dainty pieces.

"Please pass the syrup," she said.

"Which one?" Homer asked as a strawberry river ran down his pancakes.

"What does it matter? One is as sweet as the next. The resulting rise in my blood sugar may induce a few moments of light-headed giddiness but I shall still be a very large woman who lives alone and who cannot ride on a Ferris wheel. And who has never found love."

"For God's sake, Zelda, don't start with that again." Ajitabh handed her the maple syrup.

Homer wanted to ask Zelda if the reason she seemed so sad had something to do with that missed date with Mr. Snooty at Chez Bill's, but he felt too embarrassed to ask.

As he filled his belly with warm, fluffy pancakes, happiness filled him, too. Up in the mountain tower he felt close to his uncle. Gwendolyn and his father were out of jail, safe at home in their own beds. And his parents wouldn't be worried about him, believing he'd gone on a museum field trip. "Will you tell me about the Society?" he asked.

"Righteo." Ajitabh finished a spoonful of curry, then sat back on his cushion. "It all begins with Wilma von Weiner. Forty-five years ago she discovered the Lost Temple of the Reptile King and became one of the world's most famous faces. She couldn't even go to the grocery without a mob of reporters trailing her. Though quite at ease trekking through a jungle of poisonous snakes, she was shy by nature and hated public attention. So she went into hiding."

Homer knew that part, but that's where the story always ended in the history books. "Where'd she go?" he asked.

"To South America with her husband, Dr. Wortworthy, where she assisted him with his obsessive collection of rare reptiles and amphibians. But while this life kept her from the public eye, it did not satisfy her. Wortworthy had no interest in treasure hunting and Wilma discovered that she had little interest in catching and stuffing frogs. And, even though she had a young daughter for companionship, she began to feel rather lonely."

"Her daughter is Madame," Homer said.

"Yes, that's right. And it was because of her loneliness that Wilma came up with the idea for the Society of L.O.S.T.—to provide a means for likeminded treasure hunters to socialize and plan quests in secret. She handpicked the membership and each member had to swear an oath of secrecy."

"Is that why I've never read about L.O.S.T.?"

Ajitabh nodded. "It's one of the few secret societies that has actually been kept secret. Great riches pass through its hands. Imagine what would happen if a thief discovered the meeting locations."

Dog, who'd been tearing at the bone, waddled over to the coffee table and poked his nose at one of the glasses of tea. "I think he's thirsty," Homer said. Mumble appeared immediately and placed a bowl of water on the floor. Dog's long ears flopped into the bowl as he eagerly lapped. "Thanks," Homer called as Mumble left. What great service.

"Where was I?" Ajitabh asked.

"The Society of L.O.S.T.," Zelda said, helping herself to another pancake.

"Ah, yes. Along with their love of treasure hunting, the original members shared Wilma's passionate belief that the sole purpose of treasure hunting was to unearth the marvels and mysteries of the past for the education, enrichment, and enlightenment of the public. So each member swore a second oath to give all discoveries to the appropriate museum or university."

"So Wilma wasn't evil, like her daughter?" Homer asked.

"I never met her but I've been told she was charming," Ajitabh said. "Unfortunately, she died only ten years after founding the Society. Thus, the question arose, how would the Society continue to flourish as the original membership died off? It was unanimously decided that future membership would be awarded in two ways—by bloodline or by achievement. But each new member still had to swear the first oath of secrecy and the second oath to use his or her treasure-hunting skills for the greater good. Zelda and I are the newest members, as was your uncle Drake."

Homer's pancake-filled belly pushed uncomfortably against his pants, so he set his plate aside. He made room for Dog, who curled up on his pillow and started gnawing on the bone again. "How did my uncle become a member?"

"Through achievement. When he found King Tut's bathing suit he caught the Society's attention and they invited him to join."

"That's how he met Madame la Directeur," Zelda said, dabbing syrup from her lips. "She inherited her membership from her mother, of course."

"Because Dr. Wortworthy did not know about L.O.S.T. Madame only learned about it many years after her mother's death. When she had reached adulthood, the Society approached her. She had followed in her father's footsteps and had become a doctor of herpetology, but the Society opened up a whole new world for her. She caught the treasure-hunting bug and with Drake's help, they set out to find the sunken HMS *Bombastic*."

Homer couldn't believe it. He knew about his uncle's discovery, but Drake had only mentioned a "partner." He'd never called her by name. "My uncle and Madame went on a quest together? Why would he go anywhere with her? She's a monster."

Zelda repositioned herself on the cushions. Her long legs cracked as she stretched them across the carpet. "Drake didn't think she was a monster, not back then. I think he might have married her if she hadn't deceived him."

"Married her?" Homer imagined Auntie Madame la Directeur coming to the farm for Christmas dinner, choking the dogs, stealing coins from Squeak's piggy bank, shoving Gwendolyn's animals into the garbage bin.

"Using a deep-sea, seaweed-powered submersible, one of my inventions, Drake and Madame found the remains of the HMS *Bombastic* and recovered the captain's chest. Of course, you know why this was an important discovery."

"Yes. Because the *Bombastic* was the last place Rumpold Smeller was seen. They made him walk its plank."

"Exactly. Drake and Madame brought the chest to the Society but when Madame learned that everything in the chest would go to the British Museum, she left in a rage, taking most of the artifacts with her. She eventually sold them on the black market. Despite the fact that her mother had founded L.O.S.T., the membership voted to cast Madame from the Society. She had, after all, broken the second sacred vow. She's been looking for a way back in ever since."

Homer fiddled with his shoe, ashamed by his next question. His uncle had always told him that greed was the treasure hunter's worst enemy, but how could he rebuild the Milkydale library if he couldn't sell even a little treasure? "What if you want to keep a bit of treasure? I mean, I know it's best to give everything to a museum but...?"

"Not to worry," Ajitabh said. "We Society members still get paid, otherwise how could we afford to finance future quests? But what a museum can pay is a small percentage of what the black market can pay. You see?"

"Yes." Homer smiled. A small percentage was so much better than nothing.

Ajitabh reached beneath the collar of his shirt and pulled out a long golden chain. He slid the chain over his head and handed it to Homer. The chain ran through a familiar gold coin. "This is just like my coin," Homer said.

"That is the membership coin for the Society of L.O.S.T. Each member wears one at all times. The fact that Drake sent you the coin is proof that he was transferring his membership to you."

"But I don't have the coin anymore."

"That doesn't matter. You will still be granted membership. Zelda and I will bear witness that the coin was given to you."

"It might not be as easy as that," Zelda said. "Now that Madame has the coin, she will tell the membership that Drake sent it to her. There are some who want to readmit her—some, I suspect, who have received *gifts* from her. She is highly influential in the museum community. She'll do anything to get back into the Society."

"If she wants to sell her treasures on the black market, why does she want to be a member of the Society?" Homer asked.

"There are many benefits to a L.O.S.T. membership," Zelda said. "To launch a successful treasure-hunting quest, one needs the help and special talents of other members. She wants to become as famous as her mother."

Ajitabh smacked his hand on the table. Dog looked up from his bone. "They'd be bleeding fools to re-admit her. But she's a skilled manipulator and liar. And the membership knows that she and Drake were once close. They just might believe that he'd passed his membership on to her. You said she has Drake's belongings in some sort of lair?"

"Yes. She said she wanted to find a map."

Ajitabh and Zelda shared a worried look. "Then she knows." Ajitabh leaned forward, his brow furrowing. "One year ago, your uncle found Rumpold Smeller's map. Though he never brought it to a meeting, he told the membership about the map and asked for help in launching his quest. Someone in the membership must have told Madame!"

"Wow," Homer said. "I didn't know he'd found it."

Ajitabh frowned. "If she gets her greedy hands on that map, she'll say that Drake lied. She'll claim it as her own discovery and use the Society's good intentions and help to achieve the wealth and fame she desires."

"They can't help her. She killed him!" Homer cried, tipping over a syrup bottle.

Zelda's entire body stiffened. "How do you know this?"

"Mr. Twaddle, he works for her. He told me that the same thing would happen to me that happened to Uncle Drake if I kept asking questions."

Ajitabh leaped to his feet and began pacing.

"Calm yourself, Ajitabh. We have no proof," Zelda said.

He clenched his fists. "You know as well as I that she'd stop at nothing to get what she wants. I knew that man-eating tortoise sounded suspicious."

"We've got to find her lair," Homer said. "It's somewhere beneath the museum."

"Righteo!" Ajitabh smacked his hands together. "I'll take you back to the farm, then Zelda and I will go to the museum."

"No. I don't want to go back. Not yet. If she's a murderer then the police have to be told. She can't get away with it. It's not right." Homer raised himself off the pillow, certainty filling his being. He handed the coin back to Ajitabh. "My uncle sent me his most treasured possession. That's what he wrote in his letter. His *most treasured possession*. I've got to get that coin back from Madame. It's my responsibility."

Ajitabh slid the chain around his neck, then gripped Homer's shoulder. "You'd make Drake proud."

"I'm a bit confused about something." Zelda stood, her bones crackling as loudly as the fire. She gazed down at her two companions. "Why would Drake call the coin his most treasured possession? Don't you find that puzzling, Ajitabh? Certainly he valued his membership in the Society but it wasn't the most important thing to him. He rarely attended meetings. He hated all the paperwork and wasn't fond of many of the members. He didn't have much patience for all the chitchat."

"Maybe he cared about it more than we knew." Ajitabh let go of Homer's shoulder. "It's been a long night. We all need sleep. Then we shall deal with Madame."

Homer let a yawn come, wide and long. Sleep sounded good. "You won't leave without me?" he asked. "Promise?"

"My dear chap, we'll face her together," Ajitabh said. "I promise."

27

The Most Treasured Possession

The guest room was three floors down. The room was dark but Lorelei's pink hair was easy to see, poking out from under a satin quilt. "I'm afraid you'll have to share the room," Ajitabh whispered. "I have only two guest rooms and Zelda requires the one with the extra-long bed."

"No problem," Homer said, too tired to worry about sharing a room with a girl. He threw his jacket onto a chair.

Ajitabh put an arm around Homer's shoulder. A light

scent of engine oil drifted from his skin, reminding Homer of the way his father smelled after tinkering with the tractor. Ajitabh's fingertips were stained with blueprint ink—the true mark of an inventor. "I know you've made a new friend, but remember you must not tell her about the Society. You must not tell anyone."

"I won't."

"Then let's get a good sleep. We'll need our wits about us to deal with Madame." Ajitabh smiled warmly, then walked back up the spiral stairs.

"Come on, Dog," Homer whispered. Clutching the bone between his teeth, Dog pranced into the room. Homer's entire body ached with exhaustion. He sat on the bed and took off his shoes. His mother would be really upset if she found out that he hadn't packed any clean socks. Or a toothbrush or hairbrush. He shrugged. Treasure hunters don't have time to worry about personal hygiene. A quest won't wait while the treasure hunter shops for underwear at Walker's Department Store.

"Urrrr." Homer pulled Dog onto the bed and as he did so, the bone landed on the floor with a *thunk*.

Lorelei bolted upright. "What's going on?" Daisy the rat poked her black nose from under Lorelei's pillow, her whiskers twitching with annoyance.

"Everything's okay," Homer said. He pulled back his quilt. "Ajitabh and Zelda were my uncle's friends. We can trust them. They're going to help me get my uncle's stuff from Madame. And they said they'll take you back to the warehouse."

"Oh." She scratched her head. "That's good. Pancakes sure make you sleepy."

Homer yawned. "Yeah." He plumped up his pillow and was about to climb under the quilt when Dog slid off the bed and began sniffing along the floor.

"It's sure weird how he does that," Lorelei said. "Even though he can't smell."

Dog sniffed around the edge of Lorelei's bed, then stood on his hind legs and stuck his nose under Lorelei's pillow. "Urrrr." Daisy the rat crept out from the pillow and stared at Dog. Dog stuck his nose deeper, rooting around like a pig.

"Hey," Lorelei said. "Go away. I'm sleepy."

"Urrrr." Dog clamped his teeth on Lorelei's pillow and pulled it off the bed.

A glint of silver shone where the pillow had been. Homer leaned forward, squinting through the darkness. "Is that a spoon?" he asked.

"That's odd," Lorelei said, picking up the spoon. "Where did that come from?"

"I think the cook is looking for that."

"Well, I didn't take it. Why would I want a spoon?"

An awkward silence hung between them. Homer didn't want to accuse Lorelei's rat of stealing, but it seemed pretty obvious that's what had happened. Dog whined until Homer helped him back onto the bed.

"Weird dog," Lorelei said, collecting her pillow.

Homer stretched out on his back. Dog stretched beside him, his breath tickling Homer's ear. Maybe Lorelei had known that the spoon was under her pillow. Maybe she needed that spoon. Maybe she was tired of using the plastic ones that came with the soup cart. "Lorelei? Don't you want to live somewhere else? I mean, you could come live with me."

"And be a goat farmer? No offense, Homer, but that's not what I want to do with my life."

"Oh. I understand. But if I tell my mom about you—"

Lorelei leaped out of her bed and pointed a finger in Homer's face. "DON'T tell your mom. Don't tell anyone. I'm not going to an orphanage, Homer. You got that?"

"Okay." Though he couldn't see her very well through the darkness, he could feel her powerful gaze. "I won't tell anyone."

"Good." She got back into bed and as silence settled, her breathing slowed and deepened.

Homer looked across the room and out a little window where the ridge of mountains stood in silhouette against the starry sky. Everyone in Milkydale would be asleep. His mom and dad curled beneath goose down. Squeak, sleeping sideways in his bed the way he always did. And Gwendolyn, sleeping beneath the flying squirrel that hung from her ceiling. They seemed so far away. Even his old self seemed far away. He was going to become an official member of the Society of Legends, Objects, Secrets, and Treasures. Homer Winslow Pudding was going to become a real treasure hunter.

He closed his eyes. Though sleep beckoned him toward its depths, his mind continued to pick over the day's details. He'd come to The City to find out why his uncle had hidden a coin on Dog's collar. The mystery had been solved—Uncle Drake had wanted Homer to join the Society of L.O.S.T. But Zelda's question tugged at him.

"Why would Drake call the coin his most treasured possession?" Zelda had asked. "He rarely attended meetings. He hated all the paperwork and wasn't fond of many of the members."

"I've found something amazing," Uncle Drake had told Homer on that last night in Homer's room.

"Something more amazing than Rumpold Smeller's map?"

"Yes, even more amazing."

Dog began to snore, his jowls vibrating with each

expulsion of air. Homer ran his hand down Dog's long back. "I'm glad Uncle Drake gave you to me," he whispered. "If it hadn't been for you I would never have found my decoder ring. And I probably would have lost the coin on the train. And Mr. Snooty wouldn't have his brooch. And Lorelei wouldn't have her Galileo Compass. And Mumble…"

Homer's eyes flew open and he sat up straight. Dog groaned.

Could it be? Was it possible? Had the answer been at his feet this entire time?

"Is it you?" Homer asked.

Dog opened one eye.

Homer lay back down and looked at Dog's droopy face. *He found my ring, he found the coin. He found Snooty's brooch and he found Lorelei's compass and the silver spoon. All those things were lost and someone wanted them found.*

"You can't smell regular things, can you?" Homer whispered. "But you can smell…" Homer grabbed Dog's face and turned it so they were looking into each other's eyes. "You can smell lost treasures."

"Urrrr." Dog's tail whacked against the quilt.

Homer hugged Dog as hard as he could. "You're the most treasured possession, aren't you? It wasn't the coin at all. That was just a distraction in case someone nabbed you." Then he remembered his uncle's letter. *Keep it close. Keep it secret.*

He glanced worriedly at Lorelei's bed. She lay still, a small snore rising from beneath her quilt. Homer sighed with relief.

This was why his uncle had been so happy. Dog was going to be his greatest asset, his secret weapon, better than anything Ajitabh could ever invent. With a treasure-smelling dog and Rumpold Smeller's map, Uncle Drake's quest would have been a certain success. But while Madame knew about the map, she didn't know about the dog. No one knew.

Only Homer knew.

Together, Dog and Homer would finish what Uncle Drake had begun. Homer Winslow Pudding, the chunky kid from Milkydale who liked to read maps, who wasn't any good at sports, who carried a compass and day-dreamed about treasure hunting, had been given the gift of a lifetime. But if anyone else found out, Dog wouldn't be safe. He'd become the most wanted dog in the entire world. Everyone had to believe that he was just a sad, droopy dog who couldn't smell.

Somehow, some way, Homer would have to convince his father to let Dog stay on the farm. As sure as he'd gone to The City, as sure as he'd solved Dog's mystery, he'd figure out a way to keep him.

Homer hugged Dog again and, with a grin stretching from ear to ear, fell asleep.

☙

Homer felt as warm as a pancake right off the griddle. He stretched his legs and arms. Sunlight trickled through the guestroom window. *How long have I been asleep?* he wondered. He sat up and rubbed crusty bits from his eyes. Lorelei's bunk was empty, the blankets thrown aside. Maybe she and Daisy were in the kitchen eating breakfast. He remembered the silver spoon and looked around for it. Perhaps Lorelei had returned it to the cook.

"Dog?" Homer called. He got out of bed and walked to the doorway. "Dog?" Dog was probably eating breakfast, too. Homer sat back on the bed and started to put on his shoes when Ajitabh rushed into the room.

"Homer!" Ajitabh's long black hair was all messed up, as if he'd also just gotten out of bed. He wore a silk bathrobe and matching pajamas.

"What's going on?' Homer asked, tucking his compass under his shirt.

"She took the cloudcopter." Ajitabh paced, his arms gesturing wildly. "Do you hear? Your friend stole one of the cloudcopters."

"Huh?" Homer's mouth fell open. Why would she

do that? Why would she leave without him? They'd made a pact that neither of them would leave without the other.

"I'm afraid that's not the worst of the news." Ajitabh gripped Homer's shoulders, his dark eyes churning with intensity. "She took your hound."

PART SIX

THE EVIL LAIR

28

A Friend's Deception

Homer watched anxiously as Ajitabh hurried around the cluttered laboratory, stuffing things into a canvas backpack. "We must be prepared for the unexpected," Ajitabh said, pausing to scratch his beard. "Now, where the blazes did I put my portable telescope? Oh, there it is."

Screwdrivers, hammers, drills, and assorted hardware lay scattered across a worktable. Boxes with labels like COMBUSTION ACCELERATORS, HYDRAULIC FEEDERS, and SOLAR

ABSORBERS stood in stacks. Bits and pieces of pipes and engine parts covered the floor.

Zelda pushed aside some greasy rags, then sat on a stool. The legs bowed beneath her bulk. "You've been busy," she said, inspecting a shovel-like contraption.

"Drake wanted a better way to dig through sand." Ajitabh grabbed a can of engine oil. "Where's that blasted Swiss army knife?"

"I have one," Homer said, reaching into his jacket pocket. "Can we go now? I'm really worried about Dog." That was the tenth time he'd asked to leave since discovering that his new friend had stolen Dog. *His* dog. Maybe the only dog in the world that could smell lost treasure. Maybe the only chance in the world that Homer could finish his uncle's quest. But Ajitabh had insisted on gathering a bunch of equipment.

Why had Lorelei left without him? Why had she taken Dog? She'd been so nice. She hadn't judged Homer when he'd told her about the library burning down. She hadn't made fun of his love of maps. She even owned a Galileo Compass. She'd seemed like the perfect friend.

What if she'd taken Dog because she now knew Dog's secret? Maybe she'd been fake-sleeping and had heard Homer when he'd figured out Dog's talent. *Why'd I have to say it out loud?*

Homer held out his little red knife. "You can have this one," he said. "Please. Let's go."

"Keep your knife, Homer. Mine has unique alterations." Ajitabh looked behind a tangle of wire. "It shoots tranquilizer darts and has a laser that can cut through steel."

About the best Homer's knife could do was to cut through string, but he figured that was probably a good thing. The way his luck was going, if he had a knife like Ajitabh's, he'd probably cut his foot off. He stuck his knife back into his pocket.

"Homer?" Zelda rested her elbows on the worktable. She was ready for the flight to The City—bag and lantern by her side, black cape tied beneath her chin, flight goggles perched on her expansive forehead. "I can tell by your sour expression that you're blaming yourself for what has happened."

"Because it's my fault," Homer said, searching for Ajitabh's knife.

"The girl's a thief, a child of the streets. Anyone can see that just from looking at her." Ajitabh shoved a headlamp into his bag.

"You know as well as I that we should never make assumptions based on appearance," Zelda said, shaking a long finger at Ajitabh.

"I stand corrected. Where the devil is that knife?" He

crawled under the table. "I've lost it. How could I lose such a treasure?"

If Dog were here, he could find it, Homer thought as he looked under some mechanical drawings.

Zelda folded her hands on her lap. "Homer? How, exactly, did you meet Lorelei?"

"Well…" He thought back to the moment he'd stepped out of the train station—the loud noises, the bad smells, how Dog had stopped to piddle on everything. "Gwendolyn and I split up so I could go to the library to research the coin. I was walking down the street and there she was. She gave Dog and me some soup. Then I saw Snooty and Snooty's office so we said good-bye. The next thing I knew I was running down the sidewalk because I thought Ajitabh was trying to kill me." Where was that stupid knife?

"Once again, I wasn't trying to kill you," Ajitabh said from under the table.

"Go on," Zelda urged.

"I ran into Lorelei and I told her I was in trouble. She took me to this warehouse to hide. I told her some…stuff. She showed me around The City." He remembered how nice the day had been—the beautiful blue reading room, the pink sprinkled doughnuts, the movie theater and the park. He'd never spent an entire day hanging out with a friend.

"What stuff did you tell Lorelei?" Zelda's voice was soft, but serious.

He grimaced. "Um…well…" He turned red. "I told her way too much. I know it. I was stupid. Uncle Drake should never have believed in me. I told her everything."

Zelda sighed. "You're not the first good person to be deceived and you won't be the last. Our hearts often cloud our judgment."

Ajitabh popped up from under the table. "Found it!" He dropped a Swiss army knife into his backpack. "Shall we go?"

"Yes!" Homer cried, heading for the stairway.

"One moment. Something has just occurred to me." Zelda rose from the stool. "Did you tell this girl about the coin? That it was in your pocket, in a matchbook?"

Homer's face fell. Gwendolyn hadn't known about the matchbook. Zelda obviously knew, but she hadn't told Madame. "Lorelei's the one who told Madame?"

"It would appear that Madame hired a street urchin to do her dirty work," Ajitabh said, shaking his head.

Zelda pressed a finger to her chin. "It all seems clear now. Madame wanted Rumpold Smeller's map. Someone in the Society told her that Drake had found it. After she killed Drake and searched through his belongings with no success, she learned from Mr. Twaddle that Drake had sent something to Homer."

"So she lured me to the museum with a party invitation," Homer realized.

"She set Lorelei in your path to get information, knowing a boy would be much more likely to confide in someone his own age," Zelda said.

"The girl is most likely on her way back to Madame. But why would she take the hound?" Ajitabh asked. "Why not just steal the cloudcopter and be done with it?"

"It's obvious why she took Dog," Zelda said. "She knows Homer loves the creature so she'll use it for ransom. Homer told us that she is a child without a family. She is simply trying to survive. Unfortunately, she has fallen under the influence of a very wicked woman."

Homer bit his lower lip. They still didn't suspect that Dog was Drake's most treasured possession. There was still a chance that Lorelei didn't know the secret either—a small chance, but a chance nonetheless.

"It doesn't add up," Ajitabh said. "Why didn't she stay to get more information? And how the devil will she find her way back?"

Uh-oh. Homer reached into his pocket. "She's taken my map."

"What map?" Zelda asked.

"The map of the Museum of Natural History. During the ride here, Lorelei read her compass and I wrote down the coordinates. If she gives those to Madame..."

He looked desperately at Ajitabh. "She'll be able to find this place. I'm sorry. I've ruined everything."

"Do not apologize. Writing the coordinates was a brilliant maneuver," Ajitabh said. "You were thinking like a treasure hunter. However, I do not intend to let that woman find my tower."

"And I'm not letting her have Dog!" Homer cried.

"Then, there's no time to waste." Ajitabh swung the backpack of equipment over his shoulder. "Everyone to the cloudcopter!"

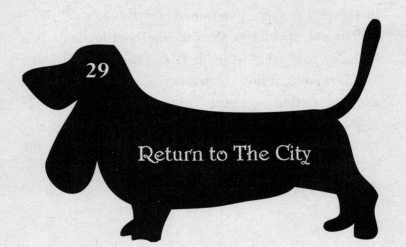

29

Return to The City

As Homer stepped onto the tower's roof, cold air, fresh with the scent of snow, tingled his nostrils. His gaze followed the jagged mountains from the skyline to where they disappeared into the foggy valley, far, far below. One misstep and he'd plummet to his death. He moved away from the edge.

"Uncomfortable with heights?" Zelda asked.

"I guess so," he said, trying not to look down. "How about you?"

She raised her eyebrows.

"Oh." He smiled apologetically. "I guess that was kind of a stupid question."

"At least the girl didn't steal the customized 'copter," Ajitabh said. It turned out that Lorelei had stolen the same cloudcopter that they had arrived in. Zelda's 'copter, specifically designed for her comfort, sat on the platform.

"You drive," Zelda told Ajitabh. "I'm no good with high-speed chases."

Ajitabh waited as Zelda climbed in. She set her bag and lantern on the 'copter's floor. "After you," he said to Homer.

Homer bent down to give Dog a boost. His heart sank as he remembered that Dog was gone. In just a few short days he'd gotten used to having the droopy fellow ambling alongside, poking him with his cold nose when he wanted something, wedging himself between Homer's shins when he got scared. Was he scared now, flying through the clouds with Lorelei and her thieving rat? Would Lorelei remember to watch what Dog ate? Homer climbed in and sat in the back next to Zelda. He fidgeted nervously. *Come on, let's get going.*

"Better button up that jacket," Zelda told him. "Night air's terrible for creaky bones."

While Homer didn't have creaky bones, he buttoned his jacket anyway, then slid the goggles over his eyes. Ajitabh loaded the backpack into the 'copter, then climbed into the cockpit. As he flicked some switches, Mumble the cook hurried onto the roof. "Dinner," he said, holding out a basket.

"Thanks." Homer took the basket. Was it dinnertime already? They had slept through most of the day. But what day was it? He drew a mental map of the events and realized that it was now Wednesday evening.

Back on the farm, the Pudding family would be finishing up their chores and getting ready to sit down to dinner. Mrs. Pudding usually made macaroni and cheese for Wednesday dinner. *I wonder what Homer's doing right now?* his mother might say. *Doesn't that field trip sound like fun?* Not in a million years would they imagine that he was about to travel in a cloud to rescue Uncle Drake's most treasured possession. And never, in a million years, would he be able to tell them.

"Mumble, I don't know how long I'll be gone," Ajitabh said. "Keep the home fires burning. Fasten seatbelts, chaps."

Mumble stepped away as the engine roared to life. Homer strapped the belt across his lap. Zelda reached into the basket and pulled out a roasted chicken leg. The 'copter vibrated. Hissing noises crept from the metal pipes. The pipe closest to Homer spurted water. "I'm going to set it for minimal cloud cover, but as soon as we near The City, I'll have to maximize the cover. Commencing minimal cloud cover." Ajitabh pressed a blue button. With a loud whistle, a sudden surge of steam shot out of the pipes. Then silence settled over the 'copter as the steam transformed into gently rising ribbons of cloud. The mountains, the platform, and a waving Mumble, disappeared from view. But inside the 'copter, Homer could still partially see his copassenger and pilot. A sinking feeling filled his stomach as the 'copter rose.

They were off.

Zelda passed a chicken leg up to Ajitabh, then offered one to Homer. "So, what's the plan?" she asked.

Ajitabh took a bite. "First thing is to get the hound back into Homer's care. Agreed?"

"Agreed," Homer and Zelda said.

"Then we shall deal with Madame. Retrieving Rumpold Smeller's map and securing evidence that she was responsible for Drake's death is of paramount importance. If we also retrieve the coin then that will be icing on the proverbial cake."

"How will we find Dog?" Homer asked.

"The girl's two hours ahead of us. I'm guessing she's never flown before so we should be able to gain on her. There's a tracking device on the 'copter, but we need to be within fifty miles to pick it up." Ajitabh flipped more switches.

Homer put his dinner back into the basket. He didn't feel much like eating. He pictured Dog's sad, red-rimmed eyes. *If Lorelei knows the secret*, he thought, *then she'll probably try to sell Dog to Madame. But if she doesn't know the secret...*

"What if we're wrong?" he blurted out.

Ajitabh looked over his shoulder. "Beg your pardon?"

"Well, what if Lorelei left because she got scared and she just wanted to get home? What if Dog followed her? He does that sometimes." With all his heart he wanted to believe that Lorelei was back at the warehouse, feeding Dog some chicken and rice soup, wondering if she'd ever see Homer again.

"I hope you're right," Zelda said. "Deceit is a difficult pill to swallow at your tender age."

As the others ate, Homer worked the situation over in his mind. Like reading a treasure map, he approached Lorelei's actions from every angle, searching for hidden clues or secret signs that maybe, just maybe, she hadn't deceived him after all.

After she'd finished eating, Zelda told Homer all about her trinket shop in Gloomy Moor. "No one else lives in Gloomy Moor but me," she said. "I like it that way. I left The City after that horrid night..."

"At Chez Bill's?" Homer asked.

Zelda put a hand over her mouth, her eyes widening with surprise beneath the goggles. "How did you know?"

"Zelda," Homer twisted in his seat so he could look up at her wide face. "When I was at Snooty and Snooty's I…" He didn't want to talk about how Dog had dug up that brooch. "I overheard Mr. Snooty talking about how he had lost his love years ago because the elevator had broken down and he couldn't get to Chez Bill's."

Zelda's hand dropped to her lap. "His love?"

"Yes. He even had a special brooch that he was going to give to her. I'm pretty sure he was talking about you because his brother said that she couldn't fit into an elevator or ride on a Ferris wheel. Anyway, Mr. Snooty said that he was going to ask her…ask you to marry him."

The goggles' lenses fogged as tears welled in Zelda's eyes. She turned away. "I've been such a fool," she said, her low voice trembling. "It is a terrible, unspeakable thing to try to force yourself to stop loving someone."

Ajitabh gave Homer an approving nod. They traveled in silence for some time as Zelda quietly cried. While Homer didn't want her to feel sad, her tears gave him hope. If she had misunderstood the situation with Constantine Snooty, it was possible that he had misunderstood the situation with Lorelei. It was possible she was still his friend.

"If we find Rumpold Smeller's map," Ajitabh told

Homer, "then we'll be able to register the finding with The Society and this will be considered your first official quest. You'll be the youngest member in the Society's history, I do believe. It's a pity Drake didn't live to see this."

The memory of the last visit with Uncle Drake played through Homer's mind again. While he remembered word for word the last conversation they'd had in his bedroom, Homer hadn't been the last family member to talk to Uncle Drake that night. After his uncle had left Homer's bedroom, Homer had watched from his window. His dad and uncle had stood in the driveway but soon into their conversation, their voices had risen in anger. "You shouldn't fill his head with nonsense," Mr. Pudding had said. "He's not like you. He's not cut out for adventure. He can't climb mountains or hike across deserts. You'll break his heart."

"The only way to break Homer's heart would be to keep him from pursuing his passion," Uncle Drake had said. "But I don't expect you to understand that."

"You think I've never felt passion?" Mr. Pudding had cried, tearing his cap off his head. "I had plans, or have you conveniently forgotten? This farm was yours to inherit, remember? You're the eldest son. You were supposed to take over after Dad died. But you abandoned Ma to go off on your adventures. If I hadn't stayed, Ma would have lost everything. I know what it's like to have dreams, then have them squashed. I don't want you doing that to Homer."

They had both looked up at Homer's window. Homer, realizing he had overheard something very personal, had darted behind his curtain.

Homer hadn't thought about that conversation until that moment on the cloudcopter. His father's dreams had been squashed? But he loved goat farming. It was all he ever talked about.

"Nearing The City," Ajitabh said, his voice pulling Homer from his memories. "Setting cloud cover to maximum." Fluffy puffs settled between Homer and Zelda. Ajitabh disappeared behind a blanket of whiteness. "I've picked up the 'copter's coordinates." He paused. Then with utmost seriousness he said, "She's landed at the museum."

No longer could Homer deny the truth. Lorelei was working for Madame.

Zelda's hand reached out and patted his.

❁

They landed beside the stolen 'copter on the northernmost corner of the museum's grounds, next to a grove of trees. Far from streetlights, the 'copters were well hidden by night's shadows. Homer, Zelda, and Ajitabh stripped off their goggles and climbed out.

"No sign of her," Ajitabh said, sliding his arms through his backpack straps.

Homer walked behind the 'copter. "Dog?" he called, hoping with all his heart that Dog had escaped. "Dog?" His jacket caught on a shrub. As he pulled it free he stepped on something. It was the bone that Mumble had given to Dog. Lorelei had probably used it to coax Dog into the 'copter. He reached into his jacket pocket. The rope leash was also missing. She'd thought of everything.

"Any idea where we can find this lair?" Ajitabh asked from the other side of the 'copter.

Homer had promised Lorelei that he'd never tell anyone about her secret entrance. But things had changed. She no longer deserved his promises. "I know how we can get in."

Homer was just about to step around the copter, when someone shouted, "There they are!" A flashlight beam landed on Zelda's face. She had no chance of hiding.

Ajitabh reacted swiftly. "Stay back," he whispered. Homer flung himself under the 'copter's belly. Fortunately, the cloudcopter was still in minimal cloud cover mode so it looked like a thick bank of fog had settled. Pressing himself against the ivy-covered ground, Homer watched as Mr. Twaddle and two policemen charged at Ajitabh.

"Halt!" The police officers pulled clubs from their holsters. Zelda dropped her bag and held up her hands.

"Officer," Ajitabh said. "This is a misunderstanding, I assure you. We are tourists, out for an evening stroll."

"Holy cow," the first officer said as he strained his neck to look at Zelda. "Get a load of this one."

"They're trespassing," Mr. Twaddle said. "They're up to no good."

"Hand over that backpack," the second officer said.

"I say, do you have a search warrant?" Ajitabh asked.

The second officer pointed the club at Ajitabh's face. "Hand it over."

Mr. Twaddle yanked the backpack from Ajitabh. He reached in and pulled out the Swiss army knife, a hatchet and some pliers. "Evening walk, my foot! These are the thieves, officers. No doubt about it." Then he pulled out Ajitabh's sword.

"Thieves?" Zelda asked.

"Someone's been stealing from the Museum of Natural History," the first officer said, still gawking at Zelda.

"Looks like you've caught the perpetrators," Mr. Twaddle said, a smug smile settling on his face.

"You're both under arrest," the second officer said. "Come with us."

"What about my personal belongings?" Ajitabh asked.

Mr. Twaddle handed the backpack to the first officer, but he kept the sword behind his back. As the officers led Ajitabh and Zelda away from the grove of trees, Ajitabh said, loudly, "Sometimes it is best to go home and wait." Although he didn't turn around when he spoke, Homer knew that the words were meant for him. "I repeat, sometimes it is best to go Homer, I mean, go home and wait."

"You're not going home," the second officer said. "You're going down to the station for questioning." Then he waved his club at Mr. Twaddle. "You'll have to come, too, to press charges."

"Of course. Got a few business obligations to tend to. I'll be there as soon as I can," Mr. Twaddle called after them as they headed for the street. "Be sure to lock them up nice and tight. No telling what they might steal next." He snickered, then hurried back toward the museum, floodlights gleaming in the sword's blade.

He hadn't noticed Homer.

Homer waited until the coast was clear, then crawled out from under the 'copter. He wiped dirt from his chin and anxiously looked around. Ajitabh wanted him to go back home, but that would accomplish nothing. There was only one person who could save Dog now.

"You must face the final test of endurance and intellect on your own," Uncle Drake had said.

So be it.

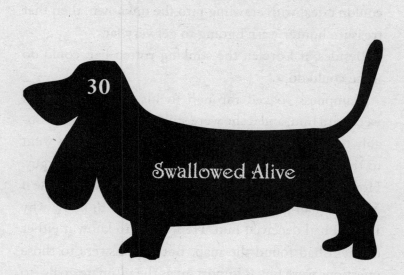

30

Swallowed Alive

Lorelei's secret entrance smelled like mildew and maybe something dead, but Homer didn't want to think about that. Why hadn't he brought a headlamp? Holding his small flashlight between his teeth, he crawled as fast as he could. The fit was tight but he managed. *Hold on, Dog, I'm coming.*

Spiders scattered, disturbed by the thundering of his knees. Hopefully, any lurking rats would slink in the opposite direction. Small, dark spaces were a common component in treasure hunting. If a treasure hunter couldn't deal with crawling into the unknown, then that treasure hunter wasn't going to get very far.

Besides, if Lorelei, the stinking rotten liar, could do it, he could do it.

Dampness soaked through to his knees. If Lorelei were with him, and if she were still his friend, she'd probably tell him that this was just like when Odysseus went to the underworld to get information from a dead guy. Homer also wanted information. He wanted to know if Madame had killed his uncle. He wanted to know why Lorelei had deceived him. He wanted to know if either of them had found the map. But the answers to those questions were not as important as the ultimate goal—to save Dog.

Up ahead, light began to bleed into the tunnel. Homer crawled toward the light and just as his knees started to chafe, the tunnel ended at a metal grate. Cautiously, he peered between the bars.

The grate was set high in a wall. A hallway, dimly lit by sconces, stretched to the left and to the right of the grate. Lorelei had told him that the tunnel ended in the basement. The place was eerily quiet.

He pressed his face against the grate to get a better look. What was that thing to the right? He aimed the flashlight beam at a gigantic statue of a tortoise. It stood on its hind legs, much taller than a full-grown man, and much wider. While its head stuck out from the wall, the tortoise's shell appeared to melt right into it. Its narrow reptilian eyes caught the flashlight's beam, giving them the illusion of life. Homer shuddered and scooted away from the grate.

It's just a statue, he told himself. He turned off the flashlight and stuck it back into his pocket. Then he pushed the grate. It opened easily, just as Lorelei had said. He swung his legs out the opening and was about to jump onto the marble floor when footsteps approached. Pulling his legs back in, Homer quickly closed the grate, then shrank into the tunnel's darkness.

Mr. Twaddle, his suit coat flapping, hurried down the hall. "I have to do everything around here," he mumbled. He must have stopped at the gift shop because he was shoving Dinookies into his mouth. Crumbs flew as he imitated Madame's shrill voice. "Get rid of the boy, Twaddle. Deal with the trespassers, Twaddle. Find the map, Twaddle. Do what I say, Twaddle, or I won't keep paying for your vacations." He threw the empty cookie package onto the floor. In his other hand he clutched Ajitabh's sword. "I hate her."

Something buzzed. Twaddle froze as Madame's voice shrieked from a wall speaker. "Twaddle! What's taking you so long? Get back down here this instant! I need you to deal with this girl and her ugly mutt."

Lorelei and Dog were in Madame's lair. Homer clenched his fists. If she did anything to Dog…

"On my way," Mr. Twaddle said through clenched teeth.

"You'd better be on your way." Then she added, "You big dummy."

"One of us is a big dummy and it's not me," Mr. Twaddle muttered.

"I heard that!"

Homer inched forward to get a better view as Mr. Twaddle stopped in front of the tortoise statue. "Why should I have to deal with the girl?" he mumbled. "I'm not the one who hired her." He reached up and poked the statue's left eye. Then he stepped back. A grinding sound rolled down the hall. Homer gasped as the tortoise's mouth slowly opened.

The mouth grew larger and larger, stretching like a grotesque sock puppet. *It's mechanical*, Homer realized as the grinding sound continued. When the grinding stopped, Mr. Twaddle took a quick look around. He slid the sword into the tortoise's mouth, then pulled himself into the cavernous hole. After his two-tone shoes had disappeared, the mouth snapped shut, then shrank back to normal size.

Of course! A secret lair had to have some kind of secret entrance. It reminded Homer of the entrance to the Reptile King's Temple, which was guarded by an enormous stone serpent. According to the biography *The Life of Wilma von Weiner*, it had taken Wilma three days to figure out that she had to crawl into the serpent's mouth to enter the tomb.

Homer opened the grate and jumped to the floor. Then he shut the grate and crept toward the statue. He reached up and pressed the tortoise's eye. The grinding sound began and the mouth cranked open, wider and wider, until Homer found himself looking into a yawning black hole. A sick feeling churned in his stomach—a mixture of nervousness and horror as he remembered that his uncle had spent his final minutes inside a tortoise's stomach. Or maybe he hadn't. But it was still a repulsive image.

But there was no time for nervousness because Dog was in trouble.

Homer took a deep breath, then stood on tiptoe and pulled himself into the mouth. As soon as his feet cleared the opening, the mouth snapped shut. Blackness engulfed Homer. The space was a tight fit. Is this how Odysseus felt when he sat inside the Trojan Horse, waiting to sneak up on the enemy? Homer didn't want to use the flashlight, just in case Mr. Twaddle was nearby. He took a deep breath. The only direction to go was forward.

And that's what he did. He crawled a few feet forward.

And that's when the ground gave way.

31

Inside the Lair

W"hoa!"

Homer slid face-first, around and around, in a dizzy corkscrew. It was just like the Whirl-a-Tron at the Milkydale County Fair. The one time Homer had ridden that contraption, he'd upchucked his curly fries. Terrified, he closed his eyes as he flew off the end of the slide and landed in a belly flop on the floor. The impact knocked the air out of him and pressed his compass into his chest. "Ow." Sitting up, his head still spinning, he tried to get his bearings and his breath.

The room was small. The end of the slide jutted out from the wall behind Homer. A narrow staircase wound back up the slide, for exiting purposes. In front of Homer, light trickled from an open doorway, as did distant voices. The room swayed as he struggled to his feet. Once the dizziness had passed, he checked his compass to make sure it wasn't broken. Then he stuck his head out the doorway.

It opened onto a balcony with a railing. The voices were too far away to understand or identify. Homer crept from the room and peered over the railing. And the first thought that came to his mind was, *I want a lair*.

He gazed down at a huge underground fortress. If he hadn't known better, he would have sworn it was the Temple of the Reptile King. How had Madame managed to build such a realistic replica? It looked exactly like the photos in Homer's treasure-hunting books. The stone walls and floor, the giant serpent and lizard statues, even the murky pool where the king had kept his treasured potbellied toads, looked authentic.

However, Madame had added some modern touches. A snazzy red speedboat was moored at the edge of the pool. Dozens of chandeliers, heavy with crystal droplets, hung from the overhead pipes. Lush oriental carpets lay here and there. A red velvet couch sat next to a red velvet throne. And there were three vending machines, one for snacks, one for espresso drinks, and one for live mice. A vending machine for live mice? The little white critters ran back and forth in their glass cubicles. A few of them sat very still, staring through the glass at a large tank in which a cobra lay curled.

A row of security monitors lined the other side of the room, revealing different parts of the museum and the museum grounds. One of the monitors was focused on a fog bank. Oh wait. It was the cloud cover for the cloud-copter. *So that's how Mr. Twaddle knew we had landed.* One of the monitors was focused on the little VIP party balloon, still floating in the Life on the Edge exhibit.

The voices seemed to be coming from beneath the balcony. Homer still couldn't catch the words or recognize the voices. And he didn't see any sign of Dog or his uncle's belongings. He'd have to take the steep stairway that led from the balcony down into the lair. But just as he worked up the courage to move, footsteps approached. Homer flattened himself on the balcony's floor, then peeked through a space in the railing.

He caught his breath. Lorelei walked out from under the balcony. Her pink hair was messier than usual and her footsteps were slow and tired. She stopped at the vending machine and punched a button, then collected a bag of potato chips. Leaning against the machine, she ate the chips, one at a time, as if she had nothing more pressing to do. As if she didn't give a hoot that Homer might be worried and missing his dog. He clenched his fists.

"Get back in there!" Madame la Directeur appeared from under the balcony and stomped toward the vending machines. "I'm not paying you to snack. We need to find that map." Her blouse had come untucked and she'd rolled up her sleeves. A few strands of her perfectly sprayed hair were out of place.

"Yeah, yeah," Lorelei said, biting a chip in half. "Hold on to your bloomers, lady. A girl's gotta eat."

"That's all you do is eat. And that ugly dog, too." Madame punched a button on the mouse vending machine. A mouse disappeared from the upper-left-hand compartment. Madame reached into the dispensing drawer and picked the mouse up by its tail. It wiggled wildly as she opened the top of the cobra's tank and tossed it in. "I don't know why you insisted on bringing that dog here. All it's doing is stinking up the back room." She ripped the potato chip bag from Lorelei's hand. "Get back in there and keep looking. The map has to be in that junk somewhere."

Homer narrowed his eyes. He'd just learned four important things: Dog was safe, his uncle's belongings were in the other room, Madame had not found Rumpold Smeller's map, and Madame clearly didn't know that Dog could smell treasure. Which meant there was still a chance that Lorelei didn't know.

Lorelei glared at Madame, then stomped beneath Homer's balcony. "Little brat," Madame snarled. Homer held his breath, pressing his body against the floor. His mouth was dry, his body sweaty. How could he get Dog's attention and make a quick exit?

As Madame ate the last of Lorelei's chips, Mr. Twaddle walked out from beneath the balcony. His suit coat was gone and his shirtsleeves were also rolled up. "This is a waste of time, I tell you. There's no map to be found. Why would he have kept it in his apartment? That's too obvious."

"Exactly. No one would suspect a priceless treasure map to be sitting in an apartment. Drake was cunning that way."

"But..."

Madame threw the potato chip bag into the pool, then pointed a finger at her henchman. "Don't *but* me, you nitwit! The map is there and we're going to find it. I need money. The self-destruct button's on the fritz again. Do you know how much it costs to replace a self-destruct button?"

"Why don't you just help yourself to another gem from the Cave of Brilliance?"

"Because I've already replaced most of them with fakes and the rest I've reported as stolen. So you see, I have no more money. I need Rumpold Smeller's treasure." She grabbed Mr. Twaddle's shirt collar. "Finding his treasure is going to make me rich and famous and I'm tired of waiting to be rich and famous. Now get back in there and keep looking."

"But I still need to go to the police station, to press charges."

"You can do that later. Ajitabh and Zelda aren't going to get in our way. They're just a couple of amateurs. I'm not worried about them. But I'll tell you who I am worried about." She leaned close to him. "I'm worried about the girl. She knows too much. As soon as we find that map, I want you to get rid of her."

"You want me to throw her out, like I did with the boy?"

"No. Read between the words, Twaddle. I want you to *get rid* of her. Just like I got rid of Drake. Feed her to the tortoise."

Homer almost cried out.

Twaddle backed up. "Hurting a child was never part of our arrangement."

Madame smiled sweetly and patted Mr. Twaddle's bald head. "Now, now, she's just a street urchin. No one will even miss her. And then, you and I can claim our glory.

Oh, and get rid of the dog, too." She walked beneath the balcony. Mr. Twaddle stood frozen, his face pale. He took a handkerchief from his pocket and wiped his brow. Then he followed Madame.

Get rid of Lorelei and Dog? Lorelei had no idea that her life was in danger. But how could Homer convince her? She'd never believe him.

Something warm brushed against Homer's cheek. Still lying on his stomach, he slowly turned his head and found Daisy's beady black eyes staring into his. Her nose twitched. "Go away," Homer whispered. Her nose twitched again. Then, she leaped onto his back and scratched at his collar. He tried to brush her off but she clung fiercely to the fabric, her nose pressed against his neck. He rolled from side to side, trying to rock her loose. Then something snapped. Daisy scurried away with Homer's beloved Galileo Compass in her teeth, its broken chain left behind.

Thieving rat!

Homer crawled toward the stairs. He hoped they weren't creaky like the ones at the Pudding farm. Another tortoise statue, large enough for him to hide behind, stood at the base of the stairs. While Madame barked orders from the other room, Homer tiptoed down the stairs, then darted behind the statue. From his vantage he had a clear view of the room beneath the balcony.

His uncle's belongings lay on the floor—books, boxes, clothing, vases, globes, parchment, shoes, pillows, all in a massive pile. Lorelei sat cross-legged, pulling socks from a drawer and sticking her hand into each one. Mr. Twaddle disassembled a pair of Extra Strong Borington Binoculars while Madame snooped through some letters, tossing them over her shoulder after reading them. But where was Dog?

"Another letter from the fat kid," Madame said. "'Dear Uncle Drake. Thank you for the book about Angus MacDoodle and his backyard treasure. I started to look for Celtic coins in our goat pasture, but Dad told me to stop digging so many holes or the goats would break their legs falling into them.'"

Homer cringed. How dare she read his letters? They'd been sent to Drake's postal box and addressed to Drake, *NOT TO HER*!

"Another letter from the kid. 'Dear Uncle Drake. I'm glad you're coming to visit on Sunday. Mom is going to bake a cherry pie because it's your favorite.'" Madame tore the letter to pieces. "Useless. I want that map. SOMEONE FIND ME THAT MAP!"

"Urrrr."

Homer's heart skipped a beat as Dog waddled into view, his rope leash dragging behind. He appeared unhurt and just as droopy as ever. He started sniffing the pile.

Homer waved his hand, trying to catch Dog's attention. Even though he desperately wanted to race in there and grab Dog, he knew he'd never be able to outrun Lorelei or Mr. Twaddle. He had to get Dog to come to him. The farm dogs would have picked up Homer's scent, no problem. They'd have been circling at his feet, ready to follow him to the ends of the earth. But not Dog.

"What's that rat got?" Mr. Twaddle asked as Daisy climbed onto the pile. "It's a Galileo Compass."

"Give me that." Madame grabbed the compass. "It's probably just a fake."

Lorelei scooped Daisy into her arms. "Daisy, where did you...?" Then she turned her head in Homer's direction. He darted behind the statue. "Um, I gotta use the bathroom. Be right back." Before Homer could get away, a pink head of hair appeared in front of his face. "Go, before she sees you," Lorelei whispered. "Hurry..." Daisy climbed out of her arms and scampered off.

There wasn't time to be angry. "You have to get out, too. She told Mr. Twaddle to get rid of you."

Lorelei flared her nostrils. "I can take care of myself. So go on." She pushed him.

"I'm not going anywhere without Dog." He pushed her back.

"What is that stupid mutt doing now?" Madame cried. "Why is it digging through the pile?"

307

Both Homer and Lorelei froze. Then they peered around the statue. Dog stood in the middle of Drake's belongings, digging. A hat flew past Mr. Twaddle, a pencil nearly hit Madame in the face.

"Stop digging! It's messing everything up. Where's the girl?"

"I'm right here," Lorelei said, running back to the room.

Madame waved her hands frantically. "Throw that dog into the pool. He's driving me crazy."

Dog pulled his head from the depths of the pile, a small book clenched between his teeth.

"For the last time, get that mutt out of here!"

Lorelei grabbed Dog's leash, then yanked the book from his mouth and ran from the room. Homer couldn't believe his eyes. Was she actually going to throw Dog into the pool? But as soon as Lorelei reached the tortoise statue, she motioned for Homer to follow and she started toward the stairs. Homer was about to take a step when Madame darted out of the back room.

"Where are you going with that book?"

Lorelei stopped in her tracks and smiled sheepishly. "What book?"

"The book that you're holding in your hand. The one the mutt dug out of the pile. I can see that it's a copy of my father's book, *Rare Reptiles I Caught and Stuffed*. Why are you carrying it?"

Lorelei glanced at the book, then smiled. "I heard it's a good book. One of the best, of course, because it was written by your father. I just wanted to look it over."

Lorelei knows, Homer realized as he peered from behind the tortoise statue. *She knows Dog's secret. That's the only reason why she'd want that book.*

"Oh." Madame's angry glare softened for a moment. Would she see through Lorelei's fake compliment? Would she confiscate the book? Homer leaned out a bit more to get a better view.

"HOWOOOOOO." The moment Dog caught sight of Homer's jacket, he pulled his leash free of Lorelei's grip and scampered behind the statue. Homer didn't dare move. He stared down at Dog, whose tail was wagging so hard it whapped against the statue. Dog whined and turned his watery eyes up at Homer. *Why aren't you petting me?* he was probably thinking. *Why did you let her take me? Don't you love me anymore?* He whined again and stuck his nose between Homer's ankles. *Was I a bad dog?*

Homer couldn't bear the huge aching feeling that filled his body. He squatted and gave Dog a fierce hug. Then he pressed his face against Dog's neck.

The moment's joy was shattered by a high-pitched

voice. "What are you doing here?" Madame grabbed Homer's sleeve and pulled him out from behind the statue.

As sure as he knew that his treasure maps were locked in the attic, as sure as he knew that his last name was Pudding and that he had a brother named Squeak and a sister named Gwendolyn, Homer knew, at that very moment, that he was a goner.

32

The Monster in the Pool

Homer looked into the eyes of the woman who had killed his uncle—dangerous eyes as dark as the lair's murky pool. He tried to hide his fear by not blinking, but her gaze was too intense. "How'd you get in here?" she asked with a sneer.

He glanced over at the stairs. Even though he wasn't a fast runner, there was a remote chance he could beat Madame to the top because she was wearing high heels. But Dog would take forever on such a steep climb.

Madame turned her anger on Lorelei. "Did you show him the secret entrance? Did you?"

"No," Lorelei insisted, her cheeks flushing crimson. "Why would I do that? I'm working for you."

"Twaddle!" Madame hollered.

"What?" Mr. Twaddle wandered into the lair. He turned one of Uncle Drake's boots upside down and shook it.

"The Pudding kid followed you. Now we've got to deal with him *and* the girl."

"Deal with me?" Lorelei clutched the reptile book to her chest. "What do you mean by that?"

Madame folded her arms. "You know exactly what I mean by that."

Mr. Twaddle tossed the boot aside and shook his head. "I told you to go home, kid," he told Homer. "You should have listened to me. Now I gotta deal with you."

Homer's gaze flew around the room. There had to be another way out. There was always another way out. He just had to look at the surroundings with a mapmaker's eye.

As Dog wandered to the side of the pool to take a drink, Homer imagined the map he had back home of the Reptile King's Temple. Until a few days ago it had been thumbtacked directly above his bed and was often the last thing he'd look at before falling asleep. The way into the Reptile King's Temple was through the snake's mouth. And, just like in Madame's lair, the obvious exit was back out the mouth. But when Wilma von Wiener had needed to bring in supplies, she'd widened the stream that fed the Temple's pool so canoes could glide in. Of course. The old City Channel. It used to run from City Lake all the way across the museum property. The lair's other exit was by water. Why else would Madame have a speedboat? But the wall around the far side of the pool looked solid. The exit had to be camouflaged.

"Um, I'm feeling kind of sleepy," Lorelei said, backing toward the stairs. "I think I'll go to the warehouse and take a nap." She fake yawned. "It's been a long couple of days."

"You're not going anywhere. Neither of you is going anywhere. *Ever again.*" Madame took a remote control from her pocket and pressed one of its buttons. A steel gate descended from the ceiling and blocked the top of the stairs.

Homer stole a long look at the remote, which was covered in buttons. One of those buttons probably opened the pool's exit.

"Hey!" Lorelei cried as the steel gate clanked into place. "What are you doing? I'm on your side, remember?"

Madame turned away. "Twaddle," she said. "Feed them to Edith."

Terror broke across Lorelei's face. Homer whipped around and stared at the glass tank. *Edith?* The snake lay curled in the tank's corner, taking a nap. The little white mouse was gone.

Mr. Twaddle ran into the back room and reemerged with Ajitabh's sword. "Get over there," he said, motioning the blade at the cobra's tank. "Both of you."

"You should just let us go," Homer said as he and Lorelei backed away from the sword. "My uncle's friends know I'm here. They'll come looking for me. They'll find me."

Madame raised her eyebrows. "You mean Ajitabh and that behemoth? Ha! They deal in trinkets and inventions. They couldn't find a secret lair if it bit them in their backsides." She tucked in her blouse. "Drake was the talented one in that group. Why he hung around with those two losers I'll never know."

Homer's face felt flaming hot. Anger pulsed through every part of his body. "Why'd you kill him? Why?"

"Because he got in my way." Madame spat those words like a snake spitting venom. "And now you two are in my way."

"You can't kill me," Lorelei cried. "I've done everything you asked. I told you about the coin. And I gave you the map with the coordinates to the tower. I could show you how to get back there."

Madame laughed. "Do you think you're the only street kid who can get information for me? Hungry kids are a dime a dozen around these parts. But you weren't supposed to know about the lair. You found it and he found it and that means you both know too much."

Lorelei stomped her foot. "But you promised that we'd be partners."

"Partners?" Madame snorted. Then she smoothed her skirt over her round hips. "I never intended to make you my partner."

"We shook hands. You gave me this compass to show how much you valued our partnership. That's what you said." Lorelei reached into her shirt and pulled out her Galileo Compass.

"You're not as smart as you think," Madame said with a chuckle. "I'd have to be insane to give you a *real* Galileo Compass. Do you know how much they're worth? That one's a fake."

Lorelei gasped, then her expression fell, weighed down by a big dose of ugly reality. "You...lied to me."

Doesn't feel too good, does it? Homer almost said. But at that moment he felt as sorry for Lorelei as he felt for himself. And their only chance of escape would be to work together. He had to talk to her.

"However, while your compass is a fake, this one is the real thing." Madame held up the compass that Daisy had

315

stolen from Homer. The compass's face sparkled with chandelier light. "I'm assuming Drake gave this to you. How else could a farm boy afford such a treasure? I'm going to sell it on the black market for loads of cash." She held the compass to the light, gazing at it as if it were a loved one. "Only the curious have something to find," she read. "That's quite poetic. I think I'll claim it as my own."

"You used me!" Lorelei yelled at Madame. "She used me." Her angry breath blew a strand of pink hair off her forehead.

Homer couldn't hold back. "Oh really?" he said. "*She* used *you?*"

Lorelei looked at him, but only for a moment.

"Get on with it," Madame said. Then she returned to the back room.

"Keep moving," Mr. Twaddle ordered, waving the sword. Dog ambled along the side of the pool, looking into the water. Homer and Lorelei took a few more steps backward, which brought them right up to the cobra's tank.

Feed them to Edith.

The snake lazily raised its head, its forked tongue darting from its mouth. Homer remembered a story in one of his treasure books about Baroness Meatpie, an avid collector of East Indian pottery. Her biographer wrote that after encountering a cobra in one of her precious pots, her agonizing screams could be heard the next village over.

"Wait…" Homer held up his hands.

"Look kid, I don't want to do this any more than you want me to do this. But she's the boss so just keep moving."

"You'll never get away with this," Lorelei said.

As Mr. Twaddle took a few more steps forward, they took a few more steps backward, passing the cobra's tank. "Keep going." Homer looked over his shoulder. Mr. Twaddle was backing them up toward the pool. But why? Edith was lying in the tank. They came to the edge. "Go on. Get in."

"What? I can't swim," Lorelei said.

"Doesn't matter. You won't need to swim," Mr. Twaddle said. Sweat beads dotted his forehead. A vein bulged in his neck.

Homer and Lorelei looked at one another, then turned and looked at the pool. Bubbles rose from the pool's dark center and something moved just below the water's surface. The hairs on Dog's back stood up and he started barking. A sick feeling grew in Homer's stomach as the top of a gigantic tortoise shell briefly surfaced, then disappeared. Lorelei squealed.

Edith.

317

It's true what they say, that an entire life can pass before someone's eyes in a single moment. Homer heard the soft bleats of the goats, felt the breeze as it rustled through the cherry trees, smelled his father's Sunday cologne. He tasted the morning porridge, felt Squeak's hand in his, and saw the golden flecks in his mother's eyes.

"WAIT!" he cried. He whipped back around. "I know what else you could sell for loads of cash." He grabbed hold of the book that Lorelei still clutched in her hands. He tried to yank it away but Lorelei held tight.

"Are you crazy?" she asked, trying to push him away.

"We've got to distract them," Homer told her between clenched teeth. He tugged but Lorelei held fast. "There's another way out. If we can get the remote control, and get into the boat, we can get out of here."

Nervous tears filled Lorelei's eyes. "Dog dug this book from the pile. You know what that means," she whispered.

"It's not important anymore." He pulled harder. She was unbelievably strong. "Lorelei, we have to work together to get out of here. You can trust me. I won't lie to you. *Ever.*"

Dog ran along the edge of the pool, following the moving bubbles. "Grrrr."

"What's going on out here? Why are they still alive?"

Madame asked, stomping back into the lair. "Shove them into the pool so we can get on with our search."

"Sorry, kids." Mr. Twaddle raised the sword and rushed toward them. Homer and Lorelei stared into each other's eyes. He expected hers to be crazed with fear—the way a goat looks when it gets stuck in a hole. But her eyes were eerily calm. She nodded and released her grip on the book.

Homer had to act quickly. "If you let us go, I'll give you the map."

Mr. Twaddle stopped in his tracks. Madame tapped her high heel. "What are you playing at?" she asked.

Homer held the book over the water. "I've got it right here but I'll throw it in if you don't let Lorelei and my dog get on that boat."

Madame scowled. "Twaddle, did you look through that book?"

"Yeah."

"And?"

"It's just a book with a bunch of stupid drawings in it."

"Drawings?" Madame's face went white. "What kind of drawings?"

"I don't know. Lines and scribbles. Stuff like that."

Madame la Directeur kicked Mr. Twaddle's shin. "You moron! There aren't supposed to be drawings in that book. My father never drew pictures of his reptiles. He only took black-and-white photographs. It's got to be the map."

Homer knew immediately what his uncle had done. During the Spanish Inquisition, when bookmakers wanted to hide forbidden books, they'd hide them within the pages of religious books, the very place where no one would think to look. Uncle Drake must have cut up Rumpold Smeller's map and stuck it into a book that no one would be interested in, and that Madame would have overlooked because she already owned a copy.

Madame's fingers twitched excitedly. "Give me that book."

Homer continued to hold it over the water. Dog growled louder as the bubbles surfaced again. "I'll give you the book if you let Lorelei and Dog get on the boat."

"Fine." Madame dismissed them with a wave of her hand. Lorelei grabbed Dog's leash and pulled him toward the boat. With a groan, she lifted him over the side and onto a seat. Then she whistled. Daisy popped out of a vending machine, where she'd been eating chips, and scurried across the floor. With a graceful leap, she landed next to Dog.

"Now open the tunnel," Homer said.

"What tunnel?" Madame asked. Homer let the book slip a bit. "Okay, okay." She pulled the remote control from her pocket and pressed a button. The wall behind the pool slid open, revealing a dark, water-filled passage.

Homer's leg began to tremble. "Slide the remote over here."

Madame put the remote on the ground, then kicked it toward him. It slid right up against Homer's foot. He reached down and his gaze left Madame for only a second. That's when something barreled into him.

Splash!

Homer's mouth filled with murky water. He fought his way to the surface and took a big breath. Mr. Twaddle stood at the pool's edge, a smile on his face. He'd dropped the sword, but he'd managed to catch the reptile book as it had flown through the air.

"Get the girl!" Madame yelled.

The boat's engine hummed to life, its propeller churned the water. Lorelei untied the line. Homer took a big breath and started to swim toward the boat. But just as he did, Mr. Twaddle broke into a run.

"I've got an idea, Homer," Lorelei cried. Mr. Twaddle reached out and grabbed the boat's railing, but he couldn't hold on because Lorelei thrust the throttle into drive. With Dog howling from the stern, Lorelei took the steering wheel and the boat sped into the tunnel and disappeared.

"Lorelei!" Homer yelled.

33

A Gentleman's
Agreement

She had an idea? Homer thought as he treaded
water, his thick coat weighing him down. *Of
course she had an idea. Her idea was, I'm going to
get out of here while I can!*

There was no time to think about Lorelei. Homer
expected, at any moment, to feel searing pain as Edith's
jaws ripped off his legs. He pumped his arms and started
toward the tunnel.

If the other kids in Milkydale had asked Homer to
go swimming with them in Frog Egg Pond, even just

one time, he might have learned how to swim. But they never asked and so he taught himself, right there and then, how to dog paddle. If you've ever dog-paddled, then you know that it doesn't get you anywhere quickly. With his hands cupped and his feet kicking furiously, the tunnel's entrance seemed miles away. Waves splashed against his face as the boat's motor faded. Lorelei had made her escape. And she'd managed to steal Dog yet again.

"What are you doing? Let go!"

Homer glanced over his shoulder. Mr. Twaddle and Madame were fighting over the reptile book. Ajitabh's sword lay forgotten at the edge of the pool.

"After all the dirty work I've done for you, I've got a right to the treasure map," Mr. Twaddle said.

"You've no right to the map. You're nothing. I'm a scientist and the daughter of Wilma von Weiner. You're just a stupid legal secretary." Madame kicked Mr. Twaddle in the shin and he kicked her right back.

As long as they kept fighting, there was a chance that Homer could escape. His arms burned as he paddled, his lungs felt like they might burst. Murky water splashed into his mouth. He coughed, struggling to find strength as the tunnel's entrance drew closer. Edith was somewhere in the pool. Would she bite off his feet? Would she swallow him before he got to the tunnel?

"Urrrr."

Dog paddled out of the darkness, his ears floating at the water's surface like fallen leaves. Homer couldn't believe it. He must have jumped out of the boat. "Dog," he called, swallowing a mouthful of slimy water. Dog's short tail wagged happily, sticking out of the water like a weird fish fin. They dog-paddled toward one another and as soon as Homer was close enough, he reached out to pat Dog's head. Dog, however, didn't stop for a greeting. He paddled right past, his eyes focused on something.

"GRRRR!"

Homer spun around. A ripple formed at the pool's edge, then moved toward them at a steady pace. "GRRRR!" Dog doubled his speed, heading right toward the ripple.

"DOG!" Homer cried, reaching out to grab his tail, but it slipped from his hand. "NO! COME BACK!"

Mr. Twaddle and Madame, each clutching an end of the reptile book, spun around like crazy ballroom dancers. "Let go, you ugly shrew."

"Over my dead body, you bald buffoon." They pushed and pulled, spun and wobbled, their eyes bulging with greed.

Dog kept swimming. Worried tears stung Homer's eyes. Dog was trying to protect him, but he'd surely get killed in the process. "DOG!" Homer screamed, his voice breaking with emotion. "Please come back."

Suddenly, Dog's ears twitched. He stopped swimming. Homer also froze as a large green head emerged from the water, followed by a long, green neck. Narrow eyes glared hungrily at Dog.

Dog pulled back his lips and showed his teeth. "GRRRR!" The mutant tortoise opened its mouth, wider and wider. Homer realized he was staring at the very creature that had eaten his uncle. Instinct told him to turn back around and swim toward the tunnel like an Olympian, but instead he swam straight for Dog. If he could just reach Dog's tail, he could pull him away. At that moment it didn't matter that Dog could smell treasure. Homer couldn't bear to lose him. He had to get to him before...before...

And that's when a roar filled the air. The red speedboat shot out from the tunnel at full speed, Lorelei at the wheel. The boat cut between Dog and the tortoise. Lorelei turned the wheel sharply, sending a huge wave into the lair. The force of the wave toppled Mr. Twaddle and Madame. The tortoise disappeared as Lorelei turned the boat again.

"Homer," she called. "Hurry. Get in."

Madame and Mr. Twaddle, still holding onto the book, struggled to their feet. Water covered the lair's floor and dripped from Madame's hair. "Let go!" Madame shrieked. And with a violent tug, she slipped in the water and fell against the cobra tank. The tank slid off its stand and shattered on the floor. Mr. Twaddle stumbled backward. He tottered at the pool's edge but then caught his balance.

"It's mine," he said when he realized that he was the only one holding on to the book.

Madame crawled away from the cobra's tank, glass shards falling from her skirt. Her high heels had floated away. "Give. Me. That."

Homer watched in agony as Mr. Twaddle held the book in the air. His uncle had died because of the map that was hidden inside. And now the bad guys had it.

"Homer, get in the boat!" Lorelei yelled.

"It's mine, it's mine, it's mine," Mr. Twaddle gleefully chanted, dancing a little jig.

Homer knew he had to let the map go. His life, Lorelei's life, and Dog's life were all that mattered. They needed to get into the boat and make their escape. He grabbed Dog's tail. "Come on."

"Noooo!" Madame cried. She stumbled forward, reaching for the sword, but Mr. Twaddle's dancing foot accidentally kicked the sword right into the pool, where it sank.

At that moment, Edith the mutant tortoise reemerged. In one perfect, graceful move, she snagged Mr. Twaddle with her enormous mouth, then pulled him and the reptile book into the murky depths.

The lair fell silent.

Homer, treading water, began to tremble all over. Dog stuck his nose against Homer's neck. "Urrrr."

Madame began to sob, her head swinging from side to side. "She ate my map. My beautiful map. My beautiful treasure."

The speedboat idled nearby. Lorelei flipped a little ladder over the side, then reached out her hand. "Come on."

Homer followed Dog to the ladder, then gave his rump a shove. Once Dog was on board, Homer pulled himself into the boat, tumbling onto the floor. Daisy the rat squealed as he landed on her tail. Dog shook water from his fur. Lorelei tried to help Homer to his feet but he recoiled.

"You only came back because you wanted Dog," he said bitterly.

"No, that's not true. I needed to get up some speed so I could make that wave." She tried to take his arm, but he yanked it away.

"You!" Madame cried from the pool's edge. "You brats have ruined everything. Well, you'll never stop me. I'm destined to become the greatest treasure hunter the world has ever seen." She was so busy yelling at them, she didn't notice the cobra sliding toward her foot. "I'll get you both. If I have to spend the rest of my life tracking you down, I'll find you and—"

"Watch out," Homer cried.

Madame screamed as the cobra sank its fangs into her heel. She crumbled to the floor.

"She'll die," Homer said.

"So?" Lorelei grabbed the boat's steering wheel. "She killed your uncle. She tried to kill us."

"We can't just leave her here."

Lorelei groaned and rolled her eyes. "I can't believe I'm saying this but... fine." She pushed the throttle forward and drove to the pool's edge. Homer tied the boat to the mooring post. Fortunately, the cobra had slithered over to the vending machines. Homer grabbed the remote control from a pile of glass. "She weighs a ton," Lorelei complained as they lifted an unconscious Madame into the boat. "Too bad the map got eaten."

Homer couldn't make sense of all the emotions that surged through his body. What he did know was that he didn't want to talk to Lorelei—not about the treasure map, not about anything. He untied the boat. "We've got to get her to a hospital."

The boat's running lights illuminated the tunnel as they sped through. When a wall came into view, Lorelei slowed the boat. Homer pushed a bunch of the remote's buttons, except the one marked SELF-DESTRUCT, until the wall opened. Then they drove out of the tunnel and emerged at a forested edge of City Lake.

Homer told Lorelei to drive to the nearest beach where they carried Madame off the boat and laid her in the grass. With her eyes closed and her face slack, she didn't look so evil. But Homer knew better. He called 911 from one of the park's payphones. He and Lorelei waited until the sirens neared, then they jumped back in the boat and drove to the center of the lake. Lorelei shut off the motor and running lights. Floating in the darkness, they sat quietly, watching as the paramedics put Madame into an ambulance and drove off.

Homer pulled Dog close. "I wonder if she'll be all right."

"Well, even if she survives that snakebite, she'll get thrown in jail for stealing gems from the Cave of Brilliance," Lorelei said.

"How will the police know that Madame stole the gems?"

Lorelei flared her nostrils. "I'll snitch on her. There are a bunch of receipts in the lair from this guy who made all the fake gemstones to replace the real ones she stole. I figure it's the least I can do. Just my way of thanking her for trying to get rid of me." She petted Daisy, who lay curled on her lap.

Homer's curiosity outweighed his anger. "Why would you work for someone like that?"

Lorelei turned away and looked out over the lake. "I

had nothing, Homer. You don't know what that's like. Mr. Twaddle found me in the library one day. I was hanging out in there 'cause I had nowhere else to go. I was reading *The Odyssey* and I told him that I liked adventure stories. He introduced me to Madame. She gave me clothes, she gave me spending money, she said I was going to be rich. She told me to pretend to be your friend and to get as much information as I could." She hung her head. "I wasn't pretending to like you, Homer. You're the best person I've ever known."

Homer didn't say anything. She was telling him what he wanted to hear, wasn't she? That's what she did to survive.

She turned back. "I'm telling the truth. I'd like to be your friend again." She reached under Daisy and pulled out a compass. "It's yours. The one Daisy stole. She's a pretty good thief. She managed to get it back when Madame wasn't looking." She handed the Galileo Compass to Homer.

Homer looked it over to make sure it was his. "Why didn't you keep it?"

"You need to rebuild that library, right? I know you were hoping that the coin would be worth a lot of money so you could sell it to a museum. But I don't know where Madame put that coin. So you could sell the compass instead."

Homer hated the idea of parting with his compass. "I guess you're right."

They sat in silence for a while. Once again, Homer found himself wide awake in the middle of the night. Distant skyscrapers twinkled beneath a spring moon. The creepy park trees cast gnarled shadows on the water. Dog stuck his nose in Homer's wet jacket sleeve. Homer, soaked from head to foot from his plunge in the lair's pool, started shivering. When Lorelei reached out to pet Dog, Homer broke the silence.

"Is that why you gave me the compass? Because you want Dog? Well, you can't have him," he said, wrapping his arms around Dog's fat middle. "Don't try to take him. I won't let you."

"I know." Lorelei draped her arm across the boat's railing. She sighed. "I won't try to take him. I shouldn't have done that. I just didn't want to be poor, ever again."

For the first time since meeting her, she seemed like every other kid, not the self-sufficient, carefree girl he'd met on the street. Maybe it wasn't so great living in a warehouse. Maybe it wasn't so great being on your own, with no one to cook for you, or help you study for spelling tests, or tuck you in at night. "What are you going to do now?"

"Well…" She tapped her feet. "I wanted to talk to you about that. I have an idea."

"What?"

"I know about Dog's secret. And you know about the lair. Why don't you come and live there with me? With Twaddle dead and Madame in jail, no one will know. We don't need Rumpold Smeller's map. There are lots of other treasures out there. Whatever we find we can keep and we'll be the richest treasure hunters in the world."

"I don't want to be that kind of treasure hunter," Homer said. "I'm going to donate all my treasures."

"Oh. That's too bad." She stroked Daisy's tail. "Then I suggest we make a gentleman's agreement. If I promise to never tell anyone about Dog, will you promise to never tell anyone about the lair?"

"Why?"

"Because I'm going to live there. I could move right in. Who's gonna stop me? Madame will be dead or she'll be in jail. But I can only live there as long as no one else knows." She smiled. "With all that equipment, I'll have a jump-start on my treasure-hunting career. And with Dog, you'll have a jump-start on your treasure-hunting career. So whadda you say?" She held out her hand. "Shall we keep each other's secret?"

"I don't know."

"Come on, Homer. I came back for you, didn't I?"

"I think you came back because you ran into that wall and you didn't have the remote so you couldn't get out."

The corners of Lorelei's lips turned up slightly. "That's not true. But I guess you'll never really know, will you?"

"If you ever try to take Dog, I'll tell the world about the lair," Homer said.

"And if you ever tell the world about the lair, I'll take Dog."

Homer reached out his hand. "You keep my secret, I'll keep yours." They looked into each other's eyes as they shook—a firm, serious shake that was tenderized by understanding.

Homer told Lorelei to drop him off at the tortoise beach, since that was the only part of the lake he was familiar with, and he figured he could find his way from there. She pulled up to the muddy bank and he and Dog climbed out. Lorelei leaned over the boat's railing. "Maybe we'll meet on the treasure trail someday. I couldn't ask for a more worthy opponent, Homer W. Pudding." Daisy climbed onto Lorelei's shoulder. "Hey, next time you come to The City, look us up. You know where to find us."

A wave crashed onto the bank as the boat sped away, but before she was out of earshot Lorelei yelled, "I'll send your uncle's stuff to your farm."

"Don't forget to send me the coin if you find it!" Homer yelled back. But the boat had disappeared into the dark. Homer looked down at Dog. "I sure hope Mrs.

Peepgrass doesn't ask me to write a report on my field trip." Dog twisted his long body and chewed an itchy spot on his hind leg. Chilly air crept through Homer's wet jacket and he started shivering again. "Let's go find Ajitabh and Zelda."

"Grrrr."

Homer whipped around. Dog's entire body went stiff as he looked at the lake. Oh no. What was happening now?

Homer and Dog backed out of the mud and up a grassy slope as Edith, the giant mutant tortoise, slowly crawled out of the lake and collapsed. She closed her eyes and moaned the moan of someone with a horrible stomachache. Her legs splayed, her chin resting in the mud, she burped. Homer grimaced. She burped again.

Then, she vomited up a book.

34

The Shape of a Hero

The moment the reptile book landed in the mud, Dog started sniffing the ground. Before Homer could stop him, he ran down the slope. Edith, eyes closed and breathing heavy, paid no attention as Dog snatched the slime-covered book and carried it back to Homer. Homer wiped the cover on the grass, then read the title: *Rare Reptiles I Caught and Stuffed*.

The map!

He looked around. Lorelei was long gone and no one else seemed to be in the park. He sat in the grass, a comfortable distance from Edith, and balanced the book on his knees. Dog leaned on Homer and watched as Homer opened the book.

Fortunately, the book hadn't been inside the tortoise long enough for her stomach acid to eat through the cover. Page one looked normal, just a bunch of writing and a black-and-white photo of a Cross-eyed Devil Frog. Page two looked normal. Page three, four, five ... "Look," Homer whispered. Dog cocked his head. Homer pointed to the upper right corner of page six. The photo's title read: PYGMY COCKTAIL LIZARD. But someone had pasted a piece of map over the lizard's photo, cut so that it fit perfectly. The little rectangle contained the map's legend and the mapmaker's initials: *R. S.* A shiver darted up Homer's spine. Just as he had guessed. His uncle had cut Rumpold Smeller's map into smaller sections and had hidden them throughout the book.

He ran his hand over Rumpold Smeller's initials. How many people had searched for this map? How many had dreamed of finding the long lost treasure? How many had lost their lives because of it? Mr. Twaddle. Uncle Drake. Rumpold himself. How many others? This was not a toy or a daydream. Possessing the map was dangerous but at least it was Homer who possessed it, rather than someone who would use it for personal gain.

He put his arm around Dog's neck. "You're the one

who found it. One day we'll be able to tell everyone the truth. But for now we'll have to find a good hiding place for it. Until we're ready to use it."

Dog licked Homer's face.

Edith moaned again. Homer might have felt sorry for her if she hadn't been a carnivorous killing machine.

Dawn trickled through the park's spindly trees. What if Lorelei came back? No telling what she'd do if she caught sight of the book. "We'd better get out of here."

They were on the wrong side of the chain-link fence so they followed it until they found a loose seam. Homer squeezed through, then pulled the fence open for Dog. Together, they hurried through the park, retracing the steps they'd taken earlier with Lorelei. A street map was posted at the park's entrance. Homer ran a finger along the map until he found the police station. With Mr. Twaddle dead and Madame la Directeur in the hospital, there was no one to press charges. The police officers would have to let Ajitabh and Zelda go.

Taxis and buses drove past, starting their morning routes. Dressed in overcoats and carrying briefcases, the first wave of office workers charged down the sidewalk. After an eight-block walk, Homer and Dog arrived at the police station just as Ajitabh and Zelda were walking down its front steps. Ajitabh's face was scruffy with stubble and Zelda's silver hair needed a good brushing.

She held out her long arms. "You're both safe," she said, wrapping Homer in a hug. "But you're soaking wet. What happened?"

What happened? What a question! If Homer had been the original Homer, the writer who had lived so very long ago, he might have spun the night's events into a ballad that would be sung for centuries. Or he might have written a best-selling novel. But how could he tell the tale without including the lair?

"Um, we got caught in some sprinklers. What happened to you?"

Ajitabh ran his fingers over his mustache, smoothing it into place. "No one from the museum showed up to file trespassing charges. And of course they had no evidence that we were involved in the museum thefts." He took off his flight jacket. "You're shivering. Put this on."

Homer peeled off his wet jacket and slid his arms through Ajitabh's, which was warm with the inventor's body heat. If only he had a new pair of pants to change into. And shoes. Dog didn't seem one bit cold and his fur had already begun to dry.

"I say, you look rather ruffled," Ajitabh said. "Why didn't you go home?"

"Well…" Homer zipped up the jacket.

"You didn't go searching for that lair, did you?" Zelda took a handkerchief from her pocket and wiped a smudge of dirt from Homer's forehead. "Not all alone. That would have been too dangerous."

"I didn't look for the lair." He hated lying to his uncle's friends. "But look what I found in…Madame's office!" He held up the reptile book.

They sat on a nearby bench. Ignoring the honks of passing cars and the stares of pedestrians who had never seen anyone like Zelda, they gazed at the pages of the book. Ajitabh took a sharp breath. "Brilliant spot to hide it, by Jove. Who would think of looking in such a boring book?"

Zelda ran a long finger over one of the map pieces. "Good thing the sprinklers didn't ruin it." She tilted her long neck and gazed down at Homer. "What made you look through a book about reptiles?"

"Um, no real reason. I just picked it up. It was kind of an accident."

Ajitabh and Zelda shared a long look. Then Ajitabh laughed. "Sometimes the best things are found by accident. I discovered that I could make cloud cover only after my self-cleaning teakettle exploded." He slapped Homer's back. "Well done, my boy. Well done."

"Yeah," Homer said, looking down at Dog, who lay across his shoes. *Well done.*

"You must keep it safe," Zelda said. "It's the most coveted map in the treasure-hunting community."

"I know." They were looking at him again, their brows furrowed. The responsibility of protecting the map suddenly overwhelmed Homer, like a math test he hadn't studied for. He shoved the book at Ajitabh. "You take it."

Ajitabh held up his palms. "Oh no, my boy. Zelda and I have too many enemies. You, on the other hand, are the perfect person to guard such a map. No one would suspect that Rumpold Smeller's map would be on a goat farm." He gently pushed the book back onto Homer's lap. "But you must keep it secret until the time is right for you to begin your quest."

"When will that be?" Homer asked.

"Ah, the impatience of youth." Ajitabh slapped Homer's back again. "It will be soon enough. Now, we'd best be getting you to your family. No need for you to ride the train. I'll take you back in the cloudcopter."

"That's great, because my train ticket's completely ruined." Homer dug the soggy slip of paper from his pocket.

Since Zelda could not comfortably fit into a taxicab or bus, they walked back to the museum. Dog trotted alongside Zelda's big black boots, his leash secure in her giant hand. Homer held the book tightly beneath his arm. He'd never had so many secrets to keep. It certainly felt as if he'd begun a new chapter in his life, like starting a new grade in school, or moving to a different town, only better.

A janitor was dragging a pair of garbage cans down the walkway just as Homer and his entourage reached the museum grounds. The janitor left the cans next to the curb. Homer spotted his sister's duffel and rescued it. He also retrieved his father's cap from the bushes. Then he walked to the fake VIP entrance and grabbed the stuffed squirrel.

"What about the coin?" Ajitabh asked.

"Madame still has it," Homer said. "I don't think I'll ever see it again."

Ajitabh nodded. "We'll be sure to get you a new one."

Both cloudcopters sat undisturbed, camouflaged by fog and shrubbery. Zelda stretched her goggles over her forehead and tied her cloak beneath her chin. Homer felt a twinge of sadness as he realized that he was going to miss her. "I almost forgot," he said. "Uncle Drake wrote in his letter that you can tell if something is a forgery. Can you tell me if this is a real Galileo Compass or a fake?"

Zelda swept her silver hair behind her shoulders, then removed a magnifying glass from her black bag. She took a long look at the compass. "This is the real thing, Homer. In fact, if I'm not mistaken, and I'm always not mistaken, this is the original. Didn't Drake tell you?"

"The original?"

"Yes. The first one. Made by Gallileo's grand-nephew."

"Wow." Homer forgot all about being cold and wet. "Can I sell it? Can I get enough money to build a new library?"

"You can get enough money to build two new libraries. I'm sure the Museum of Science and Technology would love to get their hands on this. Would you like me to handle the transaction for you?"

"Yes, please." Then Homer remembered something else. "And could you send some money to The City Public Library? Dog ate a bunch of their magazines."

"Consider it done." Zelda tucked the compass into her bag. "I'll be seeing you very soon." She hugged Homer and gave Dog's rump a good scratching. His back legs did their little happy dance.

"You going straight home?" Ajitabh asked.

"I think I'll pay a visit to the thirty-second floor of a certain office building. I may not be able to ride on an elevator, but I can certainly stick my head into an open window." She climbed in and started up the engine. Then a smile spread across her wide face. "My oh my, won't he be surprised!" After a wave good-bye, her 'copter rose into the morning sky and disappeared.

Homer, Ajitabh and Dog climbed into the other 'copter and secured their belts and goggles. This time,

Homer sat up front. "Plenty of fuel," Ajitabh said after checking the gauge. "Commencing maximum cloud cover." Homer's stomach lurched as the 'copter lifted off the ground. Homer wondered if Lorelei was exploring her new lair. And what she would do with that nasty cobra.

When they had cleared The City and had reached flying altitude, Ajitabh reduced the cloud coverage. His dark face and hair came back into view.

"So, Homer, are you ever going to tell me what really happened back there with Madame?"

Homer fiddled with his Swiss army knife. "What do you mean?"

"What I mean, dear boy, is that you are not skilled at the art of deception." Ajitabh pulled another flight jacket from under his seat and put it on. "You are a terrible liar."

"I am?" Homer tucked the knife away. "I mean...I didn't lie."

Ajitabh raised his eyebrows.

"Okay, so maybe I didn't tell you everything but I can't tell you everything because I made a promise to someone." He stifled a yawn. Even though he'd gotten a full day's sleep in the tower, the 'copter's gentle *whirr*ing was like a lullabye. His eyelids suddenly felt as if they had been painted with cement.

"A good man always keeps his promises," Ajitabh said with a knowing smile.

Without intending to, Homer fell into a deep sleep. The 'copter ride was much faster than the train, so it was still morning when Ajitabh landed on a hill just behind the Pudding Farm. Ajitabh woke Homer with a gentle nudge.

Homer turned and looked at Dog, who was asleep in one of the back seats. "My dad doesn't want to keep him," he said. "I'm going to ask him again, but if he says no..."

"Do not worry," Ajitabh said gently. "I will give Dog a home. And then you can see him whenever you come and see me. He'll still be your hound."

"You'll take good care of him? He's very...special."

"I'll take good care of him."

"You'll remember that he can't smell? That he needs to be watched so he doesn't eat anything poisonous?"

"Yes. I'll remember."

Dog opened his eyes and sat up. Homer slid into the back and hugged him, long and hard. His heart felt like it might stop beating. He didn't want to cry, so he jumped out of the 'copter. Ajitabh tossed him the duffel bag and Mr. Pudding's cap. "When will I see you again?" Homer asked as he stood in the soft, green spring grass.

"As soon as I get word of the next L.O.S.T. meeting,

344

I'll come and get you. You'll need to present yourself to make your membership official."

"Okay."

Ajitabh leaned over the side of the copter. "Excellent job and all that, Homer Pudding. You are a true treasure hunter, through and through. Keep the flight jacket and goggles. You'll be needing them the next time we meet."

"Urrrr." Dog stood at the edge of the 'copter and wagged his tail. Ajitabh reached out and grabbed his collar so he wouldn't jump. Homer couldn't bear to look at Dog.

In the beginning I said that this would not be a sad dog story. And I said that there's nothing worse than not knowing if a dog is going to live or die. Well, there's something that comes close and that's having to say good-bye to a dog.

"Would you wait, just for a bit, while I ask my father? Just in case he changes his mind?"

"Only for a moment. I can't risk being spotted."

Homer tucked the reptile book and cap under his arm, picked up Gwendolyn's duffel bag, and raced down the hill. When he caught sight of his farm, the red barn with its sagging roof, the little stone house and the red truck parked out front, he ran even faster. So much had happened, it felt as if he'd been gone for a lifetime.

The farm dogs raced up the hill, barking and wagging their tails. Homer petted them as they circled, sniffing excitedly. They couldn't believe the scents that clung to him—lair water, mutant tortoise, and rat! Mr. Pudding was just leading the goats into the lower pasture when he looked up and saw Homer running toward him. Homer waved uncertainly, a bit afraid that his father was going to start hollering.

He couldn't remember his father ever looking so tired. The rims of his eyes were as red as Dog's. His expression was neither one of anger nor happiness. He just stared as if he'd never seen Homer before.

Homer set down the duffel bag. "Dad...I...I..."

Mr. Pudding rushed forward and gathered Homer into a powerful hug. "I'm sorry," he said. "I shouldn't have put your things in the attic. Don't ever run away again. I don't know what I'd do without you."

The familiar smell of hay, soap, and engine oil, and the softness of his father's voice nearly brought Homer to tears. "I won't run away, Dad. I promise." Then he held out his father's cap. Mr. Pudding smiled and set it on his head.

"I've been missing this," he said. "I see you've brought back your sister's things. She's been right miserable since losing them." Then he looked around. "So, where's that dog of yours?"

The words flew out of Homer's mouth. His lips could barely keep up. "Dad, can I please keep him? He's a great dog. I promise he won't get into any more trouble. I'll fill in all his holes and I'll make sure he doesn't drink paint. And I won't let him sleep on the bed and—"

"Hold on there." Mr. Pudding rubbed the back of his neck. A goat stuck its head into the duffel bag. Another tried to nibble on the reptile book but Homer pushed it away. "Don't you worry none," his father said. "Your mother and I had a long talk. Taking care of that dog will be good for you. And Squeak likes him, too."

"He can stay?"

"Yep. He's not much to look at and he can't herd worth a darn but I'm sure we can find something for him to do around here." Mr. Pudding took the duffel bag and slung it over his shoulder. "So, where is he?"

Homer was already racing back across the field. *Please be there, please be there,* he thought as he pumped his arm. "DOG!" he called. The cloudcopter had landed behind a grove of birch trees, but Homer couldn't tell if it was still there. *Please be there, please be there.* "DOG!"

"Howooo!"

Dog galloped out of the birch grove, his rope leash dragging behind, his ears flapping like wings. "You can stay," Homer called out, then he crouched in the grass. "Dad's gonna let you stay." Dog licked Homer's face and Homer didn't mind one bit that the kiss was extra slobbery. He pressed his nose against Dog's soft ear and inhaled the dog scent he'd come to love. Then Homer looked to the sky and waved as a little cloud floated away.

When they'd caught up with Mr. Pudding, Homer remembered his big news. "Hey, Dad, you know that compass that Uncle Drake gave me? Well, it turned out to be a very rare compass and the Museum of Science and Technology is going to buy it and it will be enough money to build a new library."

"You sold your compass?" Mr. Pudding frowned. "But Homer, you loved that compass."

"Yeah, but I loved the library, too."

Mr. Pudding put a hand on Homer's shoulder. "I'm right proud of you, son. Giving up something you love isn't an easy thing to do."

"You gave up something you loved, too, didn't you, Dad? To run the farm."

"That was a long time ago."

"What was it?"

Mr. Pudding stopped walking and turned to look at Homer. "This may surprise you but I was going to go to college to become a cartographer."

Homer remembered the angry conversation between his uncle and his father. Mr. Pudding had given up his dream so that he could take care of the farm. So that his older brother could be free to scale mountains and search the ocean floor. It was one of the most heroic things Homer had ever heard.

"Guess you get your love of maps from me," his father said.

Homer's eyes widened. At that moment his father looked like a completely different person. Sure, he was wearing his usual overalls, and his cap, and his work boots, and sure, he still had those lines on his face from the long hours that farm life requires, but there was a little sparkle in his smile that Homer hadn't seen in a very long time.

"You want to look at some of my maps?" Homer asked.

"That sounds nice. I'm sorry I took them away. Let's get them back onto your walls where they belong." Then his gaze fell on the book in Homer's hand. "That something new?"

"Yeah. I got it in The City."

"Well, you'd better find a place for it on your shelf."

"I will."

Picking up a fox's scent, Max, Gus, and Lulu started barking as they raced across the field. Dog trotted after them, his ears swaying, his saggy skin jiggling, his tail held high.

In the back of his mind, Homer heard Lorelei's voice.

"You know, Homer, when Odysseus finally got home, the only one who recognized him was his faithful dog. He could smell him."

Homer laughed out loud.

35

Some Final Things

Did you know that if you feed lettuce, water bugs, and bits of chopped apple to a tortoise, then it will grow to be a happy, docile creature who wants nothing more than to spend a leisurely day sunning itself on a rock? But if you feed it steroids and nuclear reactor waste, which is what Madame fed to Edith, then it will become an angry, flesh-eating killing machine.

Fortunately, as Edith lay beached, her stomach uncomfortably bloated, the City Park groundskeeper, Morton

Bun, took pity upon her and from that moment on, he nursed her back to health on a strict diet of celery water and saltines. And when she returned to her normal size, she joined the other park tortoises. If you visit City Park, you can find Edith sunning with the others. She's the one with the extra saggy skin.

And did you know that if steroids and nuclear reactor waste pollute a city park's lake, then the lake water will turn murky and all the trees around that lake will turn sickly? It's true. Fortunately, Morton Bun knew that tortoise poop makes excellent fertilizer and he was able to nurse the trees back to health.

As Lorelei had promised, a bunch of boxes arrived at the Pudding Farm a few days later, filled with Uncle Drake's things. And attached to one of the boxes was a letter that Homer only read to himself.

Dear Homer,

Guess what? I made an "anonymous" call to the police station and told them all about how Madame had stolen gems from the Cave of Brilliance. They checked the security tapes and even though she's still in a coma from her snakebite, they've placed her under house arrest. Guess I won't have to worry about her for a while.

I gave my room in the warehouse and the soup cart to a homeless family. Daisy really likes our new home. I put the cobra in a basket and we dropped it off at the zoo. And we let all the mice go in the park. So now it's just the two of us. I kind of miss you but I have so much to do. You should see all the gadgets I've found!

Your friend,
Lorelei

Unfortunately, there was no L.O.S.T. coin in the boxes. *She must not have found it*, Homer thought. He wanted to trust her. Wanted to call her his friend again. So he pushed any suspicions from his mind.

And on that same day, another letter arrived.

Dear Mr. Homer W. Pudding,
The law office of Snooty and Snooty wishes to inform you that the five-day return grace period on the item that your uncle sent to you has expired. At least, we think it has expired, but since our secretary is on an extended holiday and we have been unable to find your file or anyone else's file, we are not entirely certain of anything. Because of our current

circumstances, your satisfaction is neither guaranteed nor expected.

> *Yours legally,*
> *Mr. T. Snooty and Mr. C. Snooty,*
> *Attorneys-at-Law*

P.S. If you know of a good elevator repairman, please send him posthaste.

And when Homer and Gwendolyn walked to school the day after Homer's return, Carlotta joined them.

"Hi, Homer." Homer peered over the edge of his book: *Rare Reptiles I Caught and Stuffed.* Carlotta swung her lunch basket and smiled. "Where've you been? Have you been sick? Did you do your report yet?"

"No. I've been kind of busy."

She fiddled with her hair ribbon. "Well, I never did see a screech owl so I wrote about border collies. My dad says ours will win the blue ribbon at the fair. Are you going to enter your dog in the fair?"

"I'm not sure."

"Well, I know he can't herd. Can he jump? Or fetch? Or roll over? Can he do any tricks? Can he do anything?" She looked at him with her big blue eyes, waiting for his answer.

But Homer Winslow Pudding just smiled.

Dear Reader,

If you should find yourself having to write a report on treasure hunters, you will find the following list most helpful. And if your teacher tells you that none of the people on this list actually existed, well then, you can tell your teacher that just because a person is very old, it doesn't mean that the person knows everything.

THE MOST FAMOUS
TREASURE HUNTERS OF ALL TIME

Sir Richard Borington: Designed Extra Strong Borington Binoculars. Died after being sat upon by an elephant.

Captain Ignatius Conrad: Captain of the HMS *Bombastic*. Captured the infamous Pirate Smeller. Died after being eaten by sharks.

Madame la Directeur: Daughter of Wilma von Weiner and Dr. Wortworthy. Along with Drake H. Pudding, she found the remains of the HMS *Bombastic*. Currently in a coma after suffering a cobra bite.

Sir Titus Edmund: Unearthed the only known Egyptian toaster. Who would have guessed that the ancient Egyptians loved toast? Current whereabouts unknown.

Gustav Gustavson: Discovered Aphrodite's toothbrush. Died in a sword fight.

Angus MacDoodle: Found the largest stash of Celtic coins, right in his backyard. Currently living in an undisclosed location.

Baroness Meatpie: Famous for her collection of East Indian pottery. Died from a cobra bite.

Drake Horatio Pudding: Unearthed King Tut's bathing suit. In partnership with Madame la Directeur, he found the remains of the HMS *Bombastic*. Rumored to have found Rumpold Smeller's map. Died after being eaten by a carnivorous mutant tortoise.

Homer Winslow Pudding: Skilled map reader and possessor of many secrets. Currently living in Milkydale on his family's goat farm.

Duke Rumpold Smeller: From Estonia. Said to have accumulated the greatest pirate treasure in pirate history. Died after walking the plank onboard the HMS *Bombastic*. Or did he?

Millicent Smith: Renowned for her volcano-jumping skills. Died in a house fire while trying to save her bungee cords.

Wilma von Weiner: Discovered the Lost Temple of the Reptile King. Cause of death unknown.

Dr. Wortworthy: Doctor of herpetology. Not a renowned treasure hunter but included on this list because he was married to Wilma von Weiner and assisted her in many of her expeditions. Eaten by cannibals.

Acknowledgments

Lucky for me, I've still got the same talented group of writers to call upon when I need help. They faithfully poke and prod the first draft and ask me questions like, "What kind of paper are you using?" and "Do you think it's going to rain today?" and "Are you insane?" I couldn't get through the first draft without them. They are: Anjali Banerjee, Carol Cassella, Sheila Roberts, Elsa Watson, and Susan Wiggs.

There's a fabulous new member of my team, Julie Scheina. She helped edit, along with my fabulous "old"